FOREVER THROWN

FOREVER BLUEGRASS #16

KATHLEEN BROOKS

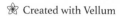 Created with Vellum

Whispered Lies

Rogue Lies

Shattered Lies

<u>*Moonshine Hollow Series*</u>

Moonshine & Murder

Moonshine & Malice

Moonshine & Mayhem

Moonshine & Mischief

Moonshine & Menace (coming Nov 2021)

Moonshine & Masquerades (coming Dec 2021)

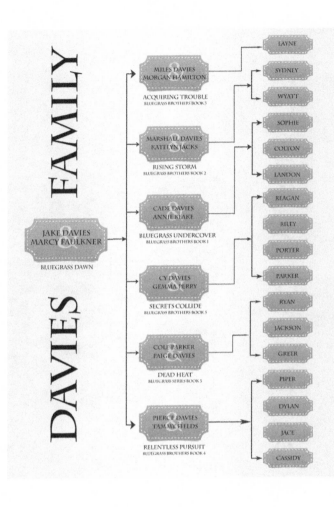

FAMILY

DAVIES

JAKE DAVIES
MARCY FAULKNER
&
BLUEGRASS DAWN

MILES DAVIES
MORGAN HAMILTON
&
ACQUIRING TROUBLE
BLUEGRASS BROTHERS BOOK 5

MARSHALL DAVIES
KATELYN JACKS
&
RISING STORM
BLUEGRASS BROTHERS BOOK 2

CADE DAVIES
ANNIE BLAKE
&
BLUEGRASS UNDERCOVER
BLUEGRASS BROTHERS BOOK 1

CY DAVIES
GEMMA PERRY
&
SECRETS COLLIDE
BLUEGRASS BROTHERS BOOK 3

COLE PARKER
PAIGE DAVIES
&
DEAD HEAT
BLUEGRASS SERIES BOOK 3

PIERCE DAVIES
TAMMY FIELDS
&
RELENTLESS PURSUIT
BLUEGRASS BROTHERS BOOK 4

LAYNE

SYDNEY

WYATT

SOPHIE

COLTON

LANDON

REAGAN

RILEY

PORTER

PARKER

RYAN

JACKSON

GREER

PIPER

DYLAN

JACE

CASSIDY

DAVIES FAMILY FRIENDS

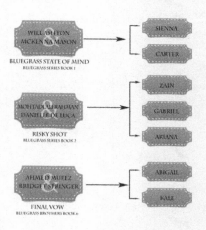

WILL ASHTON
MCKENNA MASON

BLUEGRASS STATE OF MIND
BLUEGRASS SERIES BOOK 1

SIENNA

CARTER

MOHTADI AL RAHMAN
DANIELLE DE LUCA

RISKY SHOT
BLUEGRASS SERIES BOOK 2

ZAIN

GABRIEL

ARIANA

AHMED MUEEZ
BRIDGE ESPRINGER

FINAL VOW
BLUEGRASS BROTHERS BOOK 6

ABIGAIL

KALE

1

The cheering of the crowd faded as Porter Davies slapped his cowboy hat against his chaps exactly three times before putting it on his head. A protective vest covered his flannel shirt as he got ready to enter the chute for the Saddle Bronc ride that would determine if he would be the next world champion. He'd drawn the top horse and it was going to be a hard eight seconds. This championship wasn't going to come easy.

"Next up, from Keeneston, Kentucky, Porter Davies!" the announcer shouted into the arena. "With this ride he can become this year's Saddle Bronc World Champion. Davies is two for four rides on Sinister and this championship won't be easy to win. Davies has been leading the bronc standings all year, but he's come out of left field to surprise everyone with the chance to win both the Saddle Bronc and the Bull Riding Championships."

Porter took three slow, deep breaths. The arena faded away. The sounds of the announcer and crowd faded away. His family, who'd all flown out to see him do something few had done—win two world championships the same year—

faded. All Porter heard as he entered the chute was his own breathing. Unconsciously, his head began to bob with the pace he knew Sinister would set once he started bucking.

Porter climbed down onto Sinister and felt the 1400 pound horse's muscles bunch beneath him. The gate man, the pickup riders, and even the chute itself seemed to disappear until all that was left was Porter and Sinister.

The gate opened and Sinister leapt from the chute. He bucked, and Porter, with one hand gripping the bronc rein and the other in the air, leaned back until he was almost horizontal on Sinister's back. Rolling his hips, kicking his legs up above Sinister's shoulders in a move called spurring, and moving his arm in the air, Porter kept in balance. Sinister bucked up and down, kicking out his back legs as he leapt in moves that could easily cause whiplash.

Scoring wasn't just about staying in the saddle. It was all technique. If Porter's free hand touched Sinister at all, he'd be disqualified. So instead, Porter kept it up high, even when he felt as if he were going to be flung forward over Sinister's head. The points were made by being in sync with the horse, making it look like a smooth ride when in reality it was the exact opposite. That's where Porter excelled, though. His command of the horse, his ability to feel the slightest shift so he could anticipate the next buck, and the way he synced his own breathing to Sinister's were what made him a champion.

The horn sounded and Porter grinned. He knew he'd had the ride of his life. Sinister bucked and Porter leapt off. Porter landed with a drop and roll that his military uncles and cousins would be proud of and sprang up onto his feet. He'd lost his cowboy hat during the ride and jogged over to it as the crowd cheered. He gave a celebratory wave to the masses.

The adrenaline pumping through his body from the ride and from the roar of the crowd made it hard to hear the scores as they came in. The roar of the crowd told him what he wanted to know: he was now the Saddle Bronc World Champion.

"I am so proud of you!" Gemma Davies, his mother, cried out as she flung her arms around him.

His father, Cy, was slapping him on the shoulder as his twin brother, Parker, slapped his other shoulder.

"Hell of a ride, bro," Parker said with a huge smile on his face. "Makes me miss it."

The two Davies boys had ridden rodeo together since they were teens. They'd paid their way through college on the back of a horse as they worked their way up to being professionals. Then, a couple of years ago, they started their own stock farm where they specialized in all kinds of rodeo horses—from broncos to barrel racers to ropers. But then Parker bowed out of the rodeo and became a U.S. marshal. He helped with the farm some, but it was really Porter's dream. With the money Porter earned this year on the pro circuit and the money brought in from sponsors his Aunt Morgan had set up for him, he had enough money to buy out Parker and run the farm on his own.

"How are you feeling? Any headaches, blurred vision?" his cousin, Dr. Jace Davies, asked.

"I just had the ride of my life and you're doing a med eval on me?" Porter teased his cousin.

"I cheered and didn't say anything when it looked like that horse was going to snap your neck. Now amuse me," Jace said, pulling a penlight from his jeans and flashing it in Porter's eyes. "Normal. Good."

"I'm fine," Porter said with a laugh.

"When's the bull riding?" his sister Reagan asked. His older twin sisters, Reagan and Riley, had left their children with their friends, DeAndre and Aniyah, for the weekend so they and their husbands could come to Vegas to cheer him on.

"I ride in about an hour. I need to hydrate." Jace's wife, Stella, handed him a sports drink and a power bar as if on cue.

Carter Ashton, Reagan's husband, shook Porter's hand. "What a ride!"

"Want to give up the thoroughbreds and give rodeo a try?" Porter asked with a grin.

"No way," Carter laughed.

"I'm so proud of you. My little brother is a world champion!" Riley squealed, hugging him as her husband, Matt, slapped him on the back.

"I hate to break this up, but I have no less than four major publications and three national television programs wanting a quick word with our champion," his PR guru, Aunt Morgan, said as she stepped into the family circle with her husband, Miles Davies.

"Let's do it. I'll see y'all after I come from behind and win the bull riding championship," Porter told his family. He received one more round of hugs before Aunt Morgan dragged him off while Stella shoved another protein bar in his hand.

The interviews had been brief as they knew Porter needed time to focus before the bull riding began. Porter now sat in third place of the world rankings. It would be hard to win, but the race was close. Bull riding was entirely different from bronco, but there were some similarities. Both were eight seconds, both animals were judged on their bucking, riders in both used a rope to hold onto, both animals were five feet or taller, but spurring was a bonus and not a necessity like in bronco. In fact, it was used more for gripping the bull than to spur him on. The differences were more pronounced. Porter sat upright on the bull whereas on the bronco he was reclined. He also caved to Jace's pressure and wore a helmet with a face shield when bull riding. The biggest difference was how the bull acted. They bucked slowly compared to the whiplash fast bucks of the horses. However, the bulls had more power and aggression behind each buck. They also bucked side-to-side, spun, and twisted where horses' movements were more up and down.

Porter was on deck as he watched the second-ranked cowboy go. He had a good ride, but Porter moved up to the chute knowing the door had opened. He could easily move up to second with this ride. The championship was closer than ever.

Porter's focus sharpened as he tapped his helmet against his chaps three times before securing it to his head. He was riding a bull named Outlawed Wreck and it wasn't going to be an easy ride as Outlawed Wreck was in line to win his own bovine world championship.

Everything faded away as Porter climbed the chute and positioned himself just behind the 2000 pound bull's shoulders. He gripped the bull rope and found his rhythm breathing with the bull. He felt Outlawed Wreck's sides expand as the bull breathed in deeply and they were off.

The gate was flung open. Outlawed Wreck jumped, twisted, and bucked. Porter held on as Outlawed Wreck spun so fast Porter was almost tossed off the side. This was his chance. The bull was powerful and would be scored high. If he wanted that championship . . . Porter raised his knees up and down, running the spurs along Outlawed Wreck's shoulders for extra points.

The horn sounded and only when it broke through his concentration did Porter hear the crowd roaring. He knew he'd just won the world championship in bull riding, too. He let out a whoop as he moved to dismount Outlawed Wreck.

Outlawed Wreck wasn't having it, though. He spun so fast that Porter didn't have time to counteract the force. He was flung off the bull as if he were nothing more than a rag doll. Porter knew he was airborne but he hadn't realized the metal railing was so close until his head collided with it. He felt it from the helmet down to his toes as his spine compressed with the hit. He landed hard on the dirt floor of the arena as all instincts to survive kicked in. He reached for the railing to pull himself up, but Outlawed Wreck wasn't done with him yet. Two thousand pounds of angry bull slammed into him with a bone-breaking kick.

The workers in the ring swarmed the area yelling to get Outlawed Wreck's attention away from Porter. Porter had managed to pull himself up to sitting when hands grabbed him and dragged him up and over the railing seconds before Outlawed Wreck had a chance to land another blow.

Jace's blurry face came into view as Porter struggled to breathe. "Patch. Me. Up. Doc. Have. To. Get. My. Championship," Porter said each word between gasps for air.

"You have a concussion at the very least and probably a collapsed lung. I'll have your brother accept it for you. We need to get you to the hospital now," Jace said as he took off Porter's helmet.

"I'm. Fine." Porter struggled to stand as orthopedic doctors swarmed him.

"No, you're not," Jace said with more force than he ever had before.

Everything was blurry, his head was killing him, and he was struggling to breathe. Porter knew he wasn't fine, but he would be. He always recovered. The concussions, the broken arm, the fractured clavicle, the pulled muscles, the torn ACL . . . They all healed or at least he'd managed. He'd manage this, too.

The crowd gasped and Porter tried to see the jumbo screen, but it was too blurry to read. "What. Sousa's. Time?" Sousa, the Brazilian rider, was the current number one and was in the arena now.

"7.89 seconds," Jace said matter-of-factly. "Hospital, now!"

"Won. I won." Porter grinned through the pain and the shortness of breath.

"With a giant score of 94.2, Porter Davies is a double world champion!" the announcer yelled right as Porter's family ran toward him.

Their faces were blurry and moving. Porter would have recognized the worry in them, but he couldn't see straight. Instead he reached for his brother. "Take me out there to get my trophy."

"Bro, you need to go to the hospital."

Porter shook his head, which only made it hurt more. "After."

Parker looked to Jace who was probably about to hogtie Porter and drag him to the hospital, but finally Porter felt his father and his brother slide their arms around him. "One wave of the hat and then the hospital," his father ordered as he set Porter's cowboy hat on his head. It didn't matter that

Porter was closing in on thirty. When his father used that tone there was no arguing. "Get an ambulance backed up here and ready."

Porter didn't know how he made it to the center of the arena where the awards ceremony was set up. They took one look at him and skipped the second- and third-place winners and awarded Porter his two world championships. Parker took one and held it up and his father took the other. Porter heard the cheers of the audience as he removed his hat. He only got one wave out before his father and brother practically ran from the arena with him sandwiched between him.

"See. I'm fine." Porter managed to stand on his own as he got ready to get into the ambulance. He shot his cousin a cocky grin before everything went black.

2

Keeneston, Kentucky . . .

"You shouldn't be riding," Jace called out over the fence. "It's only been two weeks since you were discharged."

Porter reined in the barrel racing horse he was training for the top women's barrel racer and trotted over to the fence. "I'm fine, Jace. My chest is a little sore, but I'm used to some degree of pain."

"How's your vision?" Jace asked, looking up at him.

"Back to normal. I mean, there are two of you, right?" Porter tried to tease, although Jace didn't laugh.

"Put up the horse. Let me examine you, Porter."

Jace wasn't in a joking mood and Porter knew why. It hadn't just been a concussion. There had also been a spinal fracture. It was healing well, but it was still there. Porter was slow to dismount. He might be injured and was pushing himself, but he was also trying to be careful, at least somewhat careful.

Jace opened the gate and motioned for Porter to take a

seat on the bench outside the barn. "At least you're wearing your brace," Jace muttered as Porter unbuttoned his flannel shirt. The bruises from the bull's hooves were still visible along his chest. The vest and helmet had saved his life.

Jace pulled out his stethoscope and listened to Porter's lungs and heart. He did a full neurological exam after that. His face was set in a frown as he put his equipment back into his medical bag.

"See, I'm fine," Porter said, trying to get Jace to lighten up. Cowboys came back from way worse injuries than this.

"You're healing well. It's actually quite remarkable for how badly you've been injured. But, as I told you, one more major injury and you'd be done. Porter, you're done," Jace said the words, but Porter didn't process them.

"Jace, aren't you being a little melodramatic? I've come back from worse injuries than this." Porter scoffed at Jace as he strapped the brace back on.

"I'm sure you can find a doctor to clear you. But it won't be me. I'm dead serious about this, Porter. I'm your cousin and your best friend. I wouldn't bullshit you. You've had too many concussions. You now have a weak vertebra that if it breaks or even has a piece of bone break off, could pinch or damage your spinal cord, leaving you paralyzed or dead. The choice is yours. But because I love you, I'm telling you it's time to hang up your spurs."

Porter shook his head as he looked around the back part of his parents' farm. These back ninety acres and the small house on it were his. He might not own them outright, but he was working on that. He'd bought Parker out of his share just three days before. He was going to approach his father next about buying the land. "I'm nothing without this," Porter admitted as fear struck him deep in his core.

Jace let out a deep breath and sat down next to him. "I'm

not talking about giving up the farm, just the competitions. You can ride. You can barrel race. You can breed horses and bulls. You just can't be on anything that bucks. I know you're fine now. I know in six weeks you could be back on a bull or a bronc, but what I'm looking at isn't your ability to ride in six weeks. I'm looking at making sure you're still alive in six years."

Porter felt it like a punch to the gut. He knew Jace spoke the truth, but that didn't mean hearing it didn't hurt like hell. "I guess it's always better to go out on top, right?"

"I'm sorry, Porter, but you are retiring as a two-time world champion. That will be big for the farm."

Porter nodded as he buttoned his shirt. "I've already sold out of all my stock for the next three years. I have the money to really expand this place now. I heard Mr. Habisher who owns the farm behind us is thinking of selling. I was contemplating buying it. I could put a path through the woods and then there's all that acreage back there. But still, not rodeoing anymore? I didn't know how Parker did it, but I guess I'll find out."

"Call him. You know your brother will help you with the transition." Jace stood up and picked up his medical bag. "I'm sorry, Porter. I know how much you love riding."

Porter nodded and watched Jace head for his SUV. Porter dug out his cell phone and called his aunt Morgan.

"How are you feeling?" Morgan didn't bother saying hello.

"Jace says I should retire. What do you think?"

"I think I've already written up a press release and have a substantial number of interviews waiting for you to announce just that. You'll go out on top while promoting your farm. You'll be set for life, Porter. And more importantly, you'll be alive for it," Morgan said bluntly.

That's why everyone in the family loved Aunt Morgan. She and Miles always told it as it was.

"Do it." Porter hung up the phone and rested his head against the side of the barn. It was done. He was retiring.

"You look great," Aunt Morgan told him as he winked at the makeup lady. "You know what you're going to say?"

"I got it," Porter said as he glanced over at the biggest sportscaster around sitting on a barstool in the middle of Porter's pasture. Above them was a tent to cast them in the perfect amount of shade. Cameras were set up, lighting was on, and it was time to announce his retirement.

Porter stood up wearing his various sponsors' jeans, boots, and hat. Morgan had gotten a bonus from them for this last bit of promotion before he was no longer marketable—those were her blunt words.

"I can't believe you're retiring," Sam Winchell said as he stood in his navy three-piece suit and pink tie. He looked completely out of place in the pasture with horses roaming in the background. However, the guy was built like a tank and was as smooth as ice in both his dress and sports knowledge. "Thanks for letting me have the interview."

"I might be a rodeo guy, but you edged out Primetime by being a Kentucky man," Porter joked as he shook Sam's hand. Sam had been a pro football player in Lexington. He'd retired ten years earlier and climbed his way up to become the best sports reporter out there. His weekly show was the highest-rated sports show in history. Plus, Porter was still doing Primetime, just not first. Aunt Morgan was a PR genius.

Sam looked around. Porter saw that his short black hair

had razor-tight edging as he turned his head. "I do miss the Bluegrass State. You ready to do this?"

"No, but I'm doing it anyway," Porter said with a smile that he didn't feel. He was supposed to be happy. He was supposed to be choosing this retirement even though it was really choosing him. But, how could he get back on a horse or bull after seeing his mother's face when he woke up at the hospital? He'd never seen her so pale or so frightened before.

"What a show we have for you tonight! I'm here in beautiful Keeneston, Kentucky, at the PD Rodeo Farm with the owner and two-time Rodeo World Champion Porter Davies," Sam said into the camera.

Porter put on his smile, answered the questions, thanked his sponsors, and pushed his farm. "This isn't the end of my career, just the first chapter in a new book," Porter said as he gestured to the farm behind him.

"What a first chapter it is," Sam said with a grin. "I hear you already have a waitlist three years out, full of the who's who on the rodeo circuit."

"It's very exciting. I'm looking forward to the future."

Sam shook hands with Porter and turned to the camera. "Thank you, Porter, for some incredible rides and all the best to your new endeavor, although you've never needed luck. You have a natural talent. Ten years on the pro circuit and now you can retire and step to the other side of the fence where I hope the grass is greener. I'm Sam Winchell. Next week I speak to basketball standout . . ."

Porter did it. He was officially retired. Sam finished with his sign-off as Porter looked out over the farm. What was he going to do with himself now? Yes, the farm was his passion, but it would never give him the adrenaline rush of those eight-second rides.

. . .

"It was a good interview," Parker said, crossing his arms over his button-down shirt. He might be a US marshal, but only his button-down shirt and tie looked the part.

"They let you wear jeans and a cowboy hat on the job? If so, maybe I should join the marshals, too," Porter said, teasing his brother.

"You'd find it boring tracking down bad guys and protecting the good ones," Parker said, knowing he was right. It really wasn't Porter's thing.

"I could become a weapons tester for Sophie," Porter said about their cousin Sophie Dagher who designed new weapons for police and military. "You may be the big tough marshal, but I shot the acid gun of death."

Porter and Parker both laughed as the video of the incident had somehow been shown to all of Keeneston. Porter had been ribbed mercilessly for accidentally melting away part of a house after tripping and shooting off a little acid bomb.

"Actually, that does sound fun. I bet she has explosives," Parker said to him.

"Nope. Don't you take my job. I called it!" Porter said, punching his brother in the arm.

"Boys," their mother said with a roll of her eyes. "Will you ever stop hitting each other?"

"They have to hit each other because they'll never beat me," their father said as he joined them. Porter shot a look to Parker. It was on.

Porter and Parker lunged for Cy and five minutes later they were covered in dirt and grass from head to toe, but they were all smiling and laughing.

"Told you so," Cy said, standing and brushing off his jeans. "The old man still has it, babe."

"Ugh, Dad," Parker groaned as Cy grabbed Gemma and kissed her way more passionately than any father should kiss a mother in front of the kids.

"When you boys are married, you'll do the same thing," Gemma said calmly after their father stopped the totally embarrassing and near-pornographic kiss. "Speaking of marriage . . ."

"Gotta go feed the horses," Porter blurted out.

"Thanks, asshole," Parker whispered as Porter bolted, leaving the marriage lecture to his brother.

Porter chuckled as he entered the barn to start the nightly chores. He might love rodeo, but he loved his family more. However, he wasn't above throwing his brother under the marriage bus.

3

Miami, Florida . . .

Willa Aldridge held her breath as her horse, Apollo, cleared the five-foot oxer jump with ease, soaring past the decorative palm trees that held up the rails. She had two more jumps to finish and the course would be clear.

Apollo could fly, but it was up to her to tell him when to spread his wings. She glanced at the clock. It was time to fly. Willa squeezed her legs and Apollo kicked it up a gear. He practically flew over the wall as they sped toward the finish line. The previous three horses had faulted on the last jump.

Willa lowered her body and tightened her thighs. The pressure encouraged Apollo as he headed for the jump. His muscles tensed under her as he got ready to explode into the jump.

Willa heard the cheers as Apollo cleared the jump and they finished the course. She sat up in the English jumping saddle and pumped her fist in the air before she patted Apollo's neck. The horse was practically bouncing with excitement. He knew he'd done well and was feeding off the crowd's energy.

The pro jumping event was just off the beach and was packed with Willa's friends and enemies. Here, on the course, she was just Willa with her horse. But as she left the ring and saw Callum Harding smirking at her, she also knew she was surrounded by enemies.

Men and women competed against each other in equestrian events. That meant her ex-boyfriend from boarding school was present at every event. He and his little horde of nightmares gave her mocking claps. As if surviving her senior year after breaking up with Callum wasn't bad enough, he'd attended university with her, too. She'd been stuck with him for another four years on the university equestrian team, before entering this elite level of jumping . . . together.

"Can you believe they're all twenty-eight or older and acting like that?"

Willa dismounted and kissed Apollo before taking off her helmet and shaking out her toffee-brown ponytail. "Thank goodness I have you, Tilly, or I'd quit riding today."

Tilly Bradford, or Matilda as her father called her, was Willa's best friend. She ran in the same circles Willa did. They had been best friends ever since they were ten years old. They had been at Marguerite Borghese's birthday party when Marguerite snatched the cupcake from Tilly's hand and declared that since it was her birthday, she got whatever she wanted. That belief system now ran to every day and not just birthdays for Marguerite. When Willa had shared her cupcake with a tearful Tilly, she'd gained a friend for life.

Tilly was "old money." Her family had made their fortune hundreds of years ago and only grown it over the centuries. So much so that even Marguerite thought twice about being a bitch to her after learning the history of the Bradford family wealth when they were all thirteen.

Tilly's house was a museum of a mansion. Well, all of her houses were. There were whole hallways filled with portraits of Bradfords who all shared the same blue eyes and various shades of blond hair.

Willa, on the other hand, was "new money." An Aldridge relative had been a duke in England a couple of centuries before. However, her father was the third son of a second son of a fifth son type thing, so all of the family wealth and fancy titles belonged to some very distant cousins Willa had never met. No, her father made his fortune by developing new technologies. Willa had gone to the best schools and had a massive trust fund. But since her father hadn't hit it big until she was almost nine years old, Willa had always thought of herself as the middle-class suburban girl she'd been raised.

She'd grown up in a split-level house where her father had converted the garage into a workroom. He started by building custom computers and then branched into software before hitting it big with a little chip that processed information a certain way to make computers run faster. Every computer made in the last twenty years had one, yet no one knew his name. Her father liked it that way. He liked flying under the radar. However, the one thing he refused to fly under the radar was his family.

Her father, Brian Aldridge, had spoiled his wife and only child. The big house, the resort-style swimming pool, and of course, a pony. Willa had had the best of everything, but even all the billions in the world hadn't kept a brain aneurysm from killing her mother when Willa was a freshman in high school.

Willa had been in a private school near their home until

that point but she had a hard time living in the house after her mother died. There were memories everywhere and so she'd begged her father to send her to boarding school. It had nearly killed him, but he'd done it for her. It was only after Willa was an adult that she realized how hard it had been on her father to lose his wife and then to send his daughter away to school. Willa decided then that she was going to make her father proud and she was going to work for him. She didn't have his ability to develop cutting edge technology, but she had a head for business.

She graduated from college with a business and finance degree and began in an entry-level job at her father's company, Anancites, as she earned her MBA. She'd been steadily working her way up since then and made it to vice president a few months ago. She'd never given up her love of riding, even through the long hours at the office. What that meant was that Willa had no life outside work or horses; she literally had no time for anything else. Several of her friends were already married and having children, but that wasn't even on her radar.

"Want to grab a bite to eat real quick before the end of the event? I assume you're driving home afterward?" Tilly asked as they walked back to the stables. Some people handed their horses off, but Willa always liked to walk Apollo back and give him a treat before the groom took him to cool down and load him into the trailer for the hour drive north to their farm near Wellington, Florida.

"That sounds great. Then you can share all the gossip you've heard today. I wish I rode first like you did so I could enjoy the rest of the event instead of being a bundle of nerves." Willa could control a boardroom with ease, but thinking about riding in front of a crowd got her nerves working overtime. But as soon as she mounted Apollo, all of the tension would disappear. All the distraction, all the pressure, and all the stress simply disappeared and she was just a woman riding a horse she loved.

"I'll grab us a table!" Tilly called out as she hurried off toward the pavilion.

"Dad!" Willa said with surprise as she approached her stall. "What are you doing here? I thought you had to work."

"I brought the helicopter and flew down to see you jump. You were magnificent." Her father was her hero. He was in his mid-fifties, but his hair was still the same toffee-brown as hers. He pulled her into a tight hug and she felt like a little girl again. "I also come with news."

"Good news I hope," Willa said as she gave Apollo his apple and nodded to his groom to take him to get cooled down and cleaned up.

Willa unbuttoned her black show coat and sighed with relief as the moisture-wicking white dress shirt began to cool her off.

"Very. We got the contract with the government. Your presentation sealed the deal," her father told her with a proud smile.

"Yes!" Willa tossed her head back in celebration. Her father had designed new multi-level mobile encryption software that would turn each phone into the most secure device in the world. A CIA operative in the Middle East would use the first level of hardware to enter his phone, such as a fingerprint, facial recognition, or passcode. That hardware was manufactured for them via another developer. Then the operative would enter a second code when accessing government information, such as searching government databases, sending or receiving secure information via email or text, and accessing secure video links.

That was where Anancites came in. That second code would trigger a five-step multi-level encryption of all information sent or received. The information sent would be encrypted with one algorithm, then that encryption would be encrypted again and again, each under a different algorithm that had its own data key, making it the most secure device in the world.

"The recent hacks from foreign states helped us get this contract, but it also puts a target on us. No one is to know what we're doing," her father said as he lowered his voice. "I want to open a second headquarters for Anancites where this will be the sole project. It will be highly classified and I want you to run it."

"Me? You're handing this over to *me* to run?" Willa asked with a mixture of shock and excitement.

"You're ready. I'll still be in charge of the software, but you'll be the point person on it. You'll run the facility and meet with the government officials. It'll be a small team at first. They're starting with phones for undercover agents. The first batch is at the office now and we'll get them set up over the next couple of weeks. Starting next month, all phones will be sent to the new office for the secure download and setup. You'll teach the agents how to use the phones, either in person or over a secure line. You're the only public face of this program. None of the tech people can have their identities known. Since they each only work on their specific level of encryption, it helps keep things confidential. It's one of the many layers I have in place to keep the intellectual property secure."

"Thank you so much, Dad. I'll make you proud."

"Oh honey, you already make me proud. You always have," Her father hugged her but then frowned. "This is the hard part. I want the headquarters more centralized. It would be too obvious if I put them in Washington or another major city like that."

"I'm going to move away from you?" Willa asked as the excitement dwindled.

"I think I found a place you'll love. You can take your horses, and it'll be a perfect cover for you. Plus, you're already going there in two weeks," her father said with a big smile.

Two weeks. She wasn't traveling for work in two weeks. No, she was going to be at a world championship horse event in . . . "Lexington, Kentucky?"

"I hope that meets with your approval. I even found a couple of farms for sale nearby that are large enough for you to build your own training center."

Okay, this wasn't horrible. "Lexington is great for me, but what about the business?"

"It's perfect. Not so big as to be an obvious location, like New York or Washington, D.C., but not so small as to lack what we need. There are plenty of office spaces to choose from and plenty of housing for our techs with an attractive cost of living for them, too. Also, the Bluegrass Airport is right there and they are used to high-profile clients flying in for horse races. Plus, it's easy for government types to arrive incognito. I want you to go to the horse event and scope out offices and look at the farms there. If you like one, buy it. You don't need to run it by me. You're the president of Anancites Mobile Encryption Division," her father said, handing her new business cards he'd printed up. They were simple. They were black with silver block letters reading Anancites, then Willa Aldridge, President underneath it. On the back was a phone number. There were no division names, no addresses, and certainly no mention of encryption.

Willa hugged her father and took a deep breath. This was life-changing. Out in the show ring, no one cared about her name. All of her self doubts, all the patronizing men she put up with in the tech industry, all the people talking about nepotism behind her back—it all went away. Now, if this company took off, it could mean one place she had to herself could be gone. She'd need to focus all she had on the job.

"Thank you for picking Lexington, Dad. I know you did it for me."

"Don't be sad, honey. You can still ride. In fact, I think it's the perfect cover. You can enter events in locales where you can meet with clients. I'd much rather have people thinking you're focused on jumping than on the top secret work you're going to be doing. Now, I have to get back. I'll see you for dinner. Love you." Her father kissed her cheek as an SUV pulled up to the stable.

"Love you too."

Willa watched as her father drove off. She looked around and saw Callum and his crew strutting back to the stables. Maybe getting out of Florida wouldn't be such a bad thing. It was time for a fresh start. It was possible people wouldn't know the Aldridge name in Lexington. She could live the kind of life she'd had before her mother died. A life where she was liked or disliked because of who she was, not because of how much money her father had or how old that money was. Yes, Lexington was sounding better and better.

4

It was four in the morning when Willa saddled Apollo at her training center in Wellington, Florida. She'd come in third last week in Miami. Good, but she felt it could have been better. The Lexington Equestrian Championship next week was even bigger than the one in Miami. That championship comprised of eight of the ten equestrian events over a series of days to determine the champions. Events included jumping, combined driving, dressage, eventing, reining, vaulting, endurance riding, and para-equestrianism.

Willa led Apollo from the barn to the outdoor practice area lit in the darkness. The sun hadn't begun to rise yet as she closed the gate to the practice ring. She felt a shiver go down her spine as she mounted Apollo. The horse sidestepped nervously, telling Willa her feeling of something being off wasn't just in her head.

Willa turned her head slowly. She saw the workers pulling in to start their day, but then she saw a shadow near the practice ring gate. As she stared at it, a person stepped forward from the shadows.

"Good morning!" the man called out.

"This is private property," Willa replied, reaching into her boot to pull out the riding crop she carried out of habit but rarely needed to use with Apollo. She sat up to her full height as she tried to keep Apollo calm.

"I made an appointment to meet with you. I just came a little early," the man said with a shrug as he leaned against the practice ring fencing. "I'm John Dickerson."

"You're five hours early, Mr. Dickerson." Willa was used to distrusting people, and everything in her said to distrust this man.

"I know, but something came up. I tried to call and reschedule, but no one got back to me. It's either now or never so I took a chance you'd let me meet with you early. It won't take long." Willa noted the easy smile and the way he bent down to try to hide his height. He was trying to make her feel safe when that was the last thing she felt.

Willa glanced around and saw more people walking around behind them. If she needed help, all she had to do was scream. "You have five minutes, Mr. Dickerson."

"I'll only need two. Care to join me?" he motioned to the small bleacher that sat outside the ring.

"No, thank you. The clock is ticking, Mr. Dickerson," Willa said coldly. She refused to show the fear she was feeling. Something about him set her on edge.

"I'll get right to the point then. Rumor has it Anancites won a government contract to encrypt all the phones of government employees." Mr. Dickerson paused to gauge her reaction. She showed none. She was used to dealing with reporters asking nosy questions. "I guess you won't confirm or deny that?"

"You guessed correctly. I will never confirm or deny any clients or even what we do. If that's all, you can be going."

The man smiled wider and all she could think of was a wolf ready to attack. "For argument's sake, let's say Anancites is encrypting those phones. Hypothetically, how much would it cost to get the skeleton key we all know you have?"

Willa fought hard to hide her surprise at his question. She had expected him to be a journalist wanting a scoop, but this wasn't a question of a journalist. "You need to leave right now."

His smile slipped as his lips thinned out. "By all accounts you're a smart woman, Miss Aldridge. Think of a price. I'll be in touch."

Apollo felt her nerves and reared. Willa hung on and when Apollo landed, the man was gone. Willa cantered Apollo around the ring once to calm him enough for Willa to be able to open the gate without dismounting. Once through, she trotted him back to the stables and dismounted as soon as she saw a groom she knew and trusted.

"Take Apollo back to his stall, please." She shoved his reins into the groom's hand before running for her car. She reached over the door of the convertible and pulled out her cell phone. Without a second thought, she opened up the back and pulled out the battery and SIM card. Tracking was too easy these days and she wasn't going to risk the man having tampered with her phone, so she disabled it.

Within twenty minutes, she was running into her father's house still in her practice clothes and boots. "Dad!" she yelled, knowing he was still asleep.

She raced up the wide staircase as her father rushed from his bedroom. "Willa, are you okay? What is it?"

"Someone wants the skeleton key to the encryption," she told him as she recounted what had just happened.

"How did they find out?" her father muttered. "There's either a leak in our company or a leak at the government. It could be either. This is why only you and I have the skeleton key. None of the other techs have the keys to any of the levels, so they aren't a threat. Especially since it's an evolving and constantly changing encryption. That puts you and me at risk. I'm getting you security right now."

Willa followed her father into his office. With a press of a button, the house filled with private security. Three men were assigned to her and took up their position outside the office door as her father talked to the lead attorney for Anancites. It seemed as if hours had passed when her father finally put down the phone and joined her in the sitting area on the other side of the room from his desk.

"Are you going to call anyone from the government?" Willa asked.

Her father shook his head as he dropped into the chair across from her. "No. I don't want to jeopardize this contract. I talked to our attorney and we both agree it's most likely a corporate spy from SynCrypt Security Group. They've been out to get us for years. Weldon is not above corporate espionage."

"What do I do now?" Willa asked.

"Pretend nothing happened. We'll tear SynCrypt apart looking for this man. You'll take your bodyguards with you to Lexington. Not a word of this incident, our encryption, or our government contract to anyone. Understand?"

"Yes, Dad."

Willa stood on wobbly legs and pulled herself together. She was not going to be intimidated. She knew there was a dark side to technology. Russia and China would do about anything to get access to their developments and then there were their competitors to think about. The number of people who would be out to get the skeleton key would be astronomical if it were widely known it existed.

"When do you leave for Lexington?" her father asked as he too stood.

"Apollo leaves late this afternoon. I'll fly to Lexington in the morning. I have a list of properties to look at and I want to get Apollo settled."

Her father hugged her tightly. "Be safe, honey. I love you."

"I will. I'll call if anything happens."

"I'm sure the worst is over. Especially when they see your bodyguards. Remember, no one can know the real reason you're in Lexington."

Willa nodded her head before kissing her father's cheek. "I know."

～

Porter grabbed the box of cereal from the grocery shelf and tossed it into his cart. He placed his hands on the shopping cart and pushed it to the end of the aisle. He was about to turn when a hand came out and clasped the end of the wire cart.

"Hello, Porter. It's been a while."

Porter looked up from the hand, to the wrinkled suit, and up to the old face staring back at him. "Eleven years, Agent Naylor. I had just turned eighteen and you asked me to join the CIA. Shouldn't you be retired by now?"

The agent, now in his mid-sixties, smiled. "I'm too valuable to cut loose. I know where all the bodies are buried. Or in your case, where all the potential agents are."

"I could have saved you the trip from DC, Agent Naylor. I wasn't interested in being in the CIA then and I'm not now." Porter moved to push his cart by him, but the agent kept his grip on it.

"I worked with your father, you know."

"You were the paper pusher behind his missions. You didn't actually work with him," Porter said, standing up to his full height and towering over the man.

"His handler retired and I was promoted. Your father just fell in love and quit before I could work with him on a new case. I hear you're retired now, too. Are you looking for something to fill your time because I have an assignment for you?"

Porter stared at him with disbelief. "I'm not working for the CIA. You can't just give me an assignment."

"I told you I would come for you one day. That day is today. It's one job. Fifty thousand dollars. Then I'll never bother you again," Naylor promised.

"Not interested," Porter said as he gave his shopping cart a little push.

"Fine, then I'll just have your brother thrown out of the US marshals," Agent Naylor said with a shrug as if it weren't a big deal.

There wasn't a doubt in Porter's mind that Naylor could do it. He could probably send a text and three minutes later Parker would be escorted from the building. "Or your sisters and brothers-in-law. I can have the government make their lives a living hell."

"You're an asshole, Naylor."

Naylor grinned in response. "You don't get to where I am in the CIA by being a nice guy. Ask your father how nice of a guy he was when he was in the agency. Whether you like it or not, Porter, you're perfect as a CIA contract employee and we don't accept 'no' as an answer."

"A hundred thousand and you get me for one month or

one case, whichever time is shorter," Porter said as a mom with three young kids in her cart pushed by them looking as frazzled as Porter felt on the inside.

"Look at you making demands. I told you that you were perfect for us. Deal." Naylor held out his hand and Porter shook it. "This is all off the books. You'll be paid in cash."

Porter's eyes narrowed. "What are you getting me into?"

"I'll meet you in the parking lot in ten minutes. Also, you're low on milk. You might want to pick some up," Naylor said before turning and strolling down the aisle.

Porter shook his head and finished his shopping. He took his time and let Naylor wait. When Porter and Parker had turned eighteen, Naylor had shown up at a rodeo. He'd tried to recruit them to join the CIA training program, but they'd both declined. Naylor had said he'd be back one day. The man was true to his word, even if everything else he said was a lie.

Porter pushed the cart out to his truck where Naylor was sitting on the tailgate. "Did you get the milk?"

"I got it. Now tell me what I'm getting myself into," Porter said as he began to unload the groceries.

"This is all top secret, so no running to that little town you love so much and blabbing it around."

Porter almost rolled his eyes. "Naylor, that little town has a spy network that would give you wet dreams. They'll know before I even get home. If you don't hurry up and tell me what the case is, one of them will text me with the details."

Naylor scoffed. Porter chuckled, he knew better than to underestimate Keeneston.

"The US government awarded a contract to Anancites to encrypt all government phones after the Russians and Chinese tried to hack us. The first people to get the encryption are undercover CIA agents. So, of course, I have surveillance on Anancites. This morning the new president of the company and head of the mobile encryption program, Willa Aldridge, was approached and offered money for the skeleton key to the encryption."

"Did she take it?" Porter asked.

"No, but she didn't not take it either. She also didn't call it in to the government. The man who approached her said he'd be in contact with her again. I need you to get close to Miss Aldridge and determine if she's a traitor who is selling out our agents or if her life is in danger," Naylor told him.

"How am I going to do that?" Porter asked.

"With horses," Naylor said with a grin. Porter raised his eyebrow and waited for Naylor to continue. "She's arriving tomorrow for the Lexington Equestrian Events. When she's not a potential traitor to the government, she's a showjumper."

"Showjumping? Isn't that the prissy sport where they parade around the ring and jump little fences? You don't expect me to do that, do you? Even you should know not all horse events are the same," Porter said, aghast at the idea of putting on those tight white pants and parading around the ring.

"Hell if I know. I'm feeling nice, though, and brought you two covers to choose from. I can get you to be a groom for her competitor, Callum Harding, who is also her ex-boyfriend. He goes through grooms on a daily basis and then usually doesn't pay them for their day's work. His stalls are on one side of Miss Aldridge's."

"And my other choice?" Porter asked. Being a groom was fine, being a groom to an asshole was something else.

"Ever heard of reining? It's an event you can enter. I can make you a competitor and there can be a convenient mix-up in stable assignments and your reining horse will be next to Miss Aldridge's jumper."

Porter pulled out his phone and searched reining. "I'm not wearing some skin-tight pants and parading around . . . wait a second." Porter watched the video of the man in jeans, a button-down shirt, and a cowboy hat work the horse in the ring. The horse spun, did some footwork, some rollbacks, and Porter's favorite, hind leg power slides. That was where the horse sprinted and then almost sat down to stop instantly. "This is cowboy stuff. I grew up training horses to do this after we moved cattle around the farm. I have a great eight-year-old mare that can do this in her sleep."

"Miss Trix?" Naylor asked. "Good choice."

Porter grew up with a former spy for a father. How Naylor knew which horse Porter would choose wasn't a surprise to him, just like how he knew Porter was low on milk. "Uh huh."

"You'll be entered by lunch. Your supplies for the competition and all the background information on Miss Aldridge, Anancites, and anyone you may come into contact with will arrive by four. Study it. Learn it. Live it. You report first thing tomorrow morning. I want you to get to know Miss Aldridge so well that you know what she's thinking before she does. It's up to you to tell us if she's a traitor or if she's in danger. Her life depends on it." Naylor hopped down from the tailgate and strode off as if a person's life weren't hanging in the balance.

Porter let out a breath and closed the tailgate. He needed to get home and find out exactly what he'd been dropped in the middle of. Tomorrow he was becoming a spy.

Porter drove up the lane of his parents' farm and forked off to the left, heading to his farm at the back of the property. He saw his father sitting on the porch to the ranch house before he even stopped the truck.

It wasn't a leap to imagine what his father was like as a spy. While he had nothing but love and support for his family, there was no doubt he could be ruthless. After all, what man in his sixties still looked like his father? His muscles were ripped and with a shaved head, he had the appearance of an MMA fighter. Well, to be fair, his uncles and family friend, Ahmed, all still looked like that. But outside of Keeneston, it would be a very unusual sight.

"Hey, Dad," Porter said, getting out of the truck and walking around to unload the groceries.

"You're low on milk."

Porter nodded. "I heard that. I picked more up."

"What did Naylor want?" Cy asked without beating around the bush. That wasn't his style.

"Why ask? Don't you know?" Porter teased his father.

Although it wasn't really a joke. There was a high probability his father did know.

"The timing is interesting. It comes right after a huge contract was awarded to Anancites to provide mobile encryption for the government. It's been called the most secure phone in the world. However, that's more of Kale's thing than yours. Of course, I don't think Naylor has the balls to blackmail Kale to work for the CIA. Ahmed would kill him on the spot," Cy said of one of his best friends.

Ahmed was the former head of security for Mo, the prince of Rahmi, who was also a family friend. His farm was down the road a bit. Prior to being Mo's head of security, he was an international badass soldier. Everyone in military organizations around the world knew and feared the name. Kale was his youngest child and only son. Ahmed's daughter, Abby, inherited the soldier badass gene and had been the only female CIA special ops agent. Kale went the other direction. He was a badass hacker, but no one knew whom he worked for. Most likely the government, but he wasn't saying and Porter wasn't asking. He was sure his dad probably knew if Porter really wanted to know.

"I heard the daughter is into horses. She'll be in Lexington tomorrow," his father added.

"It's more my thing than Kale's because Willa Aldridge is a show jumper and Naylor is having me spy on her to determine if she's a traitor or if her life is in danger. He's getting me entered into the Lexington Equestrian Event as a reining rider with Miss Trix." Porter didn't even try to keep it from his father, regardless of what Naylor told him.

"I figured. I already got Miss Trix cleaned up for you and the trailer will be ready by the morning."

"So why bother asking me if you already knew?" Porter asked as his father opened the front door for him. Porter carried in the groceries and set them down on the kitchen counter.

"I like to know what you know first. Did Naylor really think he could come onto my property, bug your house, and me not know? He's slacking then," Cy scoffed.

"I assume you took care of the bugs," Porter said as he began to put the groceries away. His father didn't answer. He just gave him a look that answered for him. "Any advice?"

"Yeah, don't get caught. My sources say Willa Aldridge is an unknown quantity, could be a wild card. Not much is known about her. Her father protected her after his wife died. Her name is only in the news for business or horses. No boyfriend, no sex tapes, no drunken nights out at the club. On paper she's a good girl, but those are the worst because you never really know how they'll react in the real world." Cy paused for a moment. "Her father is a good man." Coming from Porter's father, that was high praise. "He won't turn unless his daughter's life is in danger. The question is, what kind of person is his daughter?"

Porter drove through the early morning darkness to the Lexington Equestrian Park where the event was being held. He'd hooked Miss Trix's trailer to his truck and driven himself. A line of expensive trailers and motor coaches lined the long drive entering the park. Porter was never one to have an entourage. Instead, he simply had an enormous family that would show up at the drop of a hat.

Porter had studied the folders some CIA agent had dropped off for him. He'd gone over them and then asked his father to review them with him. Naylor had thrown him into the deep end with no official training, but what Porter had realized rather quickly was that he wasn't without training. His father had trained him his whole life without Porter even realizing it.

Porter picked up the important facts quickly in the briefings as well as noting what was not in the folder. Willa Aldridge, twenty-eight years old, equestrian and businesswoman with an MBA. She attended the best schools in the country, was well spoken, had a reputation for knowing her stuff, but there were also rumbling about not being prepared to run a company at such a young age and being a woman. Reports from competitors and from inside Anancites cited nepotism as the reason for her quick climb up the corporate ladder, although all individual reports from people she worked with showed a woman who was highly capable and well-liked by her immediate staff.

When Porter turned his research to the horse world, he found out more about her. She was not a demanding participant. She didn't request special favors and she didn't throw fits if she lost. There were no reports of her mistreating her staff, event employees, or her horses. That last one told Porter more about her than the rest of the report. You could tell a lot about a person with how they treated their horse.

Porter had also spent the night practicing with Miss Trix and reading up on the rules of reining. Through his research, he found one of the top reiners was retired rodeo star Levi Eaton. Levi would be his best angle into this world. Levi would give Porter reining credibility while Porter's cousin, Sydney Davies McKnight, would stop by later today to visit during practice to give him credibility in the ritzy side of jumping. Sydney was a former model and had her own fashion empire now. Porter had run the names of the show jumpers by her and she'd known several of them, including Willa Aldridge. Porter had smirked when he'd learned that. Take that, Agent Naylor, Keeneston's spy network for the win.

"Name," the security guard asked as he held a tablet.

"Porter Davies."

"You're in Barn A, stall 7. Here's your welcome packet with your ID, practice information, and parking passes," the guard said, handing him a thick envelope with his name printed on it.

Porter took it and followed the traffic as the sun began to rise. Apparently the CIA could pull rank. Barn A was the biggest one and was the closest to the arena.

Each barn had reserved unloading spaces for the trailers. Porter pulled into the last opening and a barn staffer jogged over to him. "I'm sorry, this is a reserved barn."

Porter handed him the ID from the package that listed his barn and gave him access to the entire event. "Reining? You should be in Barn V." He ran his finger over the list of Barn A horses and riders. "Miss Trix, Porter Davies, stall 7. That's you. Huh."

"I was a late entry. I'm guessing they put me in the only open spot," Porter said with a shrug.

"Then you're in the right place. Where are your grooms so we can get your horse unloaded?"

Porter smiled at the worker. "It's just me and I can unload her all on my own. I bet you won't hear that much today."

Porter earned a slight uptick in the man's lips. "I'll help you then, or at least show you to your stall."

"Thanks so much." Porter opened the door to his truck and held out his hand to the man. "Porter Davies."

The man looked flustered for a second but then shook Porter's hand. "Jacob Herrera."

"Nice to meet you, Jacob. Thanks for the help." Porter opened the trailer and had Miss Trix at the stall within minutes. There were two empty stalls between his area and an elegantly set area with a Cherry Blossom Farm banner overhead. Cherry Blossom Farm was Willa Aldridge's stable. He knew she'd named it in honor of her mother. Porter had read an article about how every spring they would walk through the park to see the cherry blossoms.

Miss Trix sauntered happily into her stall as Jacob set down the saddle he'd carried in. "Anything else I can help you with?"

"I've got it from here. Thanks a lot." Porter had some more equipment to bring in, but he was used to doing it all himself.

Thirty minutes later, his area was set up. He was done right in time, too, because walking by Miss Trix's stall was none other than his target.

6

Willa's bodyguards checked the area before she walked inside. Everyone there had a badge and had been cleared. She'd flown in on her private jet early that morning and now all she wanted to do was to get settled.

"Why don't you all go get breakfast?" Willa said to her security team as she stopped in front of Apollo's stall. Her area took up three stalls in a line. Her groom would sleep in the stall next to Apollo at night to guard him. Then there was all the grooming and show equipment. They also created a little sitting area between Apollo's stall and the next one.

Willa glanced to the left to find a groom in jeans and a cowboy hat sweeping up the area in front of the next stall. It was only a glance but she'd be stealing a few more. She only saw his backside and that sent a bit of a jolt to her pulse. Willa couldn't wait for him to turn around.

"If you're sure, ma'am," Reggie said, drawing her attention away from the groom. Reggie was a six-foot-three former pro football lineman and head of her security team.

Willa tried not to groan. They were doing their jobs, but

it was strange to be surrounded constantly. The lack of privacy was making her anxious and the last thing she needed was for Apollo to sense her agitation. "I'm sure."

"Deshaun will stay at the entrance to give you some space." Reggie said, realizing her need for privacy. Deshaun, a former military man turned bodyguard, was quiet and regularly took the sentry position. "Just call out if you need him. Can we bring you back anything?" Reggie nodded his head to Barry, the last of her security team. Barry was a short man with a shaved head and just a scruff of a beard. He also had shoulders wider than the stall door. He was a former MMA fighter, and while he looked preppy, he was deadly.

"I'll take an orange juice if they have any and an apple for Apollo. Thank you, Reggie."

Willa took a deep breath and her team walked away. She began checking the setup to make sure it was how she liked it. Her barn team was amazing so it was no surprise everything was right where it should be. Willa walked over to Apollo who happily stuck his head out of the stall for some snuggles.

"Hello, love. Did you have a good trip?" Willa cooed as she rubbed her hand up and down his neck, her forehead against his.

Apollo nuzzled her with his head and moved his lips over her shirt. "I don't have any treats right now, love." Willa laughed, but Apollo wasn't taking no for an answer. "Okay, I'll see if anyone has anything to hold you over until your apple arrives."

Willa turned and looked around. She saw a different groom to the right setting up and was going to ask him until she saw the banner the groom was raising—Callum. What she'd give for him to retire and never talk to her again. Willa turned back to the groom with the great butt to find him standing on a stepstool hanging his own banner.

Well, this gave her the chance to see his front. Willa headed toward him after Apollo nuzzled her again, only this time more forcefully. He wanted his treat now.

Willa walked over to her sitting area. Only a small loveseat separated her from the sexy groom. Willa didn't want to surprise the man who was standing on the stepstool with his back toward her, so she waited for him to step down.

"Have you thought about my proposal? I need a number, Miss Aldridge."

Willa's heart stopped dead in her chest. The voice was the man from Florida.

"How much for the skeleton key?" the man she thought might be Mr. Dickerson asked again.

Willa glanced down the barn to find Deshaun talking to someone. His back was to hers, but she could scream.

"Don't think about it. I'll shoot your horse before you can call out to your security team."

Willa turned slightly to her side to look at the man. If she wasn't sure about the voice, she was sure once she saw him. It was the same nondescript man from Florida, only this time he had a gun in his hand. The gun was in his folded arms mostly covered by a staff windbreaker, but was pointed at Apollo. He was wearing the official event staff polo and ball cap, complete with an all-access badge. He could blend into the crowd in a second if needed.

"There are two ways this plays out, Miss Aldridge. One, you give me a number to take back to my boss. Or two, we kill your father and take it. What's your answer?"

Willa looked into the average-brown eyes of the average-height man. She had to keep him talking in hopes Deshaun would turn around and see her in distress. "Your boss? Are you from SynCrypt? Is Weldon behind this?" Willa asked as anger began to course through her. Someone was threatening her father, her horse, and her company, and she wasn't going to stand for it.

Willa moved to step into the line of sight between the man and Apollo. The shot would be harder to make now. He'd have to shoot over her or through her.

"It doesn't matter who my boss is. What matters is if I shoot your horse now or not. Did you say goodbye to your father? He'll be dead with one text from me. Now, Miss Aldridge, which is it going to be?"

Willa's bravado was fading as her brain ran a mile a minute and none of what she was thinking was helpful. Images of her father, Apollo, the company, the work, the contract, what the skeleton key in the wrong hands could do —they all ran through her head, but not a single thing that could help her right now. She needed to tackle him, or punch him, or . . .

"Umph!"

Willa was knocked backward by a heavy weight. She stumbled and then fell right on her ass as the man threatening her was kicked in the head. The heavy weight of a man in her lap had her pinned to the ground. His legs were now tangled with hers, his bottom was in her lap, and his back was pressed against her chest.

"Dammit," the man cursed with a deep voice that vibrated through her body. "I am so sorry. Is anyone hurt?"

Willa tried to look at the man with the gun, but couldn't see him around the cowboy hat. The handsome groom had landed his sexy butt right in her lap and was blocking her from seeing anything.

"We'll discuss this later, Miss Aldridge," Willa heard the man say.

"I'm so sorry. My boot got you right in the face. Are you sure you're okay? That stupid stepstool just slid right out from under me," the groom said from where he was still sitting in her lap. He hadn't tried to move once. Willa knew this because right now she realized she had grabbed his upper arms with her hands and was currently feeling some very nice biceps. Not once had the sexy butt or the ripped arms tried to move.

"It's fine."

Willa assumed the man left since the groom's head turned slightly as if watching him.

"Miss Aldridge!" Deshaun called out as he raced forward. The man who had threatened Willa had probably walked right by him. "Get off her!"

The groom was hauled to his feet and Willa got a nice up-close look at his backside in the worn jeans. It was even better up close. "It's okay, Deshaun. Just an accident." She didn't want her bodyguard taking out the man who had inadvertently protected her.

"I'm so sorry. Are you hurt?" the groom asked as he turned around and held out his hand after Deshaun let go of him.

Willa saw brown hair with some natural dark blond streaks in it under his cowboy hat. She shifted her gaze from his head to his face. He had a strong jaw and hazel eyes that leaned more toward brown than green and were looking down at her worriedly. "I'm fine. Are you hurt?" Willa asked.

The quirk of the man's lips told her he thought it was cute she thought anything could hurt him. Willa placed her hand in his and felt the roughness of his palm and the warmth of his fingers as his large hand wrapped around hers. He gave her a little pull and Willa practically flew to a standing position. She'd felt his muscles when he was in her lap, but now she felt them in action. He was actually stronger than he looked where Deshaun probably looked stronger than he really was.

Willa was five foot eight, and this man had her looking up at him. He didn't let go of her hand as she stood chest to chest with him. Instead he smiled down at her with a mischievous grin as if he knew something she didn't.

"Miss Aldridge, what happened?" Deshaun asked. He stood at the ready to rip the man away from her at the slightest threat.

"It was my fault," the man said finally, dropping her hand and turning to Deshaun. "I was hanging my banner and thought I could reach back a little ways to anchor it, but the darn stool tipped and I landed on Miss Aldridge."

"Have we met? How did you know my name?" Willa asked suspiciously.

The man's grin widened. "Because your friend here hollered it through the barn. And no, we haven't met. However, I can remedy that. Porter Davies." The man held his hand back out and Willa shook it, feeling embarrassed at being suspicious.

"Willa Aldridge," Willa said, waiting for that moment when all the pieces fell into place and they realized she was a wealthy heiress. She waited, but it didn't come. There was no OMG moment, as she called it. Instead Porter just shook her hand.

"Nice to meet ya." Then he turned toward Deshaun. "Porter Davies."

"Deshaun Stokes."

"Military?" Porter asked.

"Yes, sir. You?"

"No, but I know the look. I have lots of friends and family in the military."

Porter's gaze then moved to Apollo. He brushed past Willa and stopped in front of her horse. He spoke softly to Apollo as she moved to join him. His hand rested on Apollo's forehead as she tried to hear what Porter was saying. Apollo tossed his head back in full show-off mode and then hit Porter's shoulder with his nose.

Porter laughed and Willa watched in wonder as her horse instantly fell in love with the groom when he pulled a sugar cube from his pocket. "Can I give him this?"

"Sure," Willa answered as she watched in wonder as her horse acted as if he and this groom had been best friends forever. Maybe she should offer him a job. "Apollo doesn't normally like strangers. I might have to hire you away from your current boss."

"That would be hard to do," Porter said, turning around as her horse tried to lick him like a dog. Apollo's big tongue came out and slurped up the side of Porter's face as Willa stood dumbfounded. Porter just laughed and hugged Apollo's head against his own.

"Whatever your boss pays you, I will double it," Willa said in wonder as Apollo went in for another kiss. Not only was this man the sexiest cowboy she'd ever seen, he clearly had a way with horses. Willa was ready to do anything it took to keep Porter Davies in her life. No, wait, her horse's life. Yeah, that was it.

7

Willa's picture in the file the CIA had on her didn't do her justice. Porter had overheard the man making threats as he was spying on Willa. Porter snapped a picture of the man with his cell phone and then thrown himself into the middle of it. Literally.

He'd thought about taking out the man, but he didn't want to put Willa's father at risk. So he'd opted to jump her, and not in the way he really wanted. But he did enjoy the feel of her beneath him. If only he were turned around and they were naked.

From that little bit of spying, Porter had learned Willa was being forced into an impossible position. She wasn't a traitor. She was being forced to choose between her father's life and the key. Yet she still hadn't answered right away and Porter had prevented her from having to do so. He knew Naylor would want clear evidence and was afraid this wasn't going to be enough for the agent.

Porter didn't know whether to be insulted or take it as a compliment that the gorgeous woman he was contemplating jumping in a whole other way thought he was a groom and was trying to hire him.

Now it was time to set it straight. He reached up to pet her horse as Apollo took his large tongue and slobbered all over Porter's cheek again. "As much as I would love to work for you, maybe I should tell you more about me. Porter Davies, owner of PD Rodeo Farm. I'm riding in the reining event." He loved the way Willa's emotions played out over her face. First there was embarrassment and then confusion. "Yeah, I know. Wrong barn. Apparently there was a mess up and they put me here." Porter shrugged and Apollo used his nose to push off his cowboy hat.

"I am so sorry. I just assumed you were the groom."

"It's okay," he said with a grin. "You'll learn we cowboys don't need any help handling a mare." Her cheeks were stained red with her blush. She'd read his grin correctly. "Want to meet my mare?"

"Your wife is here?" Willa gasped in a whisper looking around for some woman to rush out and accuse her of hitting on her husband.

Porter had to laugh. He felt bad, but it was too funny. "My actual mare, Miss Trix." Porter gestured to his stall where his sweet Trix was giving Apollo her best mane toss.

"Oh my gosh. I just keep putting my foot in my mouth with you."

Porter laughed again to show her there were no hard feelings. Plus, she was plain adorable when flustered. He had to guess she wasn't flustered often. She certainly wasn't with the man threatening her.

"Don't worry about it. In case you're wondering, there are no mares or fillies in my life besides Miss Trix."

Porter turned his back on her as he walked to Miss Trix's stall. He felt Willa behind him and Miss Trix looked out around him to see the new person coming to meet her. "She's my reining horse."

"I must admit I don't know much about the event. How did you get involved with reining?" Willa asked as she let Trix sniff her open palm.

"Through work. I did a little rodeoing and worked on my parents' farm my entire life. We work the herd and then we farm hands would have competitions. I actually didn't even know this was a thing until recently."

"A thing? You think this is just a thing?" Willa asked in amazement.

"It is a thing. It can be a big thing or a small thing. To you it may be a job. To someone else it may be a way of life. Either way, it's a thing. To me it's a fun thing. I live nearby and Miss Trix loves it. So we're here," Porter explained. "What's your story? What kind of thing is this for you?"

Willa looked as if she thought about it before answering. "I understand what you're saying. I'd say it's a big thing. My mother jumped growing up. Never anything like this. Just small shows. When she died, I used it as a way to stay connected to her. So it's a big thing to me."

"So, it's a heart thing," Porter said kindly. "Is this your career, too?"

Willa looked shocked that someone would ask her that. He only knew her name and what she did because of the CIA. Otherwise he'd have asked her the same thing, so he went with it. He wasn't about to blow his cover within the first hour. "No, I work in the family business."

"So do I. Well, kind of. My farm is part of my parents' farm. They raise cattle and I raise rodeo horses. When I'm not working my farm, I work my parents' farm with my dad."

"What about your mom?"

Porter didn't want to get into the fact his mother was a famous writer whose books were turned into blockbuster movies. Willa wouldn't be impressed. She probably met famous people all the time and probably got tired of people name-dropping. He'd let his friends and family do that for him. "She helps some. So," Porter said, running his hand through his hair. "This is embarrassing, but I've never done an event like this before. Would you mind showing me around a little?"

Willa smiled and he could see her whole body relax. "Sure. It will be fun to see it through the eyes of a newbie."

Porter pretended not to notice the bodyguard following discreetly behind them as Willa showed him the jumping ring, the warm-up area, the reining and dressage ring, the riders' only dining area, and the all the other behind-the-scenes facilities.

"Willa!" a woman shouted with excitement.

Porter turned and saw the huge smile on Willa's face as she watched the woman with blonde hair run toward her. He recognized her from the CIA packet. This was Willa's best friend. They hugged and then Willa remembered Porter was there when the woman kept glancing over at him. "Do you have a new groom?" she whispered to Willa.

Willa blushed again and finally turned to face Porter. "Porter Davies, meet my best friend, Tilly Bradford."

Porter held out his hand and shook Tilly's. "Nice to meet you, ma'am."

Tilly's eyes widened a little as she looked to Willa for an explanation on why she was with a cowboy. "Porter is a rider in the reining event. He accidentally got placed next to me in the jumper barn. It's also his first big event so I'm showing him around."

"So, do you have a girlfriend? Or a boyfriend? Or

anyone?" Tilly asked with a wink to Willa who looked ready to die on the spot.

"Tilly," Willa groaned as if begging her friend to stop the interrogation.

"Sorry, someone has to look out for your social life. You know," Tilly said, looking at Porter with a smile. "Willa doesn't have a boyfriend. She's all work and no play. I bet you'd be great at playing. So, about your love life?"

Porter grinned. Tilly reminded him of his sisters and he liked her instantly. "My previous job wasn't really conducive to relationships, so I'm single. Don't get many single men at these things?"

Tilly rolled her eyes and huffed out a breath. "Hardly ever. Or if they are, they're jerks. So a hot single guy who isn't an arrogant jerk? You're going to be swarmed. Oh Willa, we have to save the poor man from Marguerite and Valentina. They'll chew him up and spit him out before he even knows what happened."

"Thank you for your concern, ladies. I'm pretty sure I can handle anything thrown my way."

"What about slithering your way?" Tilly asked and Willa smacked her.

"Tilly, that's not nice," Willa admonished.

Tilly shrugged, then turned back to Porter. "So, do you have a brother?"

Porter laughed out loud then. "Are you sure you're not a Davies? You'd so fit into my family," he joked as they turned and headed back toward the barn. "I have two older twin sisters and a twin brother."

Tilly fanned herself. "Does he ride, too?"

"He does. He retired from the rodeo and became a US marshal," Porter told them. Tilly about swooned and Porter laughed out loud.

"Is he single? Please tell me he's single," Tilly begged.

"As far as I know he is," Porter told her, knowing Parker was going to either kill him or hug him for this.

"Is he coming to watch you ride?" Tilly asked.

Porter shrugged as they entered the barn. "Probably. My family is pretty close so he'll most likely stop by with my sisters, parents, brothers-in-law, and a whole slew of cousins. Too many to really count."

"Sweet mother, a huge family filled with men like you? Willa, did I die and go to heaven?" Tilly asked her friend before her whole attitude changed. Suddenly, sassy outgoing Tilly shrank into herself as her smile fell. Willa's back straightened and her jaw clenched. Just like Tilly, her smile fell from her face.

Porter was on instant alert as two men and two women strutted forward. He recognized them from the CIA case file. The taller man, who was still a good four inches shorter than Porter, was Callum Harding. The weaselly-looking man with the slicked-back hair and body that had never lifted weights was Cyril Van Doren. His family made their money through generations of Dutch financial leaders. The woman with the light brown slicked-back ponytail was Marguerite Borghese. Her parents were winery owners in France but raised their daughter in the US half of the year while they ran wineries in the States as well. Last was the olive-skinned and black-haired Valentina Bianchi from Italy. Her family made engines for the top luxury cars in the world and had for three generations.

Marguerite lifted her nose as if she smelled a stench. "Hanging out with the help? You two can't find any friends in our circle because you're so pathetic you have to resort to paid company." The group tittered as if they were the funniest people in the world.

Porter just smiled and rocked back on his cowboy boots. Women like Marguerite were a dime a dozen. He'd seen them on the sets of his mother's movies that starred their longtime family friend and America's Sweetheart, Taylor Everett. He'd seen it when he was in Nashville with Taylor and Trey's son, Holt, who was a country music singer. He also saw it when he'd gone to support his cousin Sydney, who had been a model.

"Look, the help thinks it's funny," Cyril said as he pointed at Porter with a smirk and a chuckle.

"I do," Porter said in his deep voice. "It's hilarious y'all don't realize I'm laughing at you. You're the ones who are so insecure about yourselves you have to put others down to make yourselves feel better. Talk about pathetic. Oh, and uh, man-to-man," Porter said, leaning closer to Cyril, "I wouldn't wear tight pants that showed what a small package you have, or at least put a sock in there or something. Ladies," Porter said to Tilly and Willa with a smile as he held an arm out to each. "Shall we?"

"We shall," Willa said with a big grin as she slipped her arm through his.

8

Porter Davies was her hero. He had fallen in her lap and saved her from someone trying to blackmail her. He hadn't treated her differently when he learned her name. He was nice to Tilly. And he'd put her ex and his minions in their place. In her mind, there was no one sexier than Porter Davies.

She and Tilly stood at the rail and watched as he practiced reining with Miss Trix. She needed to leave soon to look at both the farms her father had found and also several buildings for the mobile encryption headquarters. However, she'd noticed that Porter had watched her and Tilly practice. When the two of them saw him taking Miss Trix to his competition arena, they had rushed to watch. And ogle.

"I heard that sigh," Tilly teased as they leaned against the rail, watching Porter effortlessly put Miss Trix through her paces.

"I mean, look at him. The men in our event aren't anything like him. He's, like, real."

Tilly giggled. "There's no sock in those jeans. Have you looked him up yet?"

Willa shook her head as she heard Reggie muffle a laugh behind her. "Not yet."

"I need to look up his brother." Tilly sighed dramatically before they both broke out into giggles. "Want to grab lunch?"

"I wish. I have a meeting with a potential sponsor. Wish me luck." Willa took one last look at Porter before hugging her best friend and taking off with her three bodyguards in tow.

The drive to the newly constructed office buildings near the airport took about twenty minutes. She got to see the city of Lexington as they drove through it to meet the real estate agent.

"You guys can drop me off. I'll text you when it's okay to pick me up. I don't want to draw suspicion. Coming in with three bodyguards would be a little suspicious."

Reggie nodded but when she went to unbuckle, so did Barry. "I'll be your sole guard. You can tell her I'm your assistant."

He didn't give her time to say no as he stepped out of the car and opened the door for her. Luckily, they'd beat the agent there and didn't have to explain the SUV full of big hulking men.

"This is nice," Barry said as he looked around.

It was nice. There were several buildings spread out with green space between and around them. There even looked to be a dog park off to one side. Some of the buildings were large four-story structures while others were smaller two-story ones. Willa thought about their current needs and decided that two floors would be plenty for now.

She turned as she heard a car approaching. A peppy woman with a big smile got out of the car. "Hello! I'm Kimberly Dial with Dial Realty, where we're always dialed into the deals! You must be Miss Aldridge."

Willa shook Kimberly's hand. "I am. Thank you for showing me the property. This is my assistant, Barry."

Thirty minutes later they were off to look at more locations with Kimberly. Willa and Barry walked around more buildings than she cared to admit, but none of them compared to the first location. They'd also toured two horse farms and were almost to the third.

"And this is the farm I was telling you about earlier." Kimberly pulled up to an old cattle farm outside of town. However, it was only about twenty minutes from the first office building, so the commute wouldn't be bad.

The drive out to the farm had been beautiful too. Willa opened the door and took a deep breath of fresh air. In its current state, the farm was a blank slate and images of the horse farm of her dreams began popping up.

"It's one hundred fifteen acres in Lexington. There's a large pond over to your left that would be perfect to build a house near. Then all that land back there is pretty flat up to the property boundary," Kimberly told her. "What do you think?"

Willa took a deep breath and looked around the property. She could see the buildings in her head. "I'm ready to make an offer. I want the first office buildings and this farm. Draw up the papers and my lawyer will handle the rest. Thank you, Kimberly."

∾

Porter was brushing out Miss Trix when he felt the shadows fall over him. Callum and Cyril were without the two women and had each taken a pose leaning against the stall door with their arms crossed over their chests.

"You can never have her. You know that, don't you?" Callum asked as if it were unthinkable Willa would ever go for a man like Porter.

Porter just kept brushing Miss Trix.

"Can you imagine? An heiress and a groom?" Cyril snorted at the idea.

"She's only talking to you to make me jealous. We dated in high school and then I cut her loose and she's never gotten over it," Callum told him. "I'll take her back eventually when I'm ready to use her trust fund. But until then, it's fun to watch her trying to win me back."

Porter scoffed as he finally looked at Callum. "You're delusional. You really should see a doctor about that."

Callum shoved off the stall door and tried to tower over Porter, but it didn't work since Porter was inches taller and pounds of muscle heavier. "You're the delusional one if you think you have a chance with her. Stay away from her."

"Or?" Porter challenged in a dangerously calm tone. Willa might be his job, but damned if he didn't love talking to her too. Then there was the fact that she was stunning and all he wanted to do was peel those tight riding pants off her.

"I'll talk to your boss and have you fired. I'll make sure you never get a job in the horse industry ever again," Callum threatened as Porter just smirked.

"Porter Davies!" a deep, mature voice said from behind them. "I didn't believe it when I heard talk in the barn you were here."

"It looks like there's a party going on," Porter heard

Willa's voice call out from where she'd just arrived back. He'd lost her that morning and had been worried.

Porter set down his brush and pushed past Callum and Cyril to slap the man's back who had just arrived. "How the hell are you, Levi? I haven't seen you since the pro rodeo championship in Texas five years ago."

"I'm great. Reining is a lot easier on the body than rodeoing." Levi Eaton had been the rodeo champion that year and then announced his retirement, just like Porter had done recently. The only difference was Levi was a good fifteen years older than Porter and rodeoed up until he was forty.

"I hear that. Hey, meet my stall neighbor," Porter said, walking toward Willa and leaving Callum and Cyril behind. He felt them following along. They had to be intrigued. Everyone knew Levi. He'd made rodeo mainstream. His name had been everywhere. "Willa Aldridge, meet my friend Levi Eaton. He's the best rodeo rider in the history of the sport."

Willa smiled kindly and shook his hand. "Yes, I've heard of you. It's nice to meet you."

"You too," Levi said, releasing her hand. "Although, I was the best. This guy toppled my best scores this past year before claiming the championship in bull riding *and* bronc riding." Levi slapped Porter on the shoulder before turning to him. "Best year of rodeoing I've ever seen. How are you feeling after the throw from Outlawed Wreck?"

"I'm fully recovered, but I went ahead with retirement," Porter told him as he saw Callum and Cyril on their phones. They were probably looking him up after hearing Levi talk about him.

"I saw you on Sam Winchell's show announcing your retirement. It's a hard decision to make." Levi frowned as if thinking about his retirement. "But it was probably the right one."

"You're Porter Davies," Callum sputtered as he looked up from his phone. Porter glanced over at Willa to notice she was watching everyone with curiosity. "Sorry about thinking you were the groom, man."

Porter ignored him and turned back to Levi and Willa. "It was a tough decision. My cousin and mother talked me into it, though. Go out on top, have my health, and all that."

Levi nodded in understanding. "Miss it?"

"Every damn day," Porter answered honestly.

"Is that why you're doing reining?" Willa asked after being quiet most of the conversation.

"Part of it. My cousin is my doctor and threatened to disown me if I didn't retire. The risk of injury in reining is real low so I thought it would be a good fit." Porter felt bad for lying, but he had to talk to Naylor to find out if he should tell Willa why he was really there or not.

"Actually, I'm really glad you're here. I was going to drive out to your farm to talk to you. My daughter just turned sixteen and is getting serious about her roping. I've heard your farm is raising the best rodeo horses around now. Do you have any roping horses for sale?"

"For you, I wish I did. I have a three-year waitlist. I'm hoping to expand the farm so I can have more horses. However, if you find a horse, I'll train it for you." Porter told him.

"This man is the best," Levi said to Willa as he shook Porter's hand. "I have to get going for the night. I'll see you tomorrow and introduce you around."

"Thanks, Levi. 'Night." Porter turned to see Willa glancing behind her at Callum's setup.

The minions were there talking in hushed whispers.

Valentina caught Porter looking and smiled flirtatiously at him. "So, cowboy, want to come to dinner with us? I want to hear all about how hard you ride."

"Sorry, Willa and I already have plans." He saw Willa's eyes go wide as he smiled mischievously at her. Her back was rigid and she dared not turn around to see the reactions. But Porter saw them. Callum frowned while Valentina and Marguerite looked pissed. "Shall we?"

Porter took Willa's arm in his hand as Apollo's night groom moved to brush him down and feed him. Willa plastered on a fake smile, grabbed her things, and walked stiffly out the door with him.

"You don't have to take me out to dinner. I know you were just using me as an excuse," Willa said as her three bodyguards fell into line behind her.

"The only excuse that afforded me was the opportunity to ask you out. So, how about it? Want to taste Kentucky as only a local can show you?" Willa beamed at him and Porter felt the same heart-pounding excitement he got when he rode a bronc. "I'd love to drive you, but the choice is yours."

Willa's smile faded a bit as she cast a glance at the three men behind her. "So you noticed them?"

"They're kind of hard to miss." Porter said in a way she knew he wasn't upset.

"I'd like to ride with you," Willa said but sounded doubtful.

"Give me a sec," Porter told her before turning and headed back to the group of bodyguards.

"Can we help you?" the leader asked.

"I'm Porter Davies. I've met Deshaun already."

"Reggie Wall," the leader answered, as they shook hands.

"Barry Gruen."

Porter turned back to Reggie since he was clearly the man in charge. "I'm taking Willa out to dinner at my cousin's restaurant here in Lexington," he said, rattling off the address. "I know you don't know me, but you can trust me. You played pro football, right?" Reggie nodded. "Our really good family friends own the Lexington Thoroughbreds— Will Ashton and Mohtadi Ali Rahman. My good friends are Colt and Holt Everett. Their father is the coach and former player, Trey Everett."

Porter then turned to Deshaun. "You were military. My father and uncles own the Keeneston Training Center. My unofficial uncle is Ahmed." Porter paused and let that sink in. Every soldier learned about Ahmed. "Yes, that Ahmed. My cousin was Delta Force, my cousin-in-law was DEVGRU, another cousin is Ryan Parker, who is the special agent in charge of Lexington's FBI office, and my brother-in-law is the sheriff of Keeneston. I am very connected to this area. I am not a threat to Willa."

Porter turned to Barry and shrugged. "Sorry, I don't have any MMA connections."

Barry smirked while Reggie and Deshaun looked shell-shocked.

"So, I'm asking that you trust me and follow us to the restaurant so I can take Willa on a date. She wants to ride with me. Can you all allow that?" Porter finally asked, getting around to the point of the conversation.

"You really know Ahmed?" Deshaun asked finally.

Porter pulled up his phone and hit the call button. "Good evening, Porter. What can I do for you?"

"What are you up to, Ahmed?" Porter asked as he held the phone up for everyone to see.

"I am walking Nemi. She was a good girl and ripped the balls off a dummy at the training center today. I have to keep her trained in case your cousin hurts my daughter."

"You love Dylan," Porter reminded him.

"What do you and the three men around you need?" Ahmed asked instead of admitting he loved his son-in-law, even though it was obvious to everyone around they both loved each other very much.

"How did you know there were three of us?" Deshaun asked.

"I am Ahmed."

Porter pressed his lips together to stop from laughing. "These three are bodyguards for Willa Aldridge. I want to take her to Landon's restaurant and they need to know they can trust me. Deshaun is former military," Porter said as if that explained everything, which, for Ahmed, it did.

"You can trust Porter. You can trust any Davies from Keeneston."

"Thanks, Ahmed," Porter said, looking to the bodyguards who were whispering to each other.

"So, a date?" Ahmed asked.

"*Crrrr*. Sorry, you're breaking *crrrrshhhhh* up. I can't hear *crrrrshhh*." Porter hung up and seconds later his phone pinged with a notification a bet had been made on the Blossom Café Betting App.

The three elderly Rose sisters had always taken bets at their café. Then when their very much younger cousins came to help them out, they convinced the old bookies to switch to an app. Bets were placed and winners won part of the pot. The Rose sisters doled the rest of the pot out to the town or people in need at the end of the year.

"Okay, we'll follow you. Don't try to lose us," Reggie warned.

Porter walked back to Willa and reached for her hand.

He laced his fingers through hers and smiled down at her. "Shall we?"

Porter almost laughed at Willa's surprised glance back to the bodyguards as they got into their own SUV. However, he was too consumed with the feel of her soft, small hand in his to laugh.

9

"The bet makes so much sense now," Landon Davies whispered to Porter as he showed them to the table in the back.

"Shut up," Porter hissed back to his cousin. Landon only smirked in return.

Porter had texted Landon that he needed a private table and that he'd be at the new restaurant in twenty minutes. Landon had apparently told his staff to notify him when Porter arrived, because two seconds after Porter walked in, Landon came out of the kitchen to greet him.

"Is this table okay?" Landon asked Willa who smiled at him.

"It's great. I had no idea it was Porter's cousin who was the head chef. A rodeo rider, a US marshal, a chef . . . what an interesting family you all have. And big!" Willa said, looking like she actually wanted to know more about them.

"You have no idea," Landon muttered.

"There are three guys out front in an SUV," Porter said, ignoring his cousin's muttering. "Could you send some dinner out to them?"

"Of course," Landon told Porter before turning back to Willa. "So, how did you meet this guy?"

"His reining horse accidentally got put in the stall next to my show jumper at the Lexington Equestrian Event. Then he literally fell into my lap." Willa laughed as she told Landon the story of him falling off the ladder. The quick look Landon sent Porter said he didn't believe a word of it.

"How funny. The family can't wait to see Porter in his event. Porter starts his competition tomorrow, but when do you jump?" Landon asked.

"I start next week. Although I got some practice in today and I'll get some more in here and there. I could have flown in later, but I like to get a feel for the area. It makes Apollo more comfortable. So for these huge events, you'll usually see us jumpers here up to a week early."

"How many days do you compete?" Landon asked as the waitress filled the water glasses.

"There're three separate jumping competitions before an overall champion is named. Tuesday is the official practice day in the main arena. Wednesday is the Speed Competition. It's all about completing the course the cleanest and the fastest.

"Thursday is the start of the Team Competition that runs for two days. There's no clock, it's all about cleanest runs. I'll get scored on the number of penalties I receive, and at the end of the Team Competition, the three team members with the lowest penalties will use those scores to count as the team's total. The team with the lowest penalties wins. Also, the thirty best individual scores will move on to the Individual Competition. Hopefully, I wrap up on the following Sunday." Willa laughed at Landon's expression after finishing her schedule. "I know. It's a lot."

"I'm sure the family will figure it out and be there

cheering you on," Landon said kindly. As much as Porter dreaded the family interrogation that was sure to follow, he would be glad to have backup there if needed.

"You would come to watch me?" Willa asked, sounding surprised.

"Well, sure," Porter answered. "My family is—"

"Invested in marrying us all off," Landon said with a laugh. "I've received no fewer than six texts from the family, asking about Porter's date already."

Willa's eyes widened in surprise and both Landon and Porter watched carefully as she processed that.

"She didn't run. That's a good sign. Now how about dinner?" Landon asked.

"Porter mentioned Kentucky favorites?" Willa asked.

Landon nodded. "I know exactly what to make you then. It was great meeting you, Willa."

"You too," Willa smiled up at him. After Landon walked back into the kitchen, she turned her eyes to Porter. "He was kidding about your family, right?"

Porter groaned as he slumped back in his chair. "Normally, first dates evolve into second, third, and then there might be months before you meet the family. I'm sorry. You'll probably meet a lot of them tomorrow. It's a big family. My grandparents have six kids who all have kids and even some of my cousins now have kids of their own. I can take you home right now. You won't hurt my feelings."

Willa shook her head. "No, it's nice. It will be a pleasure if they're anything like your cousin. I was an only child. I loved it, but I'd always wondered what it would be like to have a big family."

"You won't have to wonder much longer," Porter laughed.

Kentucky Burgoo was served first. As they ate the stew

filled with meat and vegetables, Porter asked her about her job. She was vague. She worked for her father's company. She was the face of it since she'd been into business and marketing.

She didn't say who her father was and Porter didn't push. After all, he was hiding the real reason he had asked her out. However, as the date went on, Porter was forgetting the real reason he was with her. Willa had a dry sense of humor, was crazy smart, and loved horses. It was the girlfriend trifecta for Porter.

The waitress brought out Landon's signature hot brown. In Kentucky, hot browns were a classic. They were served in diners, five-star restaurants, and every place in between. Landon had wanted to take the staples of Southern cooking and elevate them. Traditionally, this open-faced sandwich was made with a piece of bread, turkey, a slice of ham, smothered in a cheesy Mornay sauce, and topped with bacon and tomato. Landon used two truffle rolls topped with shaved turkey and ham. Then he used a Mornay sauce with smoked gouda, gruyere, and provolone cheese before topping it off with a slice of tomato and applewood-smoked bacon.

Porter laughed as Willa looked at it with curiosity. "What is it?"

"Just try it," Porter urged.

Willa cut into it and moaned the second she tasted it. Porter was lost. His mind went straight to his pants. "This is divine," Willa said before digging in with enthusiasm.

The conversation never faltered until they realized they were the last two in the restaurant. Porter reached across the table and held out his hand. He smiled when she placed hers in his while they talked about horses. The empty dessert plate with two spoons was the only thing left on the table as the restaurant began to shut down.

"What are you doing back here?" Landon's raised voice caught Porter's attention a moment before the door from the kitchen to the dining area was shoved open.

The man Porter had scared off was back.

Willa froze in fear. She'd had the best first date she could have ever imagined. There was no talk about money, power, what her father was doing next, or what her family could do for him. Willa and Porter talked about growing up, family, funny stories, what she was interested in, and horses. Porter listened and asked questions. She never felt as if they were boring each other or, worse, that it was a job interview. Quite the opposite. Neither wanted the date to end.

But now Dickerson was there and he'd ruin everything. Not only was the threat to her and her father very real, she knew Porter would take one look at the danger her life was in and run for the hills. Not that she could blame him.

"Tick-tock, Miss Aldridge. My boss needs your answer now," Dickerson said as he stepped up to the table.

Willa's eyes shot to Porter, who looked rather calm, and then back to Landon who stood by the kitchen door watching with interest.

Willa shook her head, not knowing what to do or say. She couldn't hand over the skeleton key. Every undercover CIA agent around the globe would be in danger if she did. It was an impossible decision. She had thought she'd be safe with her protection detail—a detail that was apparently no longer parked in front of the restaurant. The question was, did she protect her father or protect thousands of strangers? Willa had been trying to find a way to do both. Now her time was up and an answer hadn't appeared to her yet.

"Work thing?" Porter asked casually as he glanced up at the man who had threatened her numerous times now.

"I just need something from Miss Aldridge and then I'll be out of your hair and you can enjoy the rest of your date," Dickerson said to Porter while never taking his eyes off Willa.

Think. She needed to think. She needed to buy herself more time. She needed her guards to come rushing in and save her. She needed to protect everyone.

"Gosh," Porter said with more of a country accent than she'd ever heard him use. "Your boss must be real hardcore sending you out at night to jes' to pick sum'thin' up. It must be real important like. I don't understand half of what she talks about."

Willa blinked at Porter. Why was he sounding so different?

"You wouldn't," Dickerson muttered before turning back to Willa. "The key, now."

"That almost sounds like one of them"—Porter paused and looked as if he were thinking of the right word— "ultimatums."

The man looked irritatingly at Porter. "You know, that's a good idea. The key, Miss Aldridge, or I shoot him right here over dessert."

Willa's eyes went big at the sight of a gun suddenly pressed to Porter's head. Porter didn't look nearly as panicked as she was feeling. He glanced over to Landon, but gave him a very small shake of his head. It was so small she thought maybe she imagined it.

"I'm sorry." The words tumbled from her mouth as she

begged Porter to forgive her. "I can't give it to you. Who wants it? Why?"

"All you need to know is my boss wants it, and if you don't give me the key right now, I'll kill your date. Three," he said as he began to countdown.

Willa glanced desperately around looking for a weapon. She couldn't let him kill Porter, but the only thing near her was a single spoon.

"Two."

"I'm so sorry. Thousands would die if I give it to him," Willa said as tears began to stream down her face.

She watched in horror as the man flicked off the safety and stared at her, giving her one last chance to hand over the skeleton key. Her heart broke. She thought she was going to throw up. Her whole body was shaking to the point there looked to be two Porters.

"Last chance," the man warned.

Porter moved so suddenly Willa couldn't even make a squeak of surprise. One minute, he'd been seated in his chair with a gun pointed to his head and then the next second the gun had been knocked from the man's hand and a spoon was sticking out the side of the man's throat. Willa opened her mouth to scream as Dickerson grabbed at the spoon in surprise a second before a giant cast-iron skillet slammed into the back of his head. The man was flung forward over the table where he lay motionless.

Willa stared down at the body as blood dripped onto the floor. Her mouth was open, but nothing was coming out.

"Willa, sweetheart, answer me. Willa?"

It took a moment for Porter's voice to reach her through the shock. When she finally looked up, she found Porter by her side trying to get her attention.

"You used a spoon to kill him," Willa muttered.

"I'm pretty sure Landon helped with the skillet," Porter said as if it was no big deal. "Nice hit, Landon."

"Little league," Landon said with a shrug. "I can't wait to tell Uncle Miles you stabbed someone with a spoon. He's going to be so proud. He's going to torture your father with this for years."

The front door to the restaurant was flung open as her security ran in with guns pointing at Porter and Landon.

"No!" Willa finally managed to shout. "They saved me."

"Where were you guys?" Porter asked, standing up and rounding on the security detail in a cold fury.

"A cop came by and said we had to move," Reggie said, looking a little piqued when he saw the dead body.

"Is that a spoon in his neck?" Deshaun asked, sounding puzzled from where he was bent down examining the body.

"It was the only weapon I had," Porter said with a shrug.

"Bruh, a spoon isn't a weapon," Deshaun said, standing up.

"You'd never survive a Davies family dinner if you believed that. Plus, the dead body says otherwise," Porter told him with a shake of his head.

"Our Uncle Miles was former Delta Force or something badass," Landon said, stepping into the conversation. "He swears spoons are a very versatile weapon. Porter, Ryan will be here soon."

"We have to report this. This is so not good," Reggie muttered, pulling out his cell phone.

"Stop," Porter ordered and Willa's head snapped up, tearing her gaze away from the dead man. Memories of her mother's death flooded her. This wasn't like that, but it triggered her memories of the last dead body she'd seen. Every thought in her head was a riotous mess. Flashes of old images mixing with new and a state of disbelief and acceptance of what she was seeing made for a very muddled mind.

"Ryan Parker is the head of the local FBI office. This is not to be called in. Landon, take everyone into the kitchen. Get Willa something to drink for her shock while I lock up. We can't have people wandering into a crime scene," Porter ordered and everyone snapped to attention.

Willa felt Landon pulling at her arm, trying to get her out of the chair. He gave her a little tug, but she couldn't stop looking at the dead man. Finally someone just grabbed the chair and pulled it with her in it into the kitchen.

"Why isn't he freaking out? Why aren't you freaking out? Reggie is freaking out. Barry isn't. Deshaun looks confused." Willa was out of it. She just blurted whatever was coming to mind.

"Here. Drink this. It's some special tea from our hometown," Porter shoved a straw into her mouth. "Take a nice big long drink."

Willa complied as Landon used one hand to gently rub the base of her neck in a soothing motion. The tasty liquid went down easily and a minute later she began to relax. "Landon, why aren't you and Porter freaking out?"

"Come to a Davies family dinner and you'll understand," Landon said before shoving the straw back in her mouth.

"You kill people at dinner?" Willa asked before she took another long drink.

"Not usually, but some of the spouses feel a bit tortured. Here, have more," Landon said as he refilled her glass with the special tea.

10

Porter dialed the phone and Naylor answered on the second ring. "Have you learned anything yet?" Naylor asked as Porter locked the front door.

"Yeah. I learned my Uncle Miles was right and you can kill someone with a spoon. Although the cast iron skillet to the head probably helped."

The line was quiet for a second and then Naylor spoke slowly. "I think you need to explain."

Porter spoke quickly and quietly as he laid it out for Naylor. "I can get a CIA team there in a couple of hours."

"My cousin Ryan will be here in ten minutes."

"I said no family," Naylor said, sounding pissed.

"Yeah, too late for that since my dad knew you were in my house and was a little ticked off you didn't think he'd know. I think he wants a word with you."

Naylor cursed under his breath. You did not want to piss off Cy Davies.

"Fine, but only tell Ryan what he needs to know. No one else can know about this operation, especially Willa Aldridge. We have to determine if she's a threat or not."

"I'm telling you, Naylor," Porter said, agitated that Naylor wasn't listening to him or accepting what he was saying. "This woman was about to let me be killed in order to protect this key. She is clearly the victim here and needs protection."

"We'll see. Until my people examine the body and find out who he is, you say nothing to anyone about our involvement. Got it?" Naylor asked it like a question, but it was really an order—an order Porter wasn't happy about. Willa Aldridge had no part in selling that key. Someone was clearly willing to kill to get it, though, and right now it was up to him to keep her safe.

"Got it."

"The date angle was genius. Sleep with her if you have to. Do whatever it takes to stay close to her to make sure she's not selling out our government."

"You know, Naylor, my father was right. You're an asshole."

Porter hung up the phone and let out a frustrated sigh. He headed toward the kitchen when he heard giggles.

"Shh," he heard Willa say rather loudly. "Don't tell him I said that."

Porter opened the door to see Willa still sitting in her chair from the table with her back toward him. Landon was trying not to smile while her bodyguards were doing everything they could not to laugh. Landon saw Porter and a mischievous smile spread across his face.

"Don't tell who what?" Landon asked Willa.

There was a pause and then the sound of a straw trying to suck up an empty glass. "Don't tell Porter that I like him. Shh, it's a secret." Willa's voice sounded very different than it had during dinner and her diction was wobbling between studiously clear and slightly slurred.

"I won't say a word," Landon said, pulling out his phone. Porter knew he was placing a bet and gave him the finger when Landon looked back up.

"He's a real man. He doesn't pretend to be something he's not. I also bet he doesn't have a sock in his pants. And he's so respectful. He takes good care of his horse too. That says a lot about a man. He's nice and he listens, but did you see him stab that spoon into that man's neck? Only someone really strong could do that. It was totally gross, but hot too," Willa said on a sigh. "Can I have some more of the special tea? It's yummy. Porter's yummy. He's so sexy. I could lick him. Like all over. I bet he even has that sexy V thing you only see on guys in movies. I'd totally lick that. But shh!" Willa said swaying in her chair. "Don't tell him, okay?"

"Okay," came the chorus of male voices as they all stared over her head at Porter.

He was struggling now. Knowing she liked him and the licking . . . it was a real struggle not to toss her over his shoulder and go all caveman.

A soft knock at the door had Porter turning from the kitchen to find his cousin Ryan Parker standing with his hands on his hips and a bulge from a gun clearly under his shirt.

"You drove fast," Porter said as he held the front door open for Ryan.

"I used the siren when Landon said it was an emergency." Ryan looked across the room and paused. "What killed him?"

"Either a spoon or a skillet."

"Damn," Ryan said as he pinched the bridge of his nose as if in pain. "I don't know whether to scream or be proud." He paused and then groaned. "Annoyed. I'm annoyed because every family dinner from now on, Uncle Miles will make spoon weapon references. He'll never let it die. That may be a bad choice of words."

"And, I need a favor," Porter tried to look sheepishly at Ryan, but it didn't work and he ended up smiling when Ryan rolled his eyes.

"Yeah, yeah, CIA, yeah, yeah, off the books," Ryan said exasperated.

"Everyone knows, don't they?" Porter asked, not in the least surprised.

"Grandma Marcy told everyone her grandson was taking after his father and becoming a spy. She asked not to see you naked in a movie like your father."

"I'd like to see him naked. Oh. It's a good thing I didn't say that out loud. That would be embarrassing." Porter and Ryan both turned to look up to find Willa leaning against Landon with a glass of Rose Sisters' iced tea in her hand. The three elderly Rose sisters had given Landon permission to serve their special boozy drink at his restaurant with the promise that it was named after them on the menu.

"Ryan Parker, meet Willa Aldridge. Willa, this is my cousin Ryan," Porter said, moving to put his arm around her waist. Landon was one of his best friends, but that didn't mean he wanted to see Willa in his arms.

"Hello. It's nice to meet you," Willa said, the epitome of a professional woman. Then her eyes narrowed slightly as she considered Ryan. "I bet he has a V too, but I don't want to lick it like I do Porter's. Hands down the sexiest family I've ever met," she said, looking from Porter to Ryan to Landon. "Yup." She took a deep breath, "Yum."

Landon looked away to get himself under control. Ryan's mouth dropped open and he was about to say something when Porter shook his head.

"But, they're going to look at the man spooned to death."

Willa giggled as she unknowingly continued with her running mental commentary. "And they're going to hate me. Then I'll never find out what Porter looks like naked and that makes my vagina really sad."

Landon smothered a snort. Ryan covered a laugh with a cough. Porter took some calming deep breaths and flicked Ryan off after he pulled up the betting app.

"Willa," Ryan said after placing his bet, "do you know this man?"

Willa nodded her head and, with a visible effort, pulled herself together enough to answer. "He came to my practice arena back home and threatened my father and me to turn over a business secret. That's why I have the bodyguards." She gave a nod to the bodyguards standing behind her, but the motion caused her whole body to sway. "Then he found me at the barn while I was getting Apollo settled in. Porter accidentally kicked him when he fell into my lap and I thought I would have time to figure out what to do, but then he showed up here and he put a gun to Porter's head."

"Were you going to give him the business secret?" Ryan asked.

Porter felt a tremor go through Willa's body as she remembered the incident. "No," she choked out as tears began to run down her face again. "I'm sorry. I was going to let your cousin die to protect many others. I'm sure you hate me now." She gave a loud sniffle.

"I don't hate you, Willa," Porter said gently to reassure her. "In fact, I respect you a lot more because of it. You were very brave and very strong not to fold under the pressure."

Willa looked up at Porter and his heart flipped in his chest. Her eyes shone with tears. He saw the moistened path they had taken when they rolled down her cheeks. Her eyes were red, her face blotchy, and he'd never felt so strongly for a woman in his life. That one moment changed everything for him.

The men in his family always said they fell hard and fast and that he'd know it when he felt it. Well, the feeling almost knocked him back. He wavered on his feet as he cupped her face in his hands. "I'm proud of you, Willa. You were very brave."

"That is the sweetest thing anyone has ever said to me. I wish nobody else was here so I could jump him. I bet Porter would be strong enough for up-against-the-wall sex. I've never had that before but I bet it would be amazing. I'm totally going to pull out my vibrator and think of that tonight." Willa took a deep breath and smiled up at him brightly. "Thank you. I thought you might hate me for putting you in danger. I wish I could tell you everything, but I can't."

Porter's mind was still back at the up-against-the-wall sex. Ryan cleared his throat. "We understand about secrets, Miss Aldridge."

Yeah, one very big secret. Porter was only here to find out if the woman who wanted to have sex with him up against the wall was committing treason. Although that wasn't one hundred percent anymore. He was here to protect her now. Plus, he was invested in her. He wanted Willa far more than as part of a case. For more than getting Naylor off his back. For more than sex, even though everything she said in her tipsy stream of consciousness had him thinking about that quite a bit. Now he needed to figure out how he was going to make this all work out, because when the case was over he didn't want to say goodbye to Willa Aldridge.

"Porter, why don't you take Willa home," Ryan said, all teasing from his voice gone. "Miss Aldridge, I'd feel better if Porter stayed with you overnight. Is that alright with you?"

Willa nodded her head and bit her lower lip as she finally kept her running mental commentary to herself.

"Landon, can you three get Willa into Porter's car? He'll be right there," Ryan said as Porter handed him his keys.

Landon had to half carry the stumbling Willa, and even as Ryan began to talk, Porter's eyes were only on her.

"He put a gun to your head?" Ryan asked, all business.

"Yeah, and flicked the safety off. He was going to kill me. I had no choice." Porter didn't take it lightly that he'd just killed a man. No matter the competitions the Davies family had together, actually killing someone was completely different. Not that he regretted it. He'd kill whoever put Willa in danger.

"I'm sorry. You did a good job. No wonder the CIA wanted you. Who's my contact there?"

"Agent Naylor. He's sending some agents to clean this up. I want to know who this man is before they take him away," Porter said with his hands on his hips. He watched as Landon helped Willa into the truck and all he wanted to do was protect her. "Naylor still thinks Willa is a traitor."

"After tonight? No way. That woman is as innocent as they come." Ryan sighed and ran his hand through his hair. "Look, you're like a little brother to me. Be careful, Porter. Not only is she in a dangerous situation, but also be careful with your heart. I can tell you like her, but she's Willa Aldridge. She's not going to have the quiet life you want."

"I know," he said with a sigh. "Although I don't think she wants that type of lifestyle. She's here with the elite of society, but I get the feeling she's not really a part of them."

"You've been around enough of those types to know if Willa's one of them or not. I hope she's not. I hope what I see between you can survive the secrets you both have." Ryan slapped his shoulder as a sign of support. "I'll clean this up with the CIA. Call me if you need anything. The whole family has your back, especially after this."

"Thanks, Ryan." Porter kept his eyes on Willa as he left the restaurant.

Landon moved away from the truck and met him on the sidewalk. "I like her for you. I like you for her. Take care of each other. Tonight was ... hard."

"Thanks for having my back," Porter told his cousin and gave him a hug and thumped his back.

"Anytime. I'm sure we'll all see you tomorrow. After tonight you're not going to keep anyone away."

"I ran from the Davies and Keeneston overbearingness long enough. I guess I've matured because I'm kind of excited to have them meet Willa," Porter admitted.

Landon smiled and pulled up the betting app. "Let me just place a second bet a lot sooner than my first. You're a total goner and I couldn't be happier for you. See you tomorrow."

Yeah, tomorrow. When he had to participate in the reining event. Now to get Willa home and in bed. Then he could think about tomorrow and exactly how he was going to explain his presence in Willa's life with all that was said and done.

11

Willa groaned in pain even as she and Tilly cheered on Porter at his reining event. She'd woken with a killer headache and just hoped to goodness she hadn't embarrassed herself. That worry grew when Parker joined her to watch Porter and gave her a sympathetic look.

"He did well. Let's meet him back at the barn," Parker said as Porter exited the arena. "How is this different from jumping?"

They walked back to the barn as Tilly explained about jumping and when their events would start. Callum and his minions did a double take when they walked in together and that made Willa smile with amusement.

"Here's Apollo," Willa said with pride as the groom moved away to give them privacy.

"He's magnificent," Parker said quietly as he slowly introduced himself to the horse. Yup, Willa was right. These Davies men were something else. Parker began asking her questions and they were deep in a discussion about horses when Callum rudely interrupted them.

"Chickened out on such a big stage, huh, Porter?" Callum asked with a smirk. "Is that why you're back early?"

"This must be the asshole my brother told me about," Parker said to Willa, completely at ease with insulting the powerful Callum Harding.

Callum sputtered. Cyril taunted him to fight and Callum began to posture as if he were really going to throw a punch. "You need to learn how to speak to your betters."

Parker laughed. It was so surprising Callum and Cyril froze as Tilly came over to hold Willa's hand. They might be two strong women in the real world, but here, with that horrible group of people who had tormented them growing up, they were still those shy teenage girls. It was something they were both working on.

"Betters? What century do you live in?" Parker laughed as he turned to Willa and Tilly. "These guys are a riot."

The second Parker looked away Callum swung a haymaker.

Willa and Tilly didn't have time to scream a warning. Parker deflected the punch and at the same time landed one in Callum's gut. He doubled over, trying to catch his breath as Willa gasped in shock.

Parker reached into his back pocket and pulled out a brown leather wallet. He crouched down so Callum could see him and flipped it open. "Let me introduce myself. I'm Parker Davies and you have just assaulted a federal agent."

Cyril cursed and Marguerite and Valentina suddenly got real interested in something back in Callum's area of the barn.

"So, this is how it's going to work. You're going to leave Willa and Tilly alone or I'll file charges. Got it?" Parker asked with a steely tone so deadly serious it made Willa shiver.

"Willa, I think I might have to marry that man," Tilly whispered.

"I see my brother is making friends," Porter called out, entering the barn with a herd of bunnies trailing after him and Miss Trix.

Callum struggled to stand upright and sent Willa a knowing smirk. Damn that man. He could find the chink in her armor in seconds.

"Good ride, Porter," Marguerite called out. "I see your fans loved it too."

She also sent a smirk to Willa twisting the knife Callum had stabbed her with years ago when he slept with Marguerite while dating her.

Porter tossed Miss Trix's reins to his brother and pulled Willa against his chest. "It was your good luck kiss that did it."

"Or the other kisses you got," Willa whispered, embarrassed she'd let her insecurities show.

"Nope. Yours are the only ones that matter," Porter leaned down and kissed her in front of everyone. All thoughts of humping bunnies transformed into thoughts of her and Porter, well, humping like bunnies.

"I'd like to think I matter too," a drop-dead gorgeous redhead said from behind him.

"Yeah, Porter. I matter too," a tall leggy blonde said, coming to stand next to the redhead.

"What's this about?" a second redhead asked.

"Porter says she's the only one who matters to him," the first redhead said, crossing her arms over her chest as she nodded her head at Willa. Willa flushed with a mix of embarrassment and anger. Who were these women and what did they mean to Porter? No matter how well he kissed, Willa was not sharing him.

"We'll see what he says at dinner when he wants my dessert," the second redhead said.

"You're too good to him," an exotic-looking woman with dark hair and big brown eyes said. "I never share my dessert with him."

"Oh my gosh," Marguerite laughed. "He has a harem."

"Poor Willa, she's like number eight on this list. Maybe she'll get to see him for an hour a day," Valentina laughed.

"You look familiar," Callum said, looking at the blonde. "Did I sleep with you?"

The blonde crossed her arms over her chest and narrowed her gaze at him. "Hardly, though not for your lack of trying, Mr. Harding. And you three, Cyril Van Doren, Marguerite Borghese, and Valentina Bianchi. You're all blacklisted."

"Blacklisted?" Valentina said with a snort of amusement. "How can some country bumpkin blacklist us?"

Willa watched them laugh and then she took a real good look at the blonde. "It's nice to see you again," Willa said around Porter's shoulders with a slow smile at the surprise connection.

"You remember?" the blonde asked with a smile.

"I do. We met at Fashion Week and I bought several of your designs. They're my favorites," Willa said to mega designer and former model Sydney Davies. Porter said he had a large family. The last name couldn't be just a coincidence.

The minions stopped laughing as one of them gasped.

"You're Sydney Davies. The supermodel," Callum sputtered as he instantly tried to pull himself up to full height and send her his trademark grin.

"And designer," Marguerite said. "I am so sorry. We were

just teasing an old family friend. It wasn't anything personal, Sydney."

"It's Mrs. McKnight. And my cousin is right, you're all assholes. You're also not the kind of people I want to wear my clothes," Sydney said before turning back to Willa. "You two on the other hand, I would love you to see what I'm working on now."

"I would love that," Tilly said, holding out her hand. "Tilly Bradford."

Sydney shook her hand with a kind smile on her face. Willa had liked Sydney when she'd met her years ago. She'd always seemed down-to-earth and today she liked her even more.

The redheads stepped forward next. "I'm Reagan Ashton, this one's older sister," Reagan said with a nod of her head toward Porter.

"And I'm Riley Walz, his other older sister. It's nice to meet you."

Willa shook their hands and introduced Tilly to them as well.

"Why do I know the name Reagan Ashton?" Tilly asked out loud. Willa wanted to shush her, but it was no good. Tilly usually spoke her mind, just not around the minions who were currently eavesdropping, all while trying to suck up to Sydney.

"She doesn't like to brag," Riley said, shooting some serious side-eye at the minions that made Willa laugh. "But her husband is Carter Ashton and together they own some of the best thoroughbreds around."

"This year's Derby winner," Tilly exclaimed delightedly as the minions almost tripped over themselves to hear.

"That was us," Reagan said with a proud smile.

"Okay, you got enough time. It's my turn now," the

stunning woman with dark hair said, pushing the twins apart. She held out her hand and glared. "I'm the best friend and I need to make sure you're good enough for Porter."

"Ari!" Porter groaned from where he stood talking to Parker.

Willa didn't know what to say. It was usually the reverse —her father asking if the man she was dating was good enough for her.

"Well, I'm Willa Aldridge," Willa said, shaking the woman's hand. She rolled her eyes at Willa and Willa was afraid she'd said something wrong.

"I know that. My brother gave me your file. I already know about your education, including the B-minus you got in sixth grade history, your career, your show stats, why you're really in Lexington, the date last night, and the speeding ticket you got when you turned sixteen. Those are just facts. I want to know about *you*," the woman Porter called Ari said, staring her down.

How? Who? What? This woman couldn't know those things. "Who *are* you?" Willa blurted.

"Ariana Ali Rahman-Duke," she said as if it should tell Willa everything she should know. And it did. The only thing she was confused about was how someone like Porter was best friends with Ariana. Cowboys and princesses didn't usually run in the same circles.

"Of course she's not good enough," Marguerite said with a mocking little laugh. "I am, though. Marguerite Borghese. I think we have some friends in common, your highness."

"None of the ones I like," Ari said with a roll of her eyes before turning back to Willa. "So, are you good enough for my best friend?"

There was an element to Ariana that reminded her of Marguerite—the confidence in knowing who they were and where they stood in the world. It was intimidating, but while Willa wasn't royalty, she was far from a nobody. She was an intelligent, kind, and compassionate person and that was enough.

"I am," Willa said with a confidence she used only in business negotiations, because that is what it felt like. It felt as if she were in a boardroom for a hostile takeover. "I'm a good, trustworthy person and so is Porter."

Ariana stared at her for a moment. "Are they your friends?" she asked, nodding to the minions.

"No," Willa answered immediately. "Tilly is, though. She's my best friend."

Ari nodded again as if she were taking that information and processing it. "Okay. I like you . . . for now. But you hurt Porter . . . I'll make you live to regret it," she whispered.

Willa was beginning to get used to threats and that thought alone made her giggle. Ari narrowed her eyes at her. "Sorry, it's not the first time my life has been threatened in the past twenty-four hours."

Ari wrinkled her nose. "I heard about that. Are you okay? Seriously, I know people who can fix that problem." Gone was the mean Ari and in her place was a friend.

"Totally," Riley said as her sister nodded in agreement.

"Our dad could—" Reagan started to say but Porter cut her off.

"Is the whole family here?" Porter asked as he joined them.

"Oh, yes. Everyone is here." Sydney said.

"Goodness. Who are they?" Tilly blurted out. Everyone turned to look at the group of men walking into the barn.

"Out of my way," Valentina said, shoving Marguerite aside as she leapt out into the aisle to intercept the group of tall, sexy men.

"Those are our husbands," Ari said, her voice full of warning.

Valentina stuttered in her steps, turned, and walked back to Callum's setup.

"Hey, guys," Porter said, welcoming the growing group. "Willa, meet my friends. This is Matt, he's Riley's husband. And this is Carter, he's Reagan's husband," Porter said as Willa shook each man's hand. "And that's Deacon, he's Sydney's husband. And last is Jameson, Ari's husband."

"It's nice to meet you all," Willa said with a smile.

"You say that now," Matt said with a shake of his head. "Wait until later. So, a word of warning for the newbie. Run. Run real fast because Gemma is on her way with a dinner invite. If you can't disembowel someone with a spoon or shoot a target from three hundred yards, you'll be eaten alive."

"What is it with your family and spoons? And who is Gemma?" Willa asked Porter as everyone laughed in response, but Porter didn't. Instead, his face was slightly pale and he looked more nervous than when he'd had a gun pointed at his head.

12

"My mom is on her way? Here? With a dinner invite?" Porter asked the men. No, no, no. He loved his mother, but this was bad, very bad. They'd send Willa running for the hills.

"Yup. You have less than thirty seconds to hightail it out of here," Deacon said with a shudder. "I still have nightmares from my first family dinner."

Sydney patted his arm. "It's okay, honey. You survived."

"Barely," he muttered.

Willa laughed, clearly thinking they were teasing her, but they weren't. A Davies family dinner was akin to a CIA interrogation at a black site.

"The axes," Matt shuddered.

"The hand-to-hand," Deacon shivered.

Reagan rolled her eyes at them. "They don't do that with the girlfriends."

"They do now," Ari said. "I'm not a Davies, but Abby told me she went through the course because her mom and the Davies moms said it was sexist to not treat the women the same as the men. Jace's sweet Stella ran from her dinner.

Wyatt and Camila military crawled. And Layne and Walker climbed out a window."

"That was more over babysitting," Porter said, remembering that night.

"Yeah, but Tammy did interrogate Stella at that dinner," Parker pointed out.

"Exactly how big is your family?" Willa asked after hearing all the names bandied about. "And is that Gemma?"

"Crap," Porter cursed. "That's my mom."

"Why does she have a bodyguard?" Willa asked as she looked at the intimidating man walking beside her.

The group laughed, except Porter groaned. "That's my dad." It was too late now. There was no escape.

"Sweetie, you were amazing out there!" Gemma cried, holding out her arms for her son who obediently bent down to hug his mother.

"Thanks, Mom," Porter said as he stood up. She'd supported him in every crazy thing he'd wanted to do in his life. He loved her with all his heart, but right now he just wanted to get her away from Willa.

"So nice watching you do something where you're not about to be killed every second." His mother stopped and then shrugged. "Well, except for dinner last night. But who hasn't been held at gunpoint every now and then?" His mother turned to Willa and flashed a large smile. "You must be my son's girlfriend. I'm his mother, Gemma Davies."

"Um, I, we," Willa stuttered. They'd had one date. He didn't know if that qualified them as boyfriend and girlfriend. Not that he would mind. He liked Willa. A lot. But he had a job to do and his mother scaring his target off wasn't a good start.

"Mom, it was one date. Let's see if Willa even wants to go

out with me for a second one before you turn her into my girlfriend," Porter said dryly as Parker hid his laughter behind a cough.

"Wait, did you say Gemma Davies?" Valentina asked, poking her head back up. "As in the Gemma Davies, the famous author whose books have all been made into huge blockbusters?"

Porter saw the puzzle piece click into place for Willa. Porter wasn't just some poor cowboy. His mother was famous. His friend was a princess. His cousin was a famous model and designer.

Willa suddenly burst out laughing.

"They've broken you, haven't they?" Porter asked. "You're in hysterics."

Willa shook her head. "I thought you didn't know who I am. I thought you didn't know about my job, the money, the power . . . but you did, didn't you? You just didn't care. Heck, you're more connected than I am."

"Of course I knew. I live in Kentucky, not a cave. But why would I care?"

Willa looked at him and then around at his friends. He tried to see what she was seeing. He saw that no one cared who she was or what family she came from. Not a single one of them. They didn't care what she did for a living or who her father was. The men had joked about the family dinners, but they were all hugging his mother and father and laughing with each other as they talked as a group. This was his family. They only cared if you were a good person.

"You wouldn't. I'm sorry. I'm just shell-shocked," Willa admitted after a moment.

"I know. My family is overwhelming."

"They're great," Willa said with a kind smile. "What other secrets are you keeping, Porter Davies?"

"What secrets are you keeping, Willa Aldridge?" Porter asked in return.

Willa gave a little gulp. She's told him some last night, but not all. It didn't matter. No matter how much sexual chemistry they had, she wasn't going to trust him with that information anytime soon. Instead of answering, she smiled and stepped away from Porter and in between Valentina and Gemma.

"We got interrupted earlier. I'm Willa Aldridge," Willa said, holding out her hand for Gemma. Gemma didn't shake it, though. She wrapped Willa up in a motherly hug instead.

"It's so nice to meet you. Come meet Porter's father."

"Your husband?"

"When he's good," Gemma joked. "Honey, this is Porter's girlfriend, Willa Aldridge. Willa, this is my husband, Cy Davies."

"Just because you call her his girlfriend doesn't make it so, Gem," Cy said to his wife before turning to look seriously at her and holding out his hand to her. Willa shook it, but he didn't let go. "Or are you his girlfriend?"

Oh no. Porter knew exactly what his father was up to.

"I am interested in learning more about the position," Willa said just as seriously. Porter thought he saw his father's lip quirk, but he couldn't be sure.

"You're Willa Aldridge, daughter of Brian Aldridge?" Cy asked.

"Yes."

"You were just named company president, correct?" Cy asked, leaving no time between questions.

"Yes."

"You must keep a lot of secrets in a company that deals with technology."

"Yes. What are—" Willa started to say, but Cy shushed her.

"Are you loyal to the United States?"

"Of course, why?"

Cy shushed her again. Gemma rolled her eyes. Porter wanted to rescue her, but he didn't. He needed to see if his father found the same thing he had—that Willa Aldridge was innocent of treason.

"I'm a patriot. I'm kind. I'm loyal. I love horses. I hate cilantro."

"And you'd let my son be shot in order to protect whatever secret you are keeping."

"Yes. I'm so sorry. I would have let him be killed in order to prevent the knowledge I have from getting into the wrong hands. I understand if you don't want me to date your son."

Cy's lips tilted up. Tilly sucked in a breath next to him and started fanning herself. "Not date him? Hell, that makes you the only one good enough to date him." He dropped her hand and turned to Porter. "Tell Naylor he's an idiot."

Porter nodded in agreement. Willa wasn't guilty. Her life was clearly in danger and he was going to do everything he could to protect her.

"Oh my gosh. How many hot men are in your family?" Tilly asked him.

Porter followed her gaze to the new arrivals. "The dark-haired one is Kale Mueez. He's a family friend and a computer genius. You'll remember my cousin Landon. Next to him is his brother, Colton. He's a fireman. And the last one is—"

"Holt Everett, the country singer. You know them all?" Tilly asked as the fanning increased.

"Yeah. We all grew up together in Keeneston."

"Where?" Tilly asked, crinkling her nose as if trying to place the town.

"Keeneston. It's a nearby small town."

"Do they have any houses for sale? I think I need to move," Tilly joked.

Porter chuckled, but his laughter stopped as Kale's serious face caught his attention. Why? Because Kale was never serious. "Parker, will you introduce Tilly and Willa to everyone?"

"Sure thing," Parker said, seeing the same thing Porter did. Kale nodded with his head to the side barn door and didn't stop walking while the others were greeted and brought her into the group.

Porter followed him past Callum's stalls and out the side door until they were assured of their privacy. "Ryan stopped by the farm last night after he wrapped up your spooning incident. That's just gross." Kale shuddered. "My father was impressed. Just another thing I'm not doing right."

Kale's father was the infamous Ahmed. Ahmed's daughter, Abby, was a chip off the old block, but Kale was more of a badass behind a keyboard. This summer Kale's father had ordered him home and had him in intensive physical training.

Kale had bulked up over the past three weeks but didn't look happy about it. Probably because he was bruised from the last sparring match with his brother-in-law, Dylan Davies.

"Anyway, Ryan asked me to find out everything I could on the attacker. He's the hired muscle for The Panther," Kale said in a low whisper.

"Is that supposed to mean something to me?" Porter asked.

"The Panther is a legend on the dark web. He has a sophisticated network of proxy servers that hides his location. He uses only private networks so law enforcement and other hackers can't find out what he's doing. All I know is he's an online pirate who steals government and intellectual property secrets and then sells them off to the highest bidder. At least that's what I think he does."

"Explain a little more," Porter said as he was starting to get the picture of why they were after Willa.

"Two examples, although they're both technically theoretical since nothing can be proven. One, the latest smartphone. The design was stolen and sold off to its competitor. That's the assumption anyway since their competitor came out with the phone rumored to belong to another company. Two, there was a rumored list of spies working for the British government in Russia. The list was sold and suddenly there was a mass transit accident in Russia that just happened to have every spy on that list on the train. My question is, what does Willa Aldridge have that The Panther wants to sell?"

Porter ground his teeth together. This was way worse than Naylor let on. It was clear to Porter that Willa wasn't going to hand over the key so he'd sent the man to take it. "Now that The Panther's man is dead, what's going to happen to Willa?"

"If the rumors are true, he'll send someone else and won't play nice," Kale told him. "Do you even know what he's after?"

Porter nodded.

"And it has to do with you working for the CIA."

Porter nodded again.

"Is there a way I can help?" Kale asked.

"Yes, get me everything you can on The Panther. How

can I catch him? How can I identify him?" Porter asked.

Kale shook his head. "I'm good at what I do. I'm very good. However, even I can't find him. I'll reach out to a friend. Maybe together we can get some information. For now, I'll tell you one thing. He'll be coming for her again and soon. Whatever she has, he wants and he's willing to kill for it."

"Thanks, Kale."

"You know you can trust me with your mission, right? I mean, the whole town knows you're with the CIA and it has to do with Willa, but I might be able to help more if you tell me everything."

"I know I can trust you. It has to do with a skeleton key to encryption software," Porter told him.

Kale was quiet for a second and then cursed. "It's the contract Willa got for her father's mobile encryption software that will be on every government phone, isn't it?"

"You know about that?"

Kale looked at him as if he were stupid. "Of course I do. You're not the only one with secrets. No wonder The Panther wants that. Russia, China, North Korea—they'll pay a fortune for that key. Not only them, but our allies would too. We have plenty of allied spies in the US keeping tabs on us. However, this information does help me. I'll keep an eye on the players who would bid on that and maybe find a backdoor into The Panther's network. Call me if anything develops. I'm heading back to the farm to get to work."

Porter thanked him and watched as Kale walked away while he made a phone call. "Hey, dude. I got a project for us to work on."

"Kale looked worried and Kale never looks worried. What's going on?"

Porter turned to the barn door and saw his cousin Greer

leaning against the door, quietly watching them. Greer was Ryan and Jackson's younger sister. She'd followed in Jackson's footsteps and joined the FBI Hostage Rescue Team and she was the first woman to do so. You'd never know that by looking at her, though. Greer Parker looked like the stereotypical girl next door. Her honey brown hair was in a ponytail, she wore jeans and a University of Kentucky T-shirt, and a pair of reflective aviator glasses hid her eyes. Her normal sweet-as-pie smile was missing as she was in business mode.

He could imagine she just rolled her eyes behind her glasses when he didn't answer right away. "I know you're working with the CIA. Grandma practically hung a banner and made shirts announcing it. I also know it involves that woman in there and you killed someone with a spoon last night. By the way, thanks for that. Every freaking family dinner we're going to hear Uncle Miles crowing about a spoon as a weapon."

"Someone wants something Willa has. They want to sell it on the black market. If he gets his hands on it, it would put thousands of people and the country at risk."

Greer was quiet for a moment and then nodded. "I think I know what it is, but I won't ask. Let's just say I was recently asked to upgrade my phone."

"I would hold off on that for now," Porter said. The meaning was clear and Greer gave a single nod. "What are you doing here anyway? I thought you were in DC to meet with the FBI director."

"I got back last night. The meeting went well. He's looking to retire in three years. He wants my name on the shortlist, but in order to do that I have to take a desk job and I'm not quite so sure I want that."

"Do you mean now or ever?" Porter asked as they turned to walk into the barn.

"That's what I'm trying to figure out. I have a little more time to decide my future, but the clock is starting to tick. Now, introduce me to this woman who got you trending on the Blossom Café Betting App."

13

Willa was overwhelmed by names. Cousins, siblings, friends . . . they all blurred together as Gemma Davies introduced her around. Sydney took pity on her and tried to steer the conversation toward horses instead of her love life. Riley and Reagan didn't say much. Their arms were crossed and they glared a lot. They had a strikingly similar look on their faces to their father.

"Where are all the kiddos?" yet another beautiful woman asked as she strode in with Porter.

"Cassidy," all the women answered at once.

Sydney looked a little guilty. "We did a dump and run. We all wanted to come see Porter and didn't want to juggle little ones so we showed up en masse at Desert Sun Farm and dropped them off while Cassidy was supposed to be working on translations with Mila."

"Cassidy was pissed, but Dani was thrilled. She's set up a huge nursery for when Sloane has her baby any day now," Riley told them. "Dani has offered to keep all the grandbabies, as many as they can possibly have, during the day as a way to bribe them to have more kids. Abby backed out of the room as if there were an explosive in it, while Sloane and Mila smiled that mom-smile women get when thinking of babies."

"We need to get Cassidy a really nice Christmas gift," Reagan said as the women nodded.

"Who's Cassidy?" Willa asked the group.

"She's the youngest Davies cousin," Riley answered and then paused. "Well, not counting her mother's 'oops, I thought I was in menopause' baby. But Cricket is just a toddler so she can't babysit yet."

"I can make you a flow chart," the new woman said as everyone went back to talking about someone named Sloane who was about to have a baby. "Hi. I'm Greer Parker."

"Not a Davies then," Willa said with a smile. "I'm not alone!"

Greer cringed. "My mother is a Davies."

"I should have known. How many cousins are there?" Willa asked and everyone went quiet.

"Seventeen?" Sydney said as she counted silently.

"You forgot Cricket," Greer said.

"Eighteen, then," Sydney said with a smile.

"Wait, are we counting spouses?" Riley asked.

Everyone went quiet again.

"What about children?" Reagan asked. "They're our cousins, too. Or nieces or nephews . . . wait. Now I'm confused."

"A lot." Sydney finally answered. "There are a lot of us."

As one, every cell phone went off.

"Sloane's in labor!" Ariana called out. "We're already in Lexington. This is not a drill, people. Go! Go! Go! We might have a chance at beating the Rose sisters to the hospital."

"Who is Sloane?" Willa asked Greer.

"Ari's sister-in-law. Want to see a future prince or

princess right after they're born? The food is worth the wait," Greer answered.

"Hospital food?" Willa asked Porter as Greer took off running. "I feel as if I'm missing so much information here."

"Come with me. It'll all become clear," Porter said, holding out his hand.

Willa grasped it and ran to the truck as her bodyguards leapt into their SUV to follow. People were tearing out of the parking area. Some had sirens. "You know hospitals have restrictions on the number of visitors, right?"

"Hospitals tend to look the other way on restrictions when it's a Keeneston patient. You'll see," Porter told her.

"This is a royal birth, Porter. They're not going to just let anyone in. Security is going to be tight," Willa said as Porter followed the line of cars from Keeneston.

Porter just smiled at her. "So, about that girlfriend thing."

Willa's heart instantly started beating faster. "What about it?"

"You didn't go running. You're still here with me. Does that mean my family hasn't scared you off?" he asked.

"You didn't run when a gun was pointed at you. I guess we can have crazy lives together," Willa answered as Porter's hand reached across the console. His hand cupped her knee as he broke the speed limit without blinking.

The whole Keeneston caravan was behind someone with a siren and was flying to the hospital.

"You know we have to talk before too long," Porter said into the silence. "If we really do want a relationship, then we both need to put our cards on the table."

"It's okay. Parker told me you know who I am."

"That isn't the ace in your hand, Willa," Porter said in such a way it felt like a dagger to her heart because while he didn't say it, she knew what he meant. He knew. Somehow he knew.

Willa jerked her knee out from under his hand as they turned into the hospital parking lot. "And your ace is how you know about my ace, isn't it?"

Porter gave a single nod of his head in answer. The heat left her body and Willa shivered. The warmth from Porter, the excitement of the first blush of a relationship, it all turned ice cold and froze her heart in a split second. Who was Porter Davies and how did he know about her?

Porter felt Willa pull away. A thick wall was going up around her heart and he didn't blame her. However, he wasn't lying. He wanted something more with her and he wasn't going to start off a relationship by lying. Especially when he knew she was innocent and in danger.

"I'm calling my bodyguards to get a ride home," Willa said before jumping from the truck the second Porter parked and began walking quickly away from him.

Porter got out and stalked toward her as she dug out her phone. He gently took hold of her elbow and walked her into the hospital where people were running for the elevator while some raced up the stairs to the labor and delivery room. "Not going to happen. I lost your bodyguards before we were out of the parking lot. Besides, my ace trumps yours. We're going to celebrate the birth of a new royal, meet the entire town of Keeneston, learn how to bribe nurses, and then we're laying our cards on the table."

"I'll scream," Willa threatened as she jerked her arm from his hand and tried to take off again.

"Greer, hold the door," Porter called out as his cousin

pushed the door to the stairwell open. Porter spun, grabbed Willa, and tossed her over his shoulder. She gave a little squeak and smacked his ass. "I'll return the favor when we're alone," he said to her as Greer made a TMI face.

"Help!" Willa shouted. "He's trying to kidnap me!"

Greer laughed behind him as they raced up the stairs.

"That's not what women usually say about my cousin. Usually it's 'Take me, Porter! Oh yes, yes, yes! More! More!'" Greer cried out in her best porn voice.

Porter should have told Greer the door to the labor and delivery waiting room was open, but he wasn't *that* good a cousin. He moved out of the way and Greer came face to face with their family, the royal family, the Rose sisters, and Aniyah.

"Girl, you must be getting some kind of action with those vocals," Aniyah said. Aniyah had been Riley's assistant when Riley was in the state legislature. When Riley stepped down, Aniyah won the position in a landslide. She was married to State Trooper DeAndre Drews, and had a heart of gold. Aniyah was five foot nothing with curves that her husband probably thanked God for every day. Her black hair was left natural today, except for a chunk of pink up front.

"Did you give her your oils, Aniyah?" Miss Lily Rae Rose asked. "They sure make my hoo-ha tingle."

Porter almost dropped Willa. Everyone froze at that comment. Doctors, nurses, and even a woman who was in labor stopped mid-contraction as she was being pushed through the lobby to her room.

"No, but I should," Aniyah replied. "Her hoo-ha would love them, although maybe she doesn't need them. Greer sounds just like this adult movie my Sugarbear and I watched the other night. It was all about these women who went camping and well, they got real hot sitting by the campfire. So, of course, they took off their clothes to cool down. They were playing truth or dare and one of the women was dared to go into the woods alone for fifteen minutes. Well, don't you know she's walking in the dark through the woods . . ."

"Naked?" Miss Daisy Mae Rose asked.

"You would think she would put on some clothes. I wouldn't want to get mosquito bites on my hoo-ha," Miss Violet Fae Rose said and the women all nodded their agreement.

"She was naked as the day was long," Aniyah said, picking the story back up without missing a beat. "So, she's walking and finds this nice meadow area and she stops to look up at the night sky. She sees a furry blanket laid out in the field and lies down on it to look up at the moon. Only it's not a furry blanket. It's Bigfoot! And let me tell you, Bigfoot has some skills. He had her screaming like Greer was just screaming."

Miss Lily wrinkled her nose. "How does that work exactly? Was it all furry, too? Did the girl's hoo-ha hack out a furball when they were done?"

"No more talk of hoo-has!" Greer's father, Cole Parker, roared. "I never want to hear that word again."

"You look really mad, Cole. Just like Bigfoot looked when the woman's friends came running when they heard her cries of ecstasy and he thought they were going to take her away from him," Aniyah said as she pointed at Cole's face.

"Did the friends take her away?" Miss Violet asked Aniyah, ignoring Cole's look of horror.

Aniyah laughed. "It's an adult movie, of course not. They all joined in. Haven't you seen a porno?"

"Not this century," Miss Daisy muttered.

"I'll let you borrow my copy and my oils. You can thank me later," Aniyah stage- whispered.

The room was quiet as they were all in a state of shock. From the silence, Willa finally spoke. "I'll watch the porno if someone will help me. Porter is kidnapping me."

"Just like Bigfoot did after the orgy in the woods. Your hoo-ha will be very happy tonight. I'm Aniyah, by the way."

"Willa Aldridge," Willa called out from where she was hanging over Porter's shoulder. "Can someone please call the police? Or Bigfoot? Porter is refusing to let me leave."

"Never heard a woman complain about that before. You're slacking, brother," Parker said with a smirk.

"Of course he's not letting you leave," Porter's grandma, Marcy Davies, said as she walked over in her orthopedic shoes. "You're in danger over your work and he's going to protect you."

"What? How do you know that? Who are you?" Willa asked as she placed her hands on each cheek of his ass and pushed herself up enough to see Marcy.

"Hello, dear. I'm Marcy Davies, Porter's grandmother. It's so lovely to finally meet you in person. I hear you're coming to family dinner," his grandmother said as if were a common occurrence to have an heiress thrown over his shoulder.

Willa started to wiggle and Porter smacked her bottom. "Hold still and I'll let you down."

Willa stopped wiggling and Porter plucked her off his shoulder and gently set her down in front of him.

"How did you beat us here?" Porter asked the Rose Sisters, his grandmother, and Aniyah as he gave Willa time to adapt to the new situation.

"We just happened to be visiting Dani and Mo with

Marcy when Sloane went into labor," Miss Lily said with faux innocence. They had probably been visiting every day this week to make sure they were there when Sloane when into labor. "Gabe snuck Sloane to the hospital and we didn't even know until the charge nurse called Marcy. A couple of minutes later, Dani and Mo got a text from Gabe. Dani and Mo were gracious enough to give us a ride in the helicopter."

"Suckers," Grandma Marcy said to the rest of Keeneston, not even trying to tamper her gloating at beating them all to the hospital. "Now, the nurse told us Sloane is at five centimeters, so we have some time. Come sit with us, Willa, and tell us all about what kind of danger you're in. My grandson here," Grandma Marcy said, smiling lovingly at Porter, "will keep you safe. You know he's CIA now. Just like his daddy was. My son, Cy, was a very good spy when he was younger. Now he lets his mother beat him to the hospital." She shook her head and laughed.

Porter hadn't wanted to tell Willa about his assignment with the CIA like this. He wanted them to both come clean together, and alone. Why? Because of the way Willa was looking at him right now. She was hurt, she was pissed, and she looked ready to slug him and cry at the same time.

"You're only with me because you're with the CIA?" Willa asked, her voice breaking with emotion.

"Thanks, Grandma," Porter muttered.

His grandmother rolled her eyes. "If I want more great-grandchildren, you all need to stop puttering around. It would take forever if I left it up to you two. Willa, dear, Porter was just recruited to determine if you're selling the secrets or if you're in danger. We all know you'd never sell secrets, so don't worry. Porter is more concerned with protecting you. And Porter, Willa has this thingy called a key. I don't know what it unlocks. A safe? Willa, why does everyone want this key?"

Porter gave Willa time to respond, but she just stared dumbfounded at Marcy. "That's top secret corporate information. How do you know that?"

Grandma Marcy rolled her eyes. "I raised a son and grandson who are spies, dear. I have my resources."

"The president told you in exchange for an apple pie, didn't he?" Gemma asked her mother-in-law. Grandma Marcy just smiled sweetly in response.

"I'm in a coma, right?" Willa asked Porter as she poked his chest. "Are you real? Are they real? This can't be real." She poked him again and again.

"It's real. It's just my family. Now, do you want to answer or do you want me to?" Porter asked her. "Half of them have probably figured it out already so it's not a big deal."

"How?" Willa asked them all.

"I'm on a special team with the FBI and I was just asked to upgrade my phone," Greer said.

"Us too," Porter's cousin, Dylan said as his wife, Abby, nodded her head in agreement.

"You're FBI, too?" Willa asked the dangerous looking couple.

Abby smirked. "Not exactly."

"Which agency?"

Abby just smiled again.

"I have top secret clearance," Willa said. "As you all know."

"Everyone in this room has top secret clearance, dear," Marcy said with a kindly smile. "Now, what's this key thingy?"

"My father is Brian Aldridge. He developed and owns Anancites. It's a privately held technology company. I am president of the new mobile encryption division, which just won a government contract to encrypt all government phones. Someone wants the key to the encryption so they can gain access to every government phone," Willa told them. No one looked surprised.

"The Panther," Porter said and Willa gasped.

"He's the one who is after it? How do you know that?" she asked.

"You mean, DeAndre? He's my panther," Aniyah said with a little growl. Then she paused. "Come to think about it, so is Jackson."

"You've called Kale your panther, too," Riley reminded her. "And Colton, and Landon, and I'm pretty sure Parker and Porter as well."

"I'm crushed. I thought I was your panther and I find out I'm just one of many," Ahmed said dryly.

"Don't you worry. You're my tiger, roar!" she yelled, rolling her Rs and using her nails to mimic scratching him.

Ahmed might have smiled, but then it was gone.

"The Panther is a cyber criminal. He steals valuable information and auctions it off to the highest bidder," Willa explained. "How do you know it's him?"

"Ahmed's son, Kale, is a computer genius. He told me," Porter told her. "How do you know about him?"

"We've been invited to bid on stolen property from our competitors before. We've declined each time." Willa paused and went white as a ghost. "The man you spooned to death . . ."

"Was his employee. He was to deliver the key to The Panther," Porter explained.

"So now it's going to be open season on you two," Cy said matter-of-factly.

Ahmed nodded. "Could be fun."

"Hell yeah, it will be," Cy answered. "Honey, it's time for me to pull out my big gun. Maybe a grenade or two. Did we put them in the hall closet?"

There was a squeal from the back of the waiting room. "I just got a military grade front attachment for my Humvee. I'll mow bad guys down with it."

"I got a new gun. Look at this sexy girl," Aniyah said, pulling out a new hot pink cheetah print gun.

"My sniper rifle is out in the car," Greer said with a smile. "Want me to get it?"

"Who *are* you people?" Willa cried out in alarm, and Porter figured it was a good time to get her to a private room.

"They're looking out for us. This isn't our first rodeo. You're safer with us than anywhere else in the world. You notice we lost your bodyguards but Grandma Marcy beat us here," Porter said as he dropped his voice to calm her down.

"Yes, but my guards have guns to protect us!" Willa said, nearing panic level.

"I don't mean to frighten you," Gemma said in her most motherly voice, "but everyone here has a weapon of some sort."

"There's a whole cup of plastic spoons sitting by the coffee. Do you know how many ways I could kill someone with those?" Uncle Miles asked as everyone in the room groaned.

His wife, Morgan, rolled her eyes and pointed her finger at Porter in exasperation. "You just had to kill someone with a spoon. We're never going to hear the end of this."

"It's a very versatile and underestimated weapon," Uncle Miles argued.

"I agree with my dad," his daughter Layne said with a shrug as she took a spoon and put it in her pocket. "Just in case."

"That's my girl." Uncle Miles smiled widely and slung his arm around his daughter.

Willa looked around the room and Porter could tell her head was spinning. "Come on. Let's take a stroll and have a talk. I bet there's horrible coffee downstairs."

Porter angled Willa into the elevator, snagging some cookies as he went by the nurses' station. Well, the cards were now on the table. Porter just wondered if he had a winning hand.

14

Willa stood in the elevator in stunned silence. Some old sweet grandmother in the middle of nowhere Kentucky knew about the key. Her entire career and life were at risk. Then the man she thought was so truthful and honest turned out to be a lying spy, sent to determine if she was a traitor.

Willa spun and smacked Porter on the arm. "That's why your dad asked me about my patriotism! You all thought I was a traitor!"

Porter let her hit his upper arm over and over again. "My dad's a human lie detector. Everyone knew you weren't a traitor. I knew that a minute after I met you. He verified it."

"Oh my gosh," Willa gasped again. "Falling into my lap was no accident. And here I thought it was so romantic."

Porter smiled and she felt like hitting him again. "It wasn't an accident. I saw the threat, determined you weren't a traitor and therefore in danger, then I flung myself over a bench and into your arms *while* kicking the bad guy in the face. C'mon, isn't that romantic? Maybe I just think it is because, well, you've met my father."

Okay, it was totally heroic, but she wasn't ready to tell him that. "Was everything between us an act to gather information on me?" Willa finally asked.

Porter finally moved then. In a split second, he'd hit the elevator emergency button and they came to an abrupt stop. Porter had his hands around her waist and her back pressed up against the elevator wall and was standing so close she could feel every breath he took. "Everything was very real to me. I didn't lie about a thing. I only left out the CIA bit. Every story, every conversation we had, every touch." Porter lifted a hand and traced a finger over her lips, down her neck, and feathered them over her collarbone. "And every kiss was very real."

Willa's heart rate kicked up and anger was quickly replaced with lust. Maybe the anger was still there, simmering under the surface and fueling the lust. Either way, when Willa looked up into Porter's eyes as he traced his hand down her side, she felt on fire.

"How's this for real?" Porter asked a second before dipping his head and pressing his lips to hers.

This time it wasn't gentle. It wasn't romantic. It wasn't sweet. It was hot, heavy, and hard. His lips were strong and demanding against hers as he pressed her against the wall of the elevator. Willa let that fire she was feeling loose as it roared to life inside her. She kissed back, harder and deeper as she grabbed the back of his neck and angled him just how she wanted.

Porter rocked his hips against hers and Willa exploded with need. She rocked back, lifting her leg to his hip. Porter's hand automatically grabbed it and hooked it around his waist. He read every signal she gave and when he broke the kiss to trail his lips down the side of her neck, Willa found herself pinned against the elevator wall with both legs wrapped around Porter's waist, one of his hands on her ass holding her up, and the other up her shirt. His lips left little trails of fire down her skin as he kissed along her neck. If she were in a coma, she never wanted to wake up.

Porter rocked forward again as he cupped her breast and nipped at her neck. Willa moaned as she angled her neck for him to kiss again. She'd never understood the appeal of hickeys, but she did now. Whatever he was doing to her left her a puddle of goo in his arms.

Porter's body was hard against hers as his mouth found its way back up to hers. "Is this real enough?" he asked, his lips a breath away from hers.

"Not nearly," Willa said before taking action. She closed the distance and kissed him. She let her hands explore the muscles of his shoulders as she pressed her breasts against his hard chest.

"It's okay now. I'm a fireman and I'm here to get you out."

Willa gave a little squeak as she used Porter to hide as she tugged her shirt back down at the appearance of a face above them.

"Oh, Willa," she heard Greer's voice sigh. "You just lost me a ten-dollar bet with my grandmother. I thought you'd hold out to forgive him until you reached the car."

"What's going on here?" another male voice said. "Hey, is that Porter?"

"You good?" Porter whispered to her. He didn't move until she nodded. "Willa Aldridge, meet my cousin Colton. He's the fireman. He's also Landon's older brother. The man behind him is my cousin, Wyatt. He's a veterinarian. Then next to him is his wife, Camila. She trains racehorses. Y'all, this is my girlfriend, Willa Aldridge."

Girlfriend? Did they discuss that? Willa discretely shifted her bra back into place. Yeah, she guessed they did discuss it. The anger she felt finding out he was with the CIA fizzled out. She'd been keeping secrets from him, too. She was actually relieved everything was out in the open. Willa wasn't so sure her father would like it, but she'd soon find out because if The Panther was after them, he needed to know.

"Your case," Colton said with a nod. "We know. Nice to meet you, Willa."

Willa stood blinking at them all. "How many cousins do you have again? They seem never-ending."

"I know, right?!" Camila said as she tossed her hands up. "I still get some of them mixed up and I'm married to a Davies."

Willa grinned up at the woman with the Irish accent. She liked her. She liked Greer, too, but she felt Camila understood the overwhelming feeling Willa was experiencing right now with the tidal wave of Davies cousins.

"So, if you could just push that little red button there, the Lexington Fire Department won't show up," Colton told them.

Porter pushed it as Colton leaned back from where he was looking down at them. The door slid closed as the elevator continued its way down. "Sorry about that." Porter looked a little sheepish and it just made Willa know her instincts had been right. Porter Davies was a good guy.

"How long have you been in the CIA?"

"Couple of days. My handler blackmailed me to do this. He needed someone legit to enter the horse world and I was that guy. If I didn't do it, then he'd have my brother fired from the US marshals."

That further dampened any lingering anger Willa had. "That's horrible."

"I know. So I charged him a lot for this one-time deal."

"Then you really do own a horse farm?" Willa asked.

"I do. I'm looking to expand it, too. I never wanted to lie to you and I never intended to fall for you. But I did," Porter told her as he reached out and took her hand in his.

"I did, too," Willa admitted. "If The Panther is after me, I'm putting everyone here at risk. What do we do now?"

"We find The Panther."

Porter stood off to the side of the waiting room while friends and family brought Willa into the fold. The protectiveness he felt for a woman he'd just met was insane. It was hard not to touch her constantly to make sure she was safe. Well, that and other reasons.

"You need any help?"

Porter turned to look at Greer who had come to join him on the outskirts of the waiting room. "I don't know what the hell I'm doing. Last time I was in a shootout I almost shot someone with an acid bomb of death."

"You did all right the other night when a man had a gun to your head," Greer pointed out.

"All I could think about was Uncle Miles talking about how a spoon to the throat was just one of the many ways a spoon could kill someone."

Greer smothered her laugh but turned serious. "Family dinner has trained you better than the FBI trained me. Why do you think there's such a waitlist for the uncles' training facility? You and I had that training for free every week. Get some of Piper's jackets so y'all are protected. Talk to Sophie. She'll get you some weapons. Ones that don't shoot acid,"

Greer said of their cousin Sophie Dagher, who was married to Nash, the second-in-charge of the Rahmi royal family living in Keeneston. "Then, let me tag along. You know I can ride and you know I know horses. I can be your groom. Or her groom. People regularly ignore the help, especially when they're women. It's worked to my advantage many times."

"Don't you need to get back to your team in New York City?" Porter asked. Greer was the leader of the FBI Hostage Rescue Team there.

"I'm on leave for the next two weeks. They called it a vacation. I call it punishment because DC is recruiting me over my boss." Greer let out a frustrated sigh. "It's crap like this that makes me want to leave the FBI. Can you imagine me being the director and playing this political BS game everyday?"

Porter saw the stress lines around Greer's mouth. Being a female director in the FBI would be a huge honor, but Greer didn't look like she felt honored. She looked annoyed and stressed. "Don't do it."

Greer turned her gray-green eyes toward him in surprise. Almost all the Davies kids and grandkids had Grandpa Jake's hazel eyes, but Greer got a mix of her mother's hazel eyes and her father's silver ones. "What?"

"Don't do it. You look miserable when you talk about it. So, don't become director."

"But everyone says I have to—"

"Since when do you listen to anyone?" Porter asked, cutting Greer off. "I need to talk to my dad. I'll have Willa talk to you about helping out this week. I'm all for it. You're a hell of an agent. I'm just a Davies cowboy living in a CIA world." Greer grinned at him and Porter left to give his cousin a minute to think about what he said.

Willa saw him coming and smiled up at him. "You have the most fascinating family."

"I know. Speaking of family, Greer wants to talk to you about helping us this week. Can you go talk to her while I talk to my dad?"

Willa glanced to see where Greer was and her smile faltered. "What's wrong with her? Greer looks sad and I know I've only just met her, but she doesn't strike me as the sad sort."

"She's having a career crisis."

Willa nodded. "I get it. It's hard being a woman in what's considered a man's field."

Willa left Porter without looking back. It was clear she was concerned for Greer and damned if that didn't squeeze Porter's heart.

"You know," his cousin Jace said as Colton, Landon, Parker, and Ariana joined him. This was his crew. The younger generation, although right now he didn't feel so young. "I really like her for you. I was afraid you'd end up with some buckle bunny."

"I didn't," Ari said, coming to his defense. "I always knew you had good taste. After all, we're your best friends. I think she's perfect. She's made you more serious and you're going to make her relax a little. You've only been together a couple of days and I can see you make a good team."

"Aw, just like you and Jameson," Colton said, pretending to be a smitten teenager.

Ari punched him and Porter laughed. Yup, these were his friends.

"I need to talk to my dad. I'll be right back."

Porter found his dad with his brothers and brother-in-law. Porter's cousin Dylan and cousin-in-law Walker were with them.

"Porter, good. You're here," his father said as the circle expanded and made room for him.

"Don't start this without me," Matt Walz, Porter's brother-in-law and sheriff of Keeneston, said as he joined them. "Okay, go ahead, Pop Pop."

"I'll smother you in your sleep if you call me that again," Cy growled at his son-in-law, who just grinned at him.

"Pappy Cy it is."

"Do you have a death wish?" Walker asked Matt, who just grinned in response.

"It's not bad until knives are thrown at your balls," Dylan said with a shrug. "What will little Carolina call Uncle Miles?" Dylan asked Walker about his newborn daughter.

"Sir," Walker said quickly.

Uncle Miles rolled his eyes. "I'm going to be Papa Miles. I'm already teaching her everything I know," Miles said proudly of his infant granddaughter.

"He gave her a toy spoon," Walker said as he pinched his lips together so he wouldn't laugh.

"And a grenade rattle," Miles said with a smile.

"Oh, send me a link to that," Porter's father said before turning to him. "Now, let's get Porter squared away and maybe I can get a granddaughter. What's the game plan?"

15

<hr />

"Greer?" Willa asked as she approached Porter's cousin. The woman was staring out of the window deep, in thought. "Are you okay?"

Greer turned and smiled, but it wasn't a real one. It was the one women gave when everyone expected a smile even though it was the last thing they felt. "Of course. Did Porter tell you about my idea of being your groom?"

"He said you had an idea," Willa told her as she came to stand next to her. Someone like Greer wouldn't want to be coddled, but Willa wanted to hug her. Instead, she stood next to her as they looked out the window. "I'm torn, Greer."

"How so?" Greer asked.

"I know I need the help, but if The Panther is after me, you all would be at risk. I don't think I could do that to you all."

"It's my job. The part I like to do. I like to help others," Greer said as finally her voice changed from flat to animated.

"Is that what's bothering you? Not being able to do your job?" Willa asked.

"Who said anything is bothering me?" Greer asked in a slightly annoyed tone.

Willa sighed. "It's clear as day, Greer. That doesn't make you any less strong. Sometimes it takes another woman to understand the pressures we face in male dominated fields. Do you want to talk about it?"

Willa waited as Greer looked out the window again. Finally she started talking. "I've been clawing my way to the top since I started. I'm now poised to take the lead, and I don't want it. The politics, the red tape, the BS of it all takes away from why I joined the FBI."

"To save people," Willa said with a nod of understanding.

"Exactly," Greer said, turning to her once again.

"Find your passion, Greer. Then go after it. Just because your passions change doesn't mean they aren't valid and you shouldn't go after them. It's okay to change paths to continue to grow. A tree branches out as it grows, so do people," Willa told her, and then they both turned back to the window as Greer processed it.

"So, do you want me to be your groom?" Greer asked. "I'm more than capable."

"Your capability was never in question. I have a feeling you're the most capable person I've ever met. Your safety is my concern."

"I don't want to brag, but I'm kind of an expert at that," Greer said with a little smirk.

Willa laughed and smiled at Greer. "Then I'd love your help."

"Even though I really like you, I'll still kill you if hurt Porter," Greer said with the same sweet-as-pie smile on her face as she got while talking about things she loved.

"I wouldn't expect anything less."

Porter joined Willa and Greer after hanging up with Naylor. His blood pressure was sky high, but as soon as he put his arm around Willa, it was if his whole body felt at peace.

"Naylor finally admitted you're not a threat. Their security team has been trying to catch The Panther for years and can't get close," Porter told them.

The elevator door opened and Kale rushed in. "Did I miss it?"

"Sloane just started pushing," Miss Lily told him as she handed a cookie to a nurse.

"Phew," Kale said as he looked around the room. When he saw Porter and Willa, he headed straight for them. "I'm Kale Mueez."

"He's the computer genius?" Willa asked Greer, who nodded. "I work in tech and you don't look like any computer guy I've ever met," Willa said as she held out her hand. "Willa Aldridge."

Porter watched as Kale shook her hand and smiled just a bit. He might complain about working out with his father, but Kale wasn't complaining about the increased appreciation he was getting from the ladies around town.

"Thanks, but we have an issue," Kale said, turning his phone around.

Porter looked down at it and saw his name and all his personal information listed on it. "What's this?"

"I hacked a Russian assassin's dark web account and found this. It's from The Panther, identifying you as the person protecting the key. The key being Willa," Kale explained. "He's offering a million dollars to anyone who kills you."

"What about Willa? Won't he want control of the key?" Porter asked.

"Whoever kills you gets another million for delivering Willa. That country will also get first bid at the key. If they try to take the key for themselves, they'll be eliminated and The Panther will destroy the country that betrays him."

Willa gasped and Porter cursed.

"How can he do that?" Porter asked.

"Take down their internet. Halt their shipping logistics. Take over their bombs. Turn their drones on them . . . My dad can take out a county's leader in an hour the old school way. I can take out the entire country's economy and then bomb it in an hour. The Panther is ten times better at this than I am."

"That's horrifying," Porter said as he thought of everything computers controlled as being hackable.

"And now we have countries sending assassins after us." Willa didn't ask. It was a statement. A statement made with her so far beyond panic she said it as if it were no big deal.

"Good thing you have me," Greer said with a smile. "Oh, this is going to be fun. Let me call Jackson and get his crew in on this."

"Jackson?" Willa asked Porter as Greer stepped away with her phone. "Have I met this cousin yet?"

"Not yet. He's Ryan and Greer's brother. He's FBI Hostage Rescue, too. He and two guys, Lucas and Talon, have helped us out before," Porter answered.

"Us?" Willa asked.

"Keeneston," Porter said, waving at the roomful of people. "This isn't the first time assassins have come after us and it won't be the last."

"What do we do?" Willa asked.

"We close ranks. Move you into Keeneston where we'll

have backup if we need it," Porter told her. That was the plan he'd already come up with when he was talking to his father and the rest of the family.

The double door burst open and Gabe Ali Rahman rushed out. Gone was the playboy smirk. Gone was the serious negotiator he'd turned into. Instead, there was a dopey smile on his face. "It's a boy! Mother and baby are great. We'll be out in a bit."

His parents, Dani and Mo, rushed forward and hugged him. His brother and his wife, Zain and Mila, were next and then his sister and her husband, Ariana and Jameson, were the last ones to hug him before he rushed back to Sloane and their son.

"If someone wasn't trying to kill us, this would be a very sweet moment," Willa said, taking a deep breath. "Wait, what about Tilly?"

"Tilly? What about her?" Porter asked.

"If they've been studying me, they know I'm close to my father and Tilly. They are the two most important people in the world to me."

Porter nodded as he understood what she was saying.

"I'll go get her," Greer said. "She can stay with me at the apartment."

Porter saw Willa take a deep breath and shiver as she let it out. The reality of the situation was hitting her hard. He put his arm around her and held her close to him. "Let me call your father and tell him what's going on for you."

Willa sniffled as she tried not to cry. "You have to protect him, Porter. I don't know what I'd do without my dad."

"We'll work it out," Porter promised as Willa unlocked her phone, pulled up her father's number, and handed it to him.

Greer came over and put her arm around Willa's shoulders. "So, tell me about Tilly."

Porter walked away when Kale caught up to him. "I don't want to go all fanboy, but Brian Aldridge is my hero. You all have Captain America or Superman. I have Brian Aldridge. If you want, he can stay with me and together we can work on finding The Panther."

"That does sound a little creepy fanboy-ish, but it's a hell of an idea. I'll run it past him," Porter told his friend. Two geniuses were better than one.

Porter called the number and Brian Aldridge answered at once. "Hello, honey. How is the show going?"

"Hello, sir," Porter said, intending to introduce himself, but Brian cut him off.

"Who the hell are you and where is my daughter?"

"Willa is safe. She's standing across the room from me. I'm Porter Davies. I'm the independently contracted CIA agent charged with protecting her and the skeleton key. There have been some developments you need to know about."

"Let me talk to my daughter," Brian demanded.

"One second," Porter told him as he strode across the room and held out the phone. "Your dad wants to make sure you're okay."

Willa took the phone, straightened her back, and pretended she hadn't been scared out of her mind. "Hello, Dad. I'm fine. I'm safe. All thanks to Porter. Please listen to him, okay?" Willa paused and then laughed. "No, Dad. There's no gun pointed at me. Please. It's important you listen to Porter, okay?"

Willa nodded and handed the phone back to Porter.

"What's going on?" Brian demanded.

Porter filled him in as quickly and as detailed as he could.

"The Panther. I should have known. He's coming after you and you're in danger," Brian said.

"We know. I have help here. So do you. Ever heard of Rahmi?" Porter asked about the small island country Ariana and her family were royalty.

"Yes. I've done some work with the king. Why?" Brian asked.

"You have an invitation to stay at their place in Keeneston so we can protect you. Also, a friend of mine is a bit of a computer genius. He suggested you two work together to help find The Panther," Porter told him. "And, you'll be close to your daughter."

"Every kid with a laptop thinks they're a computer genius," Brian muttered. "But I'll be there. I'll get on my plane right now."

"No, we'll send one for you. And Kale isn't some kid with a laptop. He's going to be the kid putting you out of business in five years."

"Wait, Kale Mueez?" Brian said. "The kid who hacked the NSA when he was twelve?"

Porter smiled at that memory. "Yeah, that's him."

"You're right. He's not just some kid. I look forward to meeting him. He's rather elusive in the tech world, but we all know his name." Brian Aldridge paused for a second. "Willa had you call me?"

"Yes. She wanted me to explain what was going on. She's talking to my cousin right now about protection for her friend Tilly," Porter said as he heard fingers typing on a keyboard.

"Porter Jake Davies. Twenty-nine. Son of Cyland Davies and Gemma Perry. Wow, you're a good rodeo rider. Highest earning rider for the last two years, thanks to your sponsorships. Ouch. I see why you retired," Brian said as Porter just listened, smiling. This was a trademark move of every single one of the Davies dads.

"You just bought out your brother's share of what you two have owned. You're actually financially stable, both on your own and via your parents. Hmm, interesting."

"Yes, I think I am rather interesting. Did you see the C-plus I got on that John Steinbeck paper in high school?" Porter asked.

"I did, but I got a C-minus on my Steinbeck paper, too, so I wasn't going to mention it. I do see your medical history, though. Lots of broken bones, but I don't see any hidden children or wives."

"Nope. I'm not that kind of guy."

"What kind of guy are you, Porter Davies?" Brian Aldridge asked.

"I'm the kind who doesn't get intimidated. I'm the kind who will tell you what you ask even if it's not what you want to know. I'm the kind who loves his friends and family and will do anything for them. I'm the kind of guy who will protect your daughter with his life."

"Are you the kind of guy to love her? Because, you look like you already do."

Porter paused. No one said anything about love. Like, sure. Love? Porter looked over at Willa as she talked to his family. As if sensing him, Willa glanced up and smiled at him. He was raised to tell the truth, ironic since his father had been a spy.

"I see how you're looking at her right now and how she's looking at you."

Porter glanced around and saw the hospital security

camera and gave it a little wave. "Then you don't need me to answer the question."

"Oh, I think I do. I'm putting my daughter's life in your hands. And no offense, but all I see on paper is a rodeo star. I don't see how you're qualified to protect her. If you care for her, that's something else. I would literally do anything in this world to protect my daughter. Only someone who cares about her would do the same. I could hire an army to protect her. Why should I let you do it?"

Porter kept his eyes on the camera. "I could love her. Let's just say I'm on my way. As for protecting her, pull up the security footage for Landon's on West Short Street from last night. Our friend did the security so it may take you a minute."

Porter waited as he heard Brian working on his computer. "Landon Davies owns the building." Brian was quiet for a second. "He's your cousin. You could have just given me the security password. He's standing eight feet from you."

Porter grinned into the camera. "Where's the fun in that?"

Brian chuckled as his finger flew over the keyboard. "I forgot what it's like to be challenged. Thanks for not sucking up to me."

"Not really my style, Mr. Aldridge," Porter said as he waited for Brian to find the footage.

It took him three minutes. "Jeez. Is that a spoon?"

"One thing your computer will never tell you about is Davies family dinners. I can and I will protect Willa. I'll see you soon. The plane is on the way. The man who is meeting you is named Nabi."

"Nabi what?" Brian asked.

"Umm, yeah, it's just easier to call him Nabi," he said of

Nabi's very long and difficult to pronounce last name. "I look forward to meeting you, Mr. Aldridge."

Porter hung up and handed the phone back to Willa.

"Is everything set with my dad? Was he upset?"

"He's just worried about you and he'll be here shortly. He'll stay with Kale and Kale's parents, Ahmed and Bridget."

Willa nodded as the doors opened and Gabe wheeled his wife and newborn son out into the lobby filled with Keenestonites. Sloane was grinning from ear to ear as she looked down at the bundle in her arms. "Everyone, meet Xavier. Xavier, meet your family."

16

Willa and Porter went back to the equestrian park, checked on their horses, and familiarized Greer with Willa's employees and setup. Then they'd headed to Keeneston. The drive was pretty as they wound their way over the narrow country road, cutting through crop, cattle, and horse farms. When Willa had been looking for her farm, the realtor had driven while Willa had worked on her phone the full time. Now she could really enjoy the rolling hills of the Bluegrass State.

They came around a turn and suddenly a small town appeared. "Welcome to Keeneston," Porter told her. "That's my cousin-in-law's security company."

"Aiden Creed," she read as they drove slowly by.

"This is the best, and only, place to eat. You met the founders of the Blossom Café, the Rose sisters. Now their younger cousins, Poppy and Zinnia, run it and the bed and breakfast," Porter explained.

Willa watched the rest of the town fly by. It was only one street and a couple of blocks long, but she saw where the doctor's office was, the library, the law firm, and his aunt's boutique. Then they were back onto the country roads lined with farms.

They turned into a lane and drove past a large farmhouse on the right. "That's where my parents live," Porter explained as they veered away from the house and continued driving. Soon there were only horse and cattle fields for as far as Willa could see.

They crested a little hill and there was a cottage. "This is where I live. Parker and I used to live together, but he moved into the matching cottage on the other end of the back of the property."

Porter explained to her that the house had exploded when Riley was in danger and then rebuilt. However, over the years, both Riley and Reagan had gotten married. Reagan had moved out and over to Carter's farm, and Riley and Matt had lived at that house for a while before recently buying a couple acres from their parents and building a family-sized house on the side of the farm closest to town. It also had the benefit of having its own driveway so their mom and dad couldn't monitor their comings and goings. Not that their dad hadn't already installed hidden cameras everywhere, but it made Riley feel as if she had some privacy.

"It's beautiful. The grass is so green," Willa said in wonder as she looked out over the rolling hills backing up to a heavily wooded area with a hill range that seemingly divided the land.

"These are my barns. Would you like to see them?" Porter asked after he opened the door for her.

"You know I do!" Willa couldn't wait to see the horses Porter had told her so much about.

The barns were a short walk from the house. There were training areas outside of them and the doors were open, letting the summer air flow through. Large fans circulated the air inside the clean barns and a couple of horses had fans on their stall doors as well to keep them extra cool. The barns were new and well made. They lacked the luxury touches that some of the elite show-jumping barns had, but the horses were well cared for and that's all that mattered to her. Mahogany hand-carved ceiling panels didn't matter if horses weren't cared for.

"I have state-of-the-art cushioning under the straw for them," Porter said as he stopped at an empty stall. He used his boot to push back the bedding and Willa saw the rubber mats that the expensive show stalls had. "I grow my own hay. It's all organic, fresh, and it's fed with underground limestone water. It's great for the horses," Porter explained and Willa nodded.

She loved seeing this side of Porter. He was relaxed and proud of what he'd built. "This is beautiful, Porter. The horses look so happy and healthy."

To be honest, it was a huge turn on. Callum would never think about the flooring for his horses. He had other people who did that. Seeing the care and love Porter had for his horses showed what kind of man he was under the spoon stabbing she'd seen the other night. And it even began to override the fact that he'd lied to her about the real reason he was in her life.

Porter reached out and a horse nuzzled his hand, searching for food. Porter smiled at him and Willa's anger fully melted away. "You're not a CIA super spy lying to people all over the globe. You're a horse trainer who got put in an impossible situation all because of me. How do you not hate me? I'm putting your brother's career and your life in danger."

Porter turned to face her, his brow creased. "You think

this is your fault. I can hear it in your voice. You're just as innocent in this as I am. However, if it's in my power to keep you safe, I will. Don't ever feel bad about that."

Willa looked at him and smiled as all the bits and pieces she'd learned about Porter Davies fell into place. "You'd do it just because it's the right thing to do, wouldn't you?"

"That," Porter said as he walked over to her and put his hand on her hip. The heat radiated from his hand, through her clothes and spread across her body. "And because of you. I've only known you for a few days, and I already know you're special to me. I'd never let anything happen to you when I could stop it."

"I hate to sound defeatist, but do you really think you can take on The Panther? I'll understand if it's too much. I can hide until this is over. Hell, I can hire an army to protect me," Willa told him although the thought of leaving Porter filled her stomach with lead. It didn't matter that they'd just met this week. She was falling for him hard.

"Family dinner is Sunday. Why don't you see what you think after that," Porter said, sounding very sure of himself. Willa had heard the others talking about family dinner, but she just didn't see how that could line up with military training.

Porter and Willa had already eaten dinner when the sound of tires flying over the gravel lane leading to his house echoed in the country night air. Porter had his rifle in hand before the headlights came into view.

"Who is it?" Willa asked as she came to stand beside him.

Tonight had been a taste of domestic bliss Porter hadn't

even known he'd been missing. They'd cooked dinner together, laughed as they ate, and kissed as they cleaned up. That kissing had led to them making out like teenagers on the couch until Porter had heard the crunch of the gravel.

"They're going so fast," Willa cried as she tugged on his arm. "We need to run!"

Porter lowered his rifle and shook his head. "It's Kale. Only Kale drives that fast."

"He's going to hit the house!" Willa yelled as the sports car's engine didn't let up.

"Nah, he hasn't yet," Porter said as he stepped out onto the porch as the car finally braked hard and went into a controlled spin, piling up the gravel.

The car stopped with the passenger side door even with the sidewalk leading up to the house. The door opened and a man fell out and onto the ground. His fingers curled into the grass as he groaned.

"I think I might be sick."

Willa popped her head around from where she was hiding behind Porter. "Dad?"

"Everything is spinning," her father groaned as he collapsed onto the ground. "Get it to stop."

Kale stepped out of the low slung sports car as Willa rushed forward to help her father. "I thought you'd like to see your dad as quickly as possible."

Brian Aldridge groaned again as Willa knelt down by his side. "Are you okay?"

"I will be. I've driven race cars for charity events. Nothing compared to what I just went through." Brian grabbed his daughter and looked up at her, his face sweaty and pale. "Don't ever get in the car with this man. Ever!"

"How are you doing, Willa?" Kale asked, coming around the car and smiling down at her. He reached down, grabbed her father under the arms, and hauled his tech hero to his feet. "All good, sir?"

Brian wavered on his feet and then nodded. "I think the worst of the nausea is gone. Damn," Brian said, looking up at Porter. "I had this big speech planned to intimidate you, but crawling from a car and nearly throwing up aren't very intimidating."

Porter held out his hand. "It wouldn't have worked anyway. I'm Porter Davies and it's a real honor to meet you. Willa has told me so much about you."

Brian looked at his daughter with so much love in his eyes that Porter knew why his brothers-in-law put up with so much crap from his own dad. Because they knew Cy loved his daughters and would do anything for them. Since Matt and Carter loved Porter's sisters, they put up with it, just like Porter would tolerate any hazing Brian put him through. Porter stilled as he fully thought that out. Did that mean he loved Willa? He cared for her already, but love? His family said it would hit hard and fast, but could this be it? It sure felt like it, and he was pretty sure he looked at Willa the way Matt and Carter looked at his sisters . . . fully and completely in love.

"You too?" Kale muttered to him as he took out his phone and pulled up the Blossom Café Betting App. "I'm going to be the only single guy in town soon." Kale froze and then smiled. "Actually, that wouldn't be so bad. With the battle over who runs the Belles, either Nikki or Tandy, the other members are feeling neglected. Now I just need to get Colton and Landon hooked up with someone and the field will be wide open for me."

Porter chuckled quietly at the thought of Kale surrounded by the Belles. The Keeneston Belles were technically a charitable organization comprised of the single women of Keeneston. When they married, they joined the Keeneston Women's Group, who were the real force behind the town. However, the Belles liked the attention of being a sorority-like group. They put out a yearly list of Most Eligible Keeneston Bachelors and then pursued them with all the zeal of hunters on the first day of deer season.

Nikki had been the leader of the Belles for a long time and had led with iron tits. Since Tandy moved back to Keeneston she'd been trying to get the Belles to soften a little and focus more on the charity aspect of the group than husband hunting. Right now there was a battle for leadership between the two. It would get figured out soon, but for now everyone just kept a wide berth when the two were in the same room together.

"Come on in, sir," Porter said to Brian Aldridge. "Let's talk."

Kale followed excitedly behind his nerd hero as Willa led them into the living room.

Brian took a seat on the couch next to Willa and hugged her to him. "You really think you can keep us safe? I will admit the security at Desert Sun Farm is tight. I think Willa should join me there."

Porter was about to tell him it wasn't necessary when the front door was kicked in and his father came barging in with the largest gun he'd ever seen and more ammo strapped to him than any one man should be able to carry.

Brian screamed and shoved Willa to the ground as if the coffee table would protect them.

"I saw a car. Is everything secure?" his dad asked as he scanned the room.

"Yes, Dad. Kale just brought Brian Aldridge over to see Willa," Porter said as his mother ran in the door behind his father with the Acid Gun of Death in one hand and a tray of brownies in the other.

"Do I shoot someone or feed them?" Gemma asked as she looked around the room.

"Mom! Where did you get the Acid Gun of Death?" Porter asked as calmly as he could while he raced over to her and grabbed the gun.

"Sophie thought I would need it. She also made that gun for your dad. It was my anniversary gift to him. Did I hear Willa's dad is here?"

Brian Aldridge slowly raised his head. "Are you here to kill us?"

"Kill you?" Porter's mother laughed. "No, we're Porter's parents. We thought to meet our son's girlfriend's father and welcome you to town."

Brian looked from Gemma to Cy to Porter and then to Willa. "I think it's best if we get you out of here."

Willa smiled patiently at her father as she stood up. She went over to Gemma and took the brownies from her. "Thank you for dessert, Gemma. They smell delicious. See, Dad, I'm perfectly safe here."

"Wait, wait, wait," her father said, standing up. "Let me get this straight. This crazy driver is the infamous Kale Mueez, the crazy woman with whatever an Acid Gun of Death and brownies are, is Porter's mother, and the crazy man with the biggest gun I've ever seen—"

"Thank you," Cy said with a cocky grin.

"Is Porter's father?" Brian continued. "And you're dating Porter, the CIA agent who lied to you and thought you were a traitor?"

"I never thought she was a traitor," Porter told him. If this were happening to his brother, Porter would have been laughing his ass off. As it was happening to him, it wasn't so funny.

"Dad, you can put your gun away. Although Sophie did a really nice job," Porter said, trying to regain some control of this situation.

His father slung the gun around so it rested on his hip. "Your cousin is very talented with weapons. She must get it from her mother since my brother is the worst shot of all of us. Well, except Pierce. He couldn't hit the broad side of a barn."

Brian shook his head as if in a bad dream. "Get your things, Willa. We're leaving."

"Dad. I'm staying with Porter. As you can see, I'm very safe."

Brian was still shaking his head. "His family is crazy and besides he only has a rifle. Now that I see his dad's gun, it's clear the boy can't protect you as well."

Oh no. It wasn't Cy's face that had Porter wanting to hide. It was his mother's. "Excuse me," Gemma said sweetly. "Are you saying my son isn't good enough to protect your daughter?"

Willa looked at Porter with horror. She could see where things were heading and it was like watching a burning car rolling downhill into an explosives plant. There would be no survivors.

"That's exactly what I'm saying. Willa, get your things. I knew I should have handled this myself."

"There is no one better equipped to protect your daughter than my son. My son is strong, brave, intelligent, and loyal. He is well trained in multiple fighting techniques, can outride the toughest bronc, and is a crack shot with that rifle you scoffed at. Plus, you should see what he can do with a spoon. How dare you come into his house and tell him he isn't good enough for your daughter," his mother said, her voice slowly rising as she stalked toward Brian.

Porter opened his mouth to try to diffuse the situation but his mother simply held up one finger to stop him. Porter's mouth snapped shut.

"That's exactly what I'm saying. My daughter's life is invaluable and for all I know your son is just after her money. It won't be the first time that's happened. I've chased them off just like I will your son."

"Duck and cover, son. Your mother is about to explode," Cy whispered to Porter.

"Dad!" Willa yelled, clearly angry, but Gemma held up her finger to Willa. The ultimate mom move worked because Willa's own mouth snapped shut as she moved to take Porter's hand in hers.

Cy took a giant step back and Porter thought it was a good idea. He hadn't seen his mother this angry since he and Parker had accidentally blown up her vegetable garden when they were thirteen. He had, however, also learned a valuable lesson that day about the quantities of C-4 needed to blow up things.

"How dare you?" Gemma challenged in a low voice as she stalked Brian around the living room table. "I have raised my son to be an honest, hard-working gentleman. I've raised him to only care about what's on the inside of a person, not any of the trappings of money, popularity, or fame. Obviously you think too highly of yourself. I was coming here to tell you how wonderful your daughter is. How much we enjoy her company. How talented she is. Then you insult my son and by inference, my husband and me. I should shoot you for such a narrow-minded, arrogant act. Instead, I think you need a timeout," Gemma said calmly and slowly. Porter knew that tone. It was the mother tone that sent him and Parker running for cover.

"You can't put me in a timeout!" Brian scoffed. Then his mother reached across the table, grabbed him by the shirt, and yanked him forward so that their faces were only inches apart.

"You insulted my family. You're lucky this is all you're getting."

Zap!

Brian Aldridge crumpled to the ground.

"What did you do to him?" Willa cried as she dropped Porter's arm and rushed over to where her father was halfway lying face down across the coffee table.

Braaaap. Brian Aldridge farted.

"It's a fart taser. Isn't it great?" his mother said happily as if she hadn't just tased Willa's father and as if he weren't just lying across the table unconscious and farting. "My niece, Sophie, made it. She made my husband's gun, too. Would you like me to get you one?"

"The taser or the gun?" Willa asked, and Porter busted out laughing. He had been momentarily worried Willa would be mad and leave after this, but the slight tilt of her lips told him otherwise.

"I guess either. The gun is a little bulky, though. I bet she could make you something that fit into your riding boot."

"Great idea, Aunt Gemma." Speak of the devil. Sophie was walking through the door with a smile on her face and carrying a large duffle bag. She stopped and looked at Brian farting on the coffee table. "What did he do?"

"That's Willa's father. He was a little hysterical and needed a timeout," Gemma said calmly.

Porter saw Willa frown and worry filled him again.

"Mr. and Mrs. Davies, I'm sorry for my father."

"Gemma and Cy, dear," his mother said, patting Willa's hand. "I'm sure he'll apologize when he wakes up and realizes what a good man my son is. The important question is if you realize it."

Willa turned and smiled at Porter and his whole world stopped spinning in that one moment. "I do. I think he's a great man."

17

When Willa first met Porter, she'd thought he was a groom. She didn't care then because she knew he was "a good one" as her mother used to tell her. Since then, she'd learned so much more about him. Porter Davies was a man that women only dreamed about. Even if his mother tased her father, Porter was still "a good one" and Willa wasn't about to let him go.

"Well, not the worst way it could have gone when parents meet," Sophie Dagher said with a laugh. "He's still alive. Now, I have weapons." Sophie froze. Her eyes went wide as she stared at Porter. "Sweet Mary, who gave Porter the Acid Gun of Death?"

Porter rolled his eyes at his cousin and Willa laughed. They were playing up this so-called acid gun to the point of hilarity.

"I misfired it one time and this is what I get."

"I'm pretty sure it was every time you held it. Nash still has nightmares. He wakes up screaming for someone to take the acid gun from Porter before we're all turned to goo," Sophie said as she set the duffle bag on the bar top next to the brownies.

Cy's father moved to talk to Kale, and Porter rolled his eyes again at his cousin. "Fine, here. Take it. Why did you give it to my mother in the first place?"

"She's remodeling, and it's a very easy way to take down a wall," Sophie said as if that were a common use for a gun that shot out a sticky acid bomb so strong it would melt practically anything, at least according to Porter. Willa was pretty sure he was exaggerating just a bit.

Porter held out the gun, stepped forward, and Willa's father farted so loudly that Porter stumbled. As Porter tried to catch himself, his finger slipped onto the trigger and then an acid bomb went flying.

"Whoops," Porter muttered as everyone looked around to see where the acid bomb hit.

The audible gasp behind her let Willa know when Kale saw it. The acid bomb had hit Kale's sports car dead center. The expensive black matte car was currently melting like wet paint onto the ground.

"Wow, I guess it really does melt anything," Willa said with wonder as she watched the car dissolve.

"My car!" Kale cried as he watched in horror as his sports car was reduced to a pile of goo.

Sophie grabbed the Acid Gun of Death from Porter and shook her head at him. "I defended you. I thought Nash was being dramatic. Now I owe him an apology," Sophie huffed at her cousin before turning to Willa. "Now, for your riding boots," Sophie said, reaching back into her bag. "There's not much room in them, however, I'm sure they're good leather. Leather makes the perfect sheath for a knife. If you show you me your boots, I can have Sydney make the perfect in-boot sheath for this beauty."

Willa's eyes went wide as Sophie pulled the scabbard

from a shiny knife. "I couldn't stab someone," Willa said instantly. The idea of sinking a blade into a real live person made her nauseous.

"You can do anything when your life is on the line," Sophie answered as if it were fact. Willa supposed it was. Before Porter spooned the man to death the other night, Willa had been looking for a weapon to do just that. "Now, this is made from 9260 Spring Steel. It's flexible and extremely tough. It's also extremely sharp. You can stab or slice with it. We'll practice knife skills at family dinner."

"You practice knife skills at family dinner?" Willa asked as she took the knife Sophie was handing her.

"Where do you think Porter learned how to kill someone with a spoon? I might also suggest wearing athletic clothes under a dress. You never know when you'll need to take off crawling through barbed wire or throwing an ax. The athletic wear will definitely help. Well, Porter has my number. Call anytime."

Willa's father farted and groaned. "Wait, Sophie. Where do I get one of those tasers?" Willa asked.

Sophie grinned and reached into her bag of weapons. "Here you go." Sophie tossed what looked like lipstick to her. Willa turned the bottom of the tube and out came two prongs, painted red.

"Just press the bottom of the tube," Sophie instructed.

Willa did so and sparks came to life between the two small prongs. "This is so cool," Willa said as she gave the taser a little zap.

"Let's see how dinner goes. Bring a pair of shoes you don't mind losing," Porter's father told her as he patted her back. "My wife looks sweet, but remember she was carrying the Acid Gun of Death. We'll see you tomorrow for Porter's next ride. We'll save you a seat."

Gemma smiled at her next. "Don't worry about dinner. It'll be fun. See you tomorrow," Gemma said as she hugged her.

"Hey, wait. We need a ride home," Kale called out.

"Your dad is on his way," Cy said with a little wave.

The room was quiet and Willa heard Kale give a little sniffle as he stared at the puddle of goo that had been his car. "I can't believe you melted my car."

Willa snickered and her father farted. The snicker turned into a smothered laugh, then a full-blown belly laugh. She struggled to catch her breath. "When. Your. Dad," Willa said between breaths. "Kicked in the door and your mom showed up with the brownies. And the car. Oh gosh. I can buy you a new one. Seeing it melt was so awesome."

"You are a cruel and cold woman. Do you know what a car like that means to a man?"

Willa turned to see Kale's father standing at the door.

She raised an eyebrow. "Most of the men I know who drive sports cars like that are making up for something. Or they're cheating on their wives as they go through a midlife crisis."

Willa saw the surprise on Ahmed's face and then the lip twitch that told her he was amused. "Neither. I'm the one who likes it fast, hard, and dangerous. You can ask my wife about it if you're really interested." Ahmed looked down at her father and then at his son. "Get the baggage, Kale. I promised Nemi some ice cream."

"Do I get ice cream?" Kale called out as he bent and hefted Brian Aldridge over his shoulder. "My car melted. Ice cream would soothe my broken heart. Oh, and Willa," he said after calling after his father, "I'm not old enough for a midlife crisis and well, you can use your imagination based on what you can see in my jeans."

"I already know it's all about speed for you," Willa called out. Her mouth was a runaway train. She'd never joked with people like this and certainly not about their penis size. And certainly not with her boyfriend standing there. However, Porter was grinning and the idea that she'd just called him her boyfriend in her mind was enough to make her giddy.

"The faster, the better," Kale said as he walked out the door.

"Your poor girlfriends," Willa called out and saw Kale stumble as Porter busted out laughing.

Porter closed the door, still laughing, and Willa felt her heart warm. This was fun. This wasn't a stuffy relationship all about being a trophy for your partner. The type where you were constantly judged on what you said, how you looked, and how much money you had. This was real and it was great. Acid Gun of Death, farting father, and all.

"I'm so sorry about my dad. Normally he's so laid back, but this must have really upset him."

Porter came and wrapped his arms around her. Willa tilted her head up to look into his eyes. "It's nothing to be sorry about. He's looking out for you. I understand completely. I also know this is all very sudden. I understand if you want me to take a step back. I can send you back to your bodyguards and protect you from the shadows if that's what you prefer."

Greer had pretended to be Willa tonight and taken off with Willa's bodyguards back to her rental with Tilly in tow before sneaking out the back and leaving Willa's bodyguards visibly guarding the house. For anyone who was watching, it would appear Willa and Tilly were in Lexington.

"Is that what you want? To take a step back? I know your family is pushing you on our relationship, but I won't push you." Even as Willa knew she'd be proud and giddy to call Porter her boyfriend, she wasn't going to push him. Porter didn't seem like the type of man who liked to be pushed into something he didn't want.

"If I wanted a step back, I would have taken it. Instead I moved you into my house. What does that tell you I want?" Porter asked as his eyes told her everything he wanted.

Willa blushed and licked her now dry lips. "Me?"

Porter nodded and a smirk played out on his lips. Lips she wanted to kiss.

"I guess it's good that I want you, too," Willa told him. "Even if your mother now hates my father."

Porter pushed back the hair that had fallen from her ponytail. "No parents here now. It's just you and me. No matter what our parents want, I know I want you for more than a case."

Willa's eyes fell closed as she offered up her lips to Porter. He didn't hesitate to take them in his as he kissed her slowly and seductively. His hands ran down her spine, over the curve of her hip and up her sides until they cupped her breasts.

Willa gave a little gasp of pleasure and Porter deepened the kiss. His fingers were like magic and Willa found herself melting into him. Her hands rested on his chest and she moved them to yank his shirt free. She had to feel the warmth of his skin against her palms. Only Porter shoved her away, and before Willa knew it, she was flung to the floor and Porter had the rifle in his hand.

"Identify yourself or I'll shoot!" Porter yelled.

Willa looked up at the rifle and saw a small three-inch screen above the scope. The screen showed through the wall and into the darkness of the night. A greenish-white figure could be seen clear as day and Porter had the person right in his sights.

"Just me, Porter!"

"Me who?" Porter yelled.

"Lucas," the man yelled back. "Talon is on the other side of the house and Jackson is checking out the woods."

"Try knocking next time," Porter yelled as he lowered the rifle and placed it back onto the counter.

"Who are they?" Willa asked.

"Greer's brother, Jackson, and his FBI hostage team."

A knock came at the door a second later and Porter answered it. A giant man came through, followed by a skinnier one with a big goofy smile on his face. Lastly, a serious looking man with silver eyes walked in.

"You've made the text tree blow up like Kale's car," the silver-eyed man said, finally grinning.

Porter smiled and hugged the man. "Couldn't be the boring cousin," Porter joked back. "And we all wanted that car melted. Now we're safe from Kale's driving for a couple of days."

The silver-eyed man laughed.

"He's scarier than Bertha the morning she wakes up after missing a meal," the skinnier man with the easy smile said with a chuckle.

"Who's Bertha?" Willa asked.

"She's my polar bear," the man said. "I'm Lucas. I'm from northern Alaska and Bertha lives nearby. She's the strongest, most dangerous predator, but she's also my cuddleumpkins."

"You know," Porter said with a mischievous grin, "my cousins in Shadows Landing have an alligator named Bertha. They say she's the toughest predator around."

Lucas's happy-go-lucky smile fell. "Take that back right now. A little gator has nothing on a polar bear."

"I don't know. I've seen Bertha the gator in action," silver eyes said, clearly taunting Lucas.

Lucas narrowed his eyes, opened his mouth to argue, but the mountain of a man stopped him. "Hi, I'm Talon."

"Willa Aldridge." Willa held out her hand. "Where are you from? I can't place your accent."

"I'm part Australian."

"Don't tell my mother I didn't introduce myself right away," the silver-eyed man said. "I'm Jackson Parker. My wife is Evie, and she can't wait to meet you."

"You're Greer's brother. It's so nice to meet you. All of you. You're so nice to help me out. I feel horrible putting you in this position," Willa told them.

"Taking down bad guys is what we do," Jackson told her.

"It's more fun than running from Bertha when she's feeling feisty. That old girl loves to play," Lucas said, holding up a photo for her to look at. Sure enough, there was Lucas wrestling a giant polar bear. "Let's see a gator do that," Lucas said smugly.

"Anyway, we're here to help. You'll see us out and about, so don't shoot us. We'll be at the horse event, too, but we won't be dressed like this," Jackson said, motioning to his full military gear. "Piper, one of our cousins, sent these over." Jackson dropped a backpack and opened it up. He tossed two windbreakers to her and Porter. "Wear them all the time. Sydney put decals for your farm on it. She said it would help you blend in while wearing it."

"I think she said something along the lines of bulletproof doesn't mean ugly," Talon said with a smile.

"Bulletproof?" Willa held up the light jacket.

"This is nanotechnology. This jacket is bulletproof and

stab-proof," Porter said as he looked at the PD Rodeo on the chest. "I like the decal."

"I know. I had her make FBI ones for us," Jackson told him. "I know your dad has the farm rigged, but tonight Talon will stay and patrol. Tomorrow Lucas will, then I will."

"Thank you," Willa said, feeling overwhelmed. None of these people knew her, but they were all here to help her.

"And Grandma Marcy invited us to family dinner. I can't wait. I've been practicing with the spoon Miles gave me. You're going down, Porter," Lucas taunted.

"I have my combat gear," Talon said. "I'm ready for family dinner."

Willa swallowed hard. Maybe family dinner really was something to be worried about.

18

"Oh my stars," Tilly said the second she found Willa at the event. "I'm moving to Keeneston. I have never seen so many hot men in my life."

Willa hugged her friend and enjoyed a bit of normalcy. Her bodyguards were stationed around and Greer, dressed as her groom, was hanging out near Apollo's stall.

"I met Greer's brother and his friends last night. Too bad her brother is already married," Tilly rattled on.

"I thought you liked Parker," Willa said, trying to keep up with whomever Tilly was currently lusting after. Ironically, Tilly had less of a social life than Willa did. Neither of them hardly ever dated and when they did, it usually resulted in disaster. Yet they had each other and many pints of ice cream.

Tilly sighed. "I think he thinks I'm goofy. I'm trying to be more outgoing and I just come off as silly." Tilly had been painfully shy when Willa met her as a child. She was still shy, but recently she'd forced herself to be more outgoing.

Tilly was hilarious, sweet, and good. She devoted all her spare time to charity and helping others. When they got together to hang out, they'd joke about the hot men they'd love to date but never would. Marguerite and Valentina had done a number on Tilly's self-confidence. She still saw herself as the small shy kid huddled in the corner at the party instead of the confident sexy woman she was when she wasn't around those bullies.

"I'm sure he doesn't think you're silly," Willa said, trying to reassure her friend.

Tilly shrugged. "They're all out of my league. You see how hot they are. I'm just me. But it's fun to look nonetheless."

"Tilly, you are totally in their league."

Tilly blushed and then changed the topic. "How did last night go with Porter?"

Willa laughed and filled her friend in on the acid gun, her father's bad behavior, and the way Porter had kissed her senseless and then held her all night long.

"He didn't push you to sleep with him?"

"Sleep, yes. Sex, no," Willa said, sounding disappointed.

"But you would have?" Tilly asked.

Willa didn't even think about it. "Yes. There's something there between us. I know it's soon, but Tilly, he's the one. Like, no question about it. He's the one."

"July second would be the perfect date for a wedding!" Greer called out from the stall. How she'd even heard their conversation was beyond Willa.

"Three weeks from now? We haven't even gone on a date without someone being killed or made it past some serious making out. I think it's going to take a little time," Willa said with a chuckle.

"Not with the men in my family. Once they know, they never veer from the path. They love and love hard. They don't waste time with proper dates before making a move. I can guarantee Porter is already realizing his feelings for you. If you know yours, then you two will be good to go by the next assassination attempt. Romance and gunfire. How romantic." Greer smiled to herself and gave a little sigh.

"What about you, Greer?" Tilly asked as they all joined Greer at the stall door. "Do you have a man in your life?"

Greer frowned. "Nope. The men on my team are off limits. In hostage rescue, we have to know we can trust each other completely. I can't mess that up with dating any of them. Then the rest of the FBI support and the guys I train with on different teams either think I'm a joke or are too intimated to ask me out. It doesn't help that my brothers have whispered they'll deal with anyone who hurts me. Do you know I'm twenty-nine years old and my brothers are still intimidating my dates and my dates are falling for it? Unfortunately, it works. I couldn't date someone who can't stand up to my family. So that leaves me single."

Tilly slipped her arm around Greer. "You and me both. We'll just ogle them from a distance."

Greer laughed and Willa had a feeling there was a lot going on under Greer's no-nonsense exterior. "Let's go watch Porter," Greer said to the group and they took off with the bodyguards surrounding them. Although Willa was pretty sure the most dangerous person around was the pretty woman laughing next to her.

Willa had cheered for Porter along with what appeared to be the entire population of Keeneston. Porter exited the ring and easily swung off the back of Miss Trix. He leaned forward and kissed Willa, using the brim of his cowboy hat to give them a smidge of privacy.

"I missed you," Porter whispered.

"We were only apart for thirty minutes," Willa said with a little laugh.

"That was enough. I was thinking, how about we try that date thing again? We can go to the Blossom Café tonight if you want."

Porter smiled down at her and Willa nodded. "I'd love to."

Porter got ready for his date in the guest room while Willa got ready in his room. Last night he hadn't wanted to let her out of his sight so he'd brought her back to his room. They'd lain in bed together all night. They'd kissed and talked until he curled her into him and they'd drifted off to sleep.

Waking with Willa in his arms was the best feeling he'd ever experienced. He was falling and falling hard for her. Now he had the chance to have a date with her without someone trying to kill them.

There was a knock on the front door and he rushed to answer it as he buttoned his shirt. Porter answered it with his gun in hand.

"Mr. Aldridge."

Willa's father was staring at Porter's half-buttoned shirt. Behind Brian was Ahmed, leaning against the SUV. Ahmed smirked as if he were expecting a bloodbath. He should know better. Porter wouldn't beat up Willa's father and he was certain Brian Aldridge had probably never thrown a punch in his life.

"Am I interrupting?" The meaning of Brian's question was clear.

Porter shook his head as he invited him in. "Just getting

dressed for dinner. We're going to the Blossom Café. Would you like to join us?"

Mr. Aldridge looked back toward the bedrooms.

"We got dressed in separate bedrooms," Porter told him. They hadn't slept in those separate rooms, but he didn't feel the need to tell Willa's father that.

"Willa is an adult." Mr. Aldridge took a deep breath but looked relieved nonetheless. "I'm sorry about my behavior last night. I've already apologized to your parents. I can only justify myself for being worried for my daughter's safety. I've lost her mother. I can't lose her, too."

"I understand, sir."

Brian Aldridge dropped onto a living room chair, set his elbows on his knees, and ran his hand over his head. "Kale and I worked all day today and haven't gotten anywhere with The Panther. Until his money and intelligence sources are turned off he's a constant threat to us. It's almost enough for me to end the encryption program all together."

"Kale is the smartest man I know. He'll figure something out. Until then, Willa is safe here. I promise."

"I know, but you shouldn't have to promise. You're a young man with his own life and we've come in here and messed it all up."

Porter could tell him not to worry about it. He could tell him meeting Willa was the best thing to have happened to him. He could have told him all this and more. However, the stress lines on Brian's face told him right now wasn't the time. He wouldn't be able to hear it.

"You just focus on what you do best and I'll focus on keeping Willa safe. We'll attack this together from two separate sides. The whole town is here to support you both," Porter told him.

Brian nodded and stood slowly up. "Again, I'm sorry I

said those things about you last night. I didn't mean them. You seem like a good man."

"Thank you, sir."

Brian let out a sigh and turned to look out the open front door. "That man scares me. This morning he was walking around with a dog in a baby sling and then threw a knife at his son-in-law's balls when they came over for breakfast."

Porter chuckled because he'd seen both things happen. "Ahmed Mueez is a living legend in military circles around the globe. His son-in-law is my cousin Dylan, who is almost as talented as Ahmed. Pair him with Ahmed's daughter, Abby, and you're at the safest breakfast table in the world. The knife thing is how they bond."

"Bond? I always wanted a son-in-law I could play chess with, not try to murder."

"It's more of a flinch game between Ahmed and Dylan. They try to see if they can get the other to flinch as they throw knives. If they wanted each other dead, it would be done, the body would be gone, and they would be back eating their breakfast before you could blink."

Brian's eyes were wide and then he shook his head. "I guess I'm safe then." Brian looked at him then and cocked his head just a bit to the side. "Do you throw knives or do you play chess?"

"Both," Porter said with a grin.

"We'll have to have a game soon. You can learn a lot about a man by how he plays chess."

Porter smiled at Brian as he began to walk out of the house. "Yes, my father told me the same when he taught me how to play. I look forward to it."

Porter watched as Brian and Ahmed drove off. He heard the bedroom door open and smelled a whiff of the light and airy perfume Willa favored. "Was that my father?"

"Yes, he came to apologize. He wants to play chess."

"Oh no." Willa's face fell and Porter looked at her in confusion.

"Isn't that a good thing?"

"No. He will obliterate you, humiliate your intelligence, and send you crying from the room. My father is a ruthless chess player and will comment on what type of man and how unworthy you are while playing."

Porter grinned. "I like a challenge."

"I have a feeling chess with my father is equivalent to your family dinner," Willa sighed.

Porter held open the door to the garage and smiled to himself. This was going to be fun.

19

Porter opened the door to the Blossom Café and felt at home. The memories he had eating dinner there with his family, friends, and town were some of his best. The smell of Southern cooking tempted his nose and rumbled his stomach as they took an open table for two near the door and across the way from the Rose Sisters.

"This is so unfair," Jameson Duke said from where he was sitting nearby with Ariana.

"What is?" Porter asked as Willa turned and waved at Ari.

"I walk in here and the whole place interrogates me. You walk in with Willa and nothing," Jameson complained.

Miss Lily nodded at the table across from them. "This is what Bridget was talking about. We go too easy on the ladies. Apparently, we're sexist."

"That's not true. I was thoroughly interrogated," Kenna Ashton called out.

"Me too," his Aunt Morgan added.

"Maybe we're going soft in our middling years," Miss Daisy said to her sisters. Middling, only if they planned to live to be two hundred years old and Porter was pretty sure that was the plan.

"Stella, did we interrogate you?" Miss Violet asked Jace's wife.

"No, you just placed bets on when we were going to get married," Stella called out from the table she sat at with Jace, Jackson, and Evie.

"Me neither," Evie said. "Pam just offered to mow down terrorists for me."

"Now that I'm older, my insurance rate has gone down. I can afford to hit a few more bad guys again," Pam told everyone as she rubbed her hands together. Pam handled having an empty nest with vehicular violence, but only with bad people.

"Humph. Maybe we are going soft in our middle years," Miss Lily said as she frowned.

"Well, we can't have that," Miss Daisy said, turning to Willa. Porter threw his salad fork at Jameson and gave him the middle finger, which resulted in the long reach of a broom being slammed down on his head.

"You know better than that, young man," Miss Lily chided as she thumped the handle of the broom against the floor to emphasize her point.

"Sorry, ma'am," Porter said. Sorry he was caught, that was. He was so going to get Jameson for this. A baby bet in the café app would make Jameson's life a nightmare for the next three months.

"I'll start," Miss Violet said. "What are your intentions with our Porter?"

Willa had just taken a sip of her iced tea and promptly choked on it. Poppy, the waitress, didn't seem distressed by her choking. Instead she put her hands on her hips and waited for an answer.

Willa looked around and everyone leaned forward to hear her answer. Deacon smirked and Porter decided he was going to kill him, too.

"Well," Willa started slowly, looking thoroughly perplexed and embarrassed. "I like him. Is that what you want to know?"

The Rose sisters made little harrumphs and then the interrogation was on.

"How do you plan to handle the long distance?" Miss Violet asked.

"I don't think distance will be a problem if we can solve the threat against me," Willa said, and Porter wondered if there was something she wasn't telling him because she was very careful with her wording.

"What do you think of Porter's job?" Miss Daisy asked.

"Which job? CIA or horse trainer?" Willa asked just as fast as the question was hurled at her.

Porter had to smile to himself. His girl didn't fold. She was calm and deliberate under pressure.

"Horse trainer," Miss Daisy replied just as quickly. Her eyes narrowed and Porter knew she meant business now.

"I love it. A man who treats his animals well is a good man," Willa said. "Next question?"

Porter watched as rapid-fire questions came from all over the café. They asked about her feelings, her preferences on movies and books, her thoughts on marriage, and then his aunt Morgan raised her hand. "I have a question from a call-in. How do you feel about babies?"

Call-in, yeah right. Porter knew exactly where that question was coming from. His mother.

"They're adorable," Willa answered and Porter had to smirk a little. She was the queen of answering every question without actually answering the question.

Aunt Morgan grinned. She owned her own PR firm and knew a good non-answer when she heard one. "You're a dream client. However, I need to know about your feelings on personally giving birth to a child that shares DNA with both you and Porter, specifically."

Porter almost spit out his drink. Only it wasn't his spit that was all over the table. It was the glass right in front of him. The glass had shattered and the liquid ran over his hand.

Porter blinked and then he was moving. Even as people around him yelled "Gun!" Porter leapt over the table, slamming into Willa, and crashing them onto the floor.

Porter kicked out with his booted foot and knocked the table onto its side to provide cover.

"They'll shoot through it!" Willa cried as she lay on the floor with her hands over her head.

"These tables are like a hundred years old. They're made of real wood and steel. A bomb couldn't hurt these tables," Porter told her. "Stay here."

"You're not going out there, are you?" Willa asked, but Porter was already moving. He pulled the gun with the X-ray screen and was on the move.

"Yes! I'll get my Hummer." Pam scrambled out the back door along with half the café. The other half were pulling weapons from purses, holsters, or from under the table. Spatulas, brooms, pans, knives, forks, and a soup spoon held by none other than a grinning Uncle Miles.

"I got your back," Porter heard Jackson say as he tossed the jacket Piper had made at him. Porter threw it on and glanced over his shoulder to see Willa sliding into hers while Abby and Dylan flanked her on each side.

"We got her," Abby called out. That was all Porter

needed to know as Parker joined him and Jackson sliding out the front door.

Porter was hunched over as they ran. Gunshots rang out and pinged into the concrete near his feet as he dove for cover behind a minivan.

"It's coming from the courthouse," Jackson said.

"I know where they are," Porter said after scanning the area with his gun and not finding anyone. He looked to his brother. "In our favorite spot." According to the Rose sisters, he and Parker had been "little rascals," they liked to climb and hide and their father had encouraged it. Spy training started early for the Davies twins. Later on, he and Parker became the go-to for sniper shooting from these hard-to-reach vantage points. However, this one wasn't hard to reach. It was just hard to see.

"Finally," Jackson said as his eyes took in the family moving into position on both sides of Main Street. A large engine roared to life behind the café. "We'll find your hiding spot. We could never find y'all."

"I don't think that will be necessary," Parker said, and Porter felt the familiar tug at his lips he got when they had a plan. They'd always been good at coming up with plans and never having to say a word of explanation. "You ready?"

"Ready for what?" Jackson asked.

Porter gave a nod. Parker took off his hat so they'd be hard to tell apart and then the plan was in motion. Porter shoved Jackson onto his back and the twins took off in the opposite directions.

"Not fair!" Jackson shouted.

Porter ran past his truck and grabbed the lasso from the back without slowing down. He didn't need to look behind him to know Parker was doing his part of the plan.

The gunman was confused. The twins looked enough

alike that at a distance he or she couldn't tell who was who so they had to split their shots. They'd fire a couple at Porter and then a couple at Parker. The farther apart they ran, the more time they each had to make their move.

Porter hit Aiden's office and when they turned the fire to Parker, Porter sprinted across the street and slammed himself against the side of the courthouse. As the shooter searched for him, he knew his brother was doing the same. The hiding place they had as children was actually the large bronze statue of a horse in front of the courthouse. The horse was rearing up and the rider on it was holding an arm up in victory. It was large enough that if you could get on top of it, you could hide on either side of the rider or under the mane, which, if you had a brother to boost you up, it was easy enough for a child to do it. From there it was a clear shot to the café. Plus, you had lots of exit points to slide down and run away to hide again.

Porter looked around the corner of the courthouse and didn't see a thing. He used the sight on the gun Sophie had given him and there the assassin was, clear as day. The assassin had his leg hooked around the rider's leg and was lying up and under the mane. The bronze hid most of the man, but the leg was plain as day.

Porter glanced down the side of the building and saw his brother looking at him. The sound of the engine revving, of tires squealing, and the headlights of the Hummer turning onto Main Street was enough to worry the assassin. He unhooked his foot and it was clear he was going to try to sneak off into the darkness.

Porter held up his hand and then opened and closed his fist. Together, both brothers sprinted from the sides of the courthouse to converge on the man trying to slide off the statue from behind.

"US marshal, freeze!" Parker yelled when the man got both feet on the ground.

The black clad figure turned to look at Parker and didn't see Porter closing in on him. He finally turned to see Porter and took off. He made his move as Parker fired his weapon, and sprinted toward the street.

Everything happened at once. The town erupted from every direction: Cody and Luke, the deputies, converged from behind with Porter and Parker; Jackson and his team from across the street; Miles from the north side of Main Street and Cy from the south. The man was trapped.

Then he saw the Hummer racing toward the street and jumped.

"Shit," Porter cursed as he dropped the gun and grabbed his lasso. He raised his arm and sent it spinning above his head. They needed the shooter alive to try to find The Panther.

Pam gunned her military surplus Hummer with the obscenely large grill and Porter had to move now. With a flick of his wrist he had the rope flying right to his target. The circular part of the lasso fell easily over the running man. Porter gave it a sharp tug and it tightened around the assassin's shoulders. With another big tug, the rope yanked the man backward. Pam missed hitting him by inches.

The Hummer came to a screeching halt as everyone raced to the tied-up assassin. Porter kept the rope tight as he wound it up while walking toward the groaning man.

"I almost had him!" Pam cried as she shot her arms up into the air in frustration. "Look at him. He's a little fella. I could have sent him flying a good thirty yards."

Porter had to smother a laugh as Aniyah came up and put her arm around Pam. "It's a shame. You could have gotten a new personal best. Don't worry, sugar. I'm sure another assassin will come and you'll punt him all the way to Paige's shop."

Pam frowned but nodded. "Thanks, Aniyah."

"Anytime, sugar. I have this video that will make you forget all about it. It was real educational for being a special video. What do you know about the Yeti?"

Parker picked up the man and Jackson was there to zip-tie his hands behind his back. Porter pulled the rope tighter and wound it around his captive's legs to prevent him from running.

Willa came out with Dylan and Abby on either side, both armed to the teeth. Behind her, the Rose sisters stood at the ready with a wooden spoon, a broom, and a spatula.

Porter reached down and ripped off the full head mask.

"Wang Lei," Dylan said with a dangerous smirk as he pushed the man to sit down on the curb. "What is China's top assassin doing in Keeneston going after my cousin?"

Wang Lei swallowed hard as Abby squatted down in front of him. "Wang, Wang, Wang," Abby tsked sadly. "What did I tell you I was going to do if I ever saw you again?"

Abby was talking as if Wang Lei were a child who had stolen too many cookies from the cookie jar, but the menacing look in her eyes told Porter she wasn't going to give Wang Lei a timeout.

"You would cut off my balls with a spoon and feed them to me."

The sound of a spoon clattering on the pavement echoed down Main Street as Miles tossed the soup spoon between Abby and Wang Lei.

Abby picked up the spoon and Wang Lei tried to wiggle away, but Porter had a strong hold on him.

Abby tapped the spoon on the curb between Wang Lei's

legs and looked sternly at him. "I'll let you keep one of your balls if you tell us everything we want to know."

Wang Lei shook his head, but Porter saw the sweat begin to drip down the side of his face.

Abby shoved the spoon into his groin and every man cringed. Wang Lei howled and then he pissed himself and passed out.

"I think we all know who just won the biggest badass in-law game once and for all. Boom!" Uncle Pierce said as he used his fingers to accentuate the boom. "Suck it with your spoon, Miles."

"But she did it with my spoon," Miles countered. "Besides, my son-in-law isn't even here. It's not a fair call."

"Yeah, Nash isn't here either," Uncle Cade said. "Biggest badass son- or daughter-in-law is still up for grabs."

"Are they for real?" Willa asked as she hurried to his side and looked down at the unconscious would-be assassin.

"They are. Ready to run away from us yet?" Porter asked her.

Willa turned to Abby. "Were you really going to feed him his balls?"

Abby shrugged. "I think it would be rather gross, but men's balls are their biggest weakness so I exploit it."

Willa smirked suddenly just like Abby had done a moment ago. "Why don't you pour some fake blood over his crotch and then feed him something that resembles testicles."

"Suck it, Pierce," Cy said, flicking off his younger brother. "She's not even my daughter-in-law yet and she's diabolical. Mental torture like that can break a man faster than any physical pain." Porter's father high-fived Willa, who looked as if she couldn't tell if he was joking or not. "She has my approval and we haven't even seen what she can do with an ax."

"So, your dad likes me because I can mentally torture someone and not because of my trust fund, my contacts, or my Ivy League degree?" Willa whispered to Porter.

"Yeah, that about sums it up."

"Huh," Willa said as she thought about that. "I think that's the best and most honest compliment I've ever gotten."

"I'll run back to the office and get some testicles," Wyatt called out. "I just helped castrate some goats. That should do it."

"He's a large animal vet," Porter explained to Willa who nodded.

"Good to know. That makes things slightly less weird."

"Willa! What happened?" Tilly cried out as she clung to a man's arm.

Greer looked annoyed as she joined the town. "Dang, I missed it. As soon as I heard Pam's tires, I got Tilly to safety. Who is he?"

"Chinese assassin," Porter told her.

"Why is there a spoon on the ground?" Greer asked.

"Abby was going to cut off his balls with it but he passed out and Willa suggested faking said castration and forcing him to eat goat balls," Porter said, filling her in. Greer grinned in reaction as the man Tilly clung to crossed his legs.

"I knew I liked you," Greer said with approval.

"Tilly, what are you doing with Ben?" Parker asked the tiny, sweet, and obviously smitten Tilly. It was clear she was interested in Parker, but Parker was staying mysteriously quiet on his thoughts about her, so she was doing everything she could to make him notice her. Including flirting with the very sexy man next to her, who just happened to be a priest.

"He came over to help protect me. He was former Special Forces," Tilly said, batting her eyes up at Ben who cleared his throat as if realizing exactly where this was going. "Unlike others, he's offered to come see me tomorrow night for some one-on-one time."

"Really?" Parker asked, and Porter saw he was trying not to laugh. "What are you two going to do?"

"I can think of all kinds of things," Tilly said as Porter began to cringe, realizing where she was going with this conversation.

"Um, Tilly," Porter said, trying to cut her off to save her the embarrassment he knew was coming.

"No, Porter. Your brother wants to know." Tilly walked over to Parker and went up on her tippy toes and whispered in his ear. Parker's expression turned to stone.

"Darlin', the only thing you're going to be doing on your knees with Ben is praying," Parker said with zero emotion. Anger rolled off his twin, but only Porter could tell. Parker was masking his feelings for all around him. Interesting.

"Oh, he'll see God alright," Tilly challenged back as she crossed her arms over her chest.

"Um, Tilly," Porter said again. Only this time he didn't let her stop him. He grabbed her arm and pulled her to him and then dropped his voice. "Ben is our town's Catholic priest."

Porter felt bad as her face went from white with shock to red with embarrassment. Her eyes began to fill with tears as she struggled to control her emotions. "A real one? Like a real, married only to God, not having sex, priest?"

Porter nodded and Tilly sighed. "What a waste. A man like him should be able to date."

"You could always petition the pope," Porter whispered to her before raising his voice. "That's so kind of you, Tilly. I'm sure Willa needs to have a glass of special tea at the café after the shock of everything."

"What?" Tilly asked.

"I'm helping you leave without my brother seeing your red eyes."

A little smile came across her face. "You're a good man, Porter." Tilly then raised her voice. "But I think I want in on the castration."

Greer snorted behind her. "Come on. Let's get the fake blood and torture this asshole."

Porter blinked as he quickly lost control of the scene. Wang Lei was whisked off to the basement of the security building at Desert Sun Farm where the questioning would technically be on Rahmi soil. Willa was already getting in the car with Abby and Dylan as they talked about how to best feed Wang goat balls.

"You can drive me," Parker said as he shook his head.

"Sure, and you can tell me what's going on with Tilly."

"Nothing is going, or can ever, go on with Matilda Bradford," Parker said with steel to his voice.

Porter didn't believe his brother for one second.

20

Willa didn't know how a matter of days could seem like a lifetime—in the best possible way. She had spent so much time with Porter and had so many long talks, deep kisses, and tantalizing moments that she couldn't imagine him not being in her life. Love wasn't a word she thought she'd use during a life and death situation, but she was definitely falling in love with Porter. While she wasn't sure, she would bet he was falling for her, too. The real her.

It had been two days since Willa watched Abby force-feed goat testicles to an assassin until he cried and handed everything over to Kale. Kale had infiltrated the invitation-only portion of The Panther's network but was still trying to get through multiple firewalls to access The Panther's entire network from auction items to financials. Her father and Kale were rarely seen, but Abby promised they were being fed regularly.

For two days, Willa had lived in the alternate world of Keeneston and actually felt bummed out when she had to return to the real world. Especially when dealing with Callum and his minions, like she was now.

Porter had just finished his last reining event and took second place. He was talking to the media while Willa and Greer were brushing Apollo after feeding him for the night. Willa's guards were at each exit while Reggie was getting the car ready to leave for the night.

Callum and Cyril had approached and were currently leaning against the stall door, giving her a hard time. Only something different was happening. Willa wasn't cowering. She was mad, but she wasn't running away. Instead, she looked at Greer and rolled her eyes, not letting their taunts get to her.

"With the help again. I swear, sometimes I think you'd be better off being a maid. That's why you need a strong man who will tell you what to do and the proper way to act," Callum said, stepping into the stall.

Willa saw Cyril slithering toward Greer but knew Greer could handle herself.

Instead of trying to duck out, she turned and faced Callum head-on. "Did it ever occur to you that it's not me, but you? That you're the reason I don't want to be with you? That you're the reason you can't keep any grooms around? That you're the reason your employees all leave within six months? So, instead of telling me what I need to be doing, why don't you take a hard look at the common factor that sends people running—you."

Greer smirked, but her smirk fell as Cyril pulled his patented isolation move. He slid in between her and Apollo and began to walk Greer slowly toward the back corner of the stall. Willa was about to intercede when Callum grabbed her arm.

"No one talks to me like that. You're lucky I'm letting you crawl back into my life and bed."

"Was I not clear?" Willa asked, feeling her anger boiling

up. "I am sick and tired of you, Callum. You're a spoiled bully and I will never, *ever* be in your life again. I'd rather sit on a porcupine than sleep with you again. There is no, and will never be an, us again. Understand?"

Willa saw what was going to happen a split second before Callum's hand flew at her face. But Porter and his father had been working with Willa for the past two days. She lifted her arm and blocked the slap that was coming. Then she tightened her hand into a fist and delivered a neck-snapping right cross.

Callum spun to face the stall door where Tilly stood, her face red with anger. "I am so sick of men!" Tilly shouted before she kicked Callum in the balls.

Willa didn't see what happened with Greer, but a second later Cyril flew through the air and landed in a heap on top of Callum. All the fuss had Apollo uneasy, blowing and sidestepping around in the stall.

"What the hell is going on here?" Parker demanded as he stormed toward the stall door with Miss Trix's reins in his hand. He stood just behind Tilly as he looked into the stall. Apollo started to settle down as soon as he saw Miss Trix.

"Men are assholes and we took care of it. Right, ladies?" Tilly said with her hands on her hips as she glared over her shoulder at Parker.

Willa saw Parker's jaw tighten as he looked from Tilly to Willa to Greer and then to the heap of groaning men. Cyril pushed up to his knees, wavered, and reached out to pull himself up. Although he didn't grab the stall door. He grabbed Tilly's waistband. He pulled, her pants came down, and Parker got a view of Tilly's bottom in a thong. Cyril pitched forward when he tried to stand. His face landed in Tilly's crotch. Tilly gasped, Parker growled, and punched Cyril unconscious.

"Parker!" Greer called out as she pulled her cousin off Cyril. Willa sprang forward and grabbed Miss Trix as Tilly yanked up her pants while looking completely mortified.

Greer had Parker in a headlock and dragged him off Cyril as Tilly burst into tears a second before she turned and made a run for the exit.

"Matilda!" Parker called out, but Tilly didn't slow down.

"What is wrong with you?" Greer asked as Parker's chest heaved.

"He shouldn't treat a woman like that. He needed to be taught a lesson." Parker shoved up to his feet, took Miss Trix's reins, and left.

"Well, that was interesting," Willa muttered.

Greer nodded and looked after her cousin. "So interesting it may be worth a bet. Right after I place one on your surviving family dinner tonight."

~

Porter looked nervous and that did not help Willa's nerves as they approached the large farmhouse belonging to Jake and Marcy Davies.

"Why is everyone here already? Aren't we ten minutes early?" Willa asked as she saw the field full of cars.

"It's an ambush," Porter muttered to himself. "I should turn around. We need to find higher ground."

Willa gave a little laugh. "It's dinner, Porter. It's not an attack."

"I wouldn't be so sure of that. The aunts have been on this full equal treatment kick. I'm afraid you're the first one to really be subjected to it."

"I got an A in negotiations in business school. I'm sure I

can handle some questions from your aunts. Besides, your mom is super sweet."

"Don't fall for it. It's all an act," Porter warned. "Be suspicious of everyone and everything."

Porter pulled to a stop and Willa was determined to be gracious and kind, just like her mother had taught her. Kindness was the strongest weapon of all. The door to the farmhouse opened and a sweet older couple came out.

"Hello, Mrs. Davies. It's lovely to see you again. I brought some homemade bread for dinner," Willa said as she walked up the stairs. Porter hissed at her to be careful, but Willa ignored him. He was really making too big a deal of this family dinner.

"Thank you, dear. This is my husband, Jake. Jake, this is Porter's little friend, Willa Aldridge."

"Good luck. Stay low to the ground, and remember to zigzag," Jake Davies told her.

Willa laughed but then the rest of the porch filled with the men of the family.

"What's going on?" Porter asked as he put a protective arm around Willa's waist.

"We're just going to give the women a chance to get to know each other," Cy said frowning.

"They told us we weren't allowed to play," Uncle Cade said as he, too, frowned.

"How are we supposed to get to know the in-laws if we can't see how they handle a life-or-death situation?" Miles asked.

"I have our night vision binoculars so we can watch. Hi, I'm Marshall Davies. We haven't met yet."

Willa shook his hand. "Nice to meet you. So, where are the ladies? I'd love to have a cozy little chat with them."

"Oh no. It's like a lamb to slaughter. I can't watch," Uncle Pierce said as he went back inside.

There was a whizzing sound and then an arrow landed on the ground right next to Willa's foot. She jumped and looked down at the arrow. There was a note attached.

There are five stations you must complete. You have one hour. Run.

There was a rudimentary map on the small note.

"That's the property. The first station is about four hundred yards back that way. Good luck. Remember, zigzag," Jake told her before giving her a wink a second before another arrow almost struck her foot.

"You weren't kidding about dinner," Willa said accusatorily to Porter.

"I've been telling you!"

"Good thing I'm always prepared." Willa shoved the bread into Marcy's hands and pulled off the cotton summer dress she was wearing. Underneath she was dressed in black running pants and a black long-sleeved athletic shirt.

"Your cooking better be worth it," Willa called out to Marcy.

"You survive and I'll give you the first slice of apple pie," Grandma Marcy called out encouragingly and Willa took off running.

Arrows flew as she zigged and zagged across the field behind the house toward the first station. As Willa approached, she saw women step from the shadows.

"So, you want to date my nephew?" a tall blonde who looked very much like Sydney asked.

"Willa, this is my mother, Katelyn, and my aunt Tammy," Sydney explained. "The rules are simple. You compete in each station while answering a question from each participant. Then you run to the next station."

"Okay, shoot."

"That's the next station. This one we throw," the little sprite of a woman said as she handed Willa a large ax.

Willa watched as the little woman threw the ax at a wood bullseye. "Why are you here doing this?" Tammy asked.

Willa mimicked Tammy's throw and threw the ax. It spun and landed in the dirt halfway to the target.

"First, I like Porter and I'm hoping this is worth it. Also, for as crazy as this is, I'm envious of your family's closeness. I'm close with my father, but without my mother I didn't have the traditional family feel. There are no large family cookouts. No cousins dropping by. No sweet but deadly uncles and aunts. You all have that in spades, and I like being a part of it. Even if this is the craziest thing I've ever done."

Tammy handed her another ax as Katelyn stepped up and threw. Her ax landed dead center. "Are you with Porter only to have the sense of family?"

"No. I liked him before I met you all," Willa said, shaking her head as she lined up her next shot. She'd watched Katelyn closely and threw. The ax hit the side of the board and fell to the ground. Willa smiled excitedly. "I hit the board!"

Sydney was up next and hit another bullseye. "Porter would never be happy in the kind of circles you run in. Circles someone like Callum Harding runs in. The seen to be seen thing isn't Porter and he'd be miserable. How would you work as a couple when his ranch life and your glamorous life don't mix?"

"I despise the person Callum is. I hate that part of my life—the part that is just for show. I do charity events for good causes, not for the glitz and glamour. I'd be much happier riding horses, writing checks for charity, and doing my work. And being with friends. True friends, like Tilly. Not the fake kind who want something from you." Willa lined up her last throw. She let it go and it thunked into the bottom corner of the wood. She didn't hit a target, but she's at least hit the board.

"Now what?" Willa asked. An arrow landed by her foot and she knew the answer. Run.

The next station was manned with only two people—Greer and an older woman. "What do I do here?" Willa asked as she tried to catch her breath from dodging arrows.

"Shooting," Greer said as she waved to three different guns: a rifle, a shotgun, and a pistol. "This is my mother, Paige Parker. Now, we have some questions for you."

Greer handed her the pistol and then took her own shot.

"What would you do if my cousin said he was going back into the rodeo?" Greer asked, after emptying her clip dead center of the target.

Willa lined up the pistol and pulled the trigger. Nothing. Greer reached over and flipped the safety off. "I will most likely move from showing professionally to part-time. I know how hard it is to love something so much but not be able to do it. I would understand his desire and agree to whatever the doctor recommends. However, I'd also help him find a new passion if he couldn't ride anymore. I want to be there and support Porter in anyway I can."

Willa fired off the clip. This was going much better than the axes, at least she hit the target.

Greer picked up the rifle and aimed at a target so far away Willa could barely see it. Greer fired off a series of shots as her mother watched with binoculars. "Great shot, sweetie!"

"Do you love Porter?" Greer asked.

"I believe I do. If I didn't, I wouldn't be here competing in some weird version of Girlfriends' Hunger Games."

Willa lined up her shot and fired. She hit the closer target but missed the distant one.

Paige picked up the shotgun and nodded to Greer who pulled out a clay target. Paige blasted two in a row before handing it off to Willa. Finally, an activity where she had some level of competence. Willa loaded the shells and took aim.

"What would you do if Porter got you a vacuum cleaner for a Christmas gift?"

"Like the robot kind?" Willa asked as Greer released the trap and Willa hit the clay pigeon.

"No, like the kind you push. Although it did do well at picking up pet hair," Paige answered as Greer pulled the trap again.

Willa shot and shattered the second clay pigeon. "I'd probably vacuum very early in the morning to wake him up and then maybe buy him a mop for his birthday."

Paige smiled. "You are devious. I would have never imagined it. Now, run."

The arrow flew and landed right behind her. "Who's shooting?"

"You'll find out!" Greer called out as Willa took off running.

21

"What do you think they're doing to Willa?" Porter asked from where the Davies men waited around the massive dining room table.

Cy shrugged. "Not much. I think your mother wants more grandchildren so I'm sure it'll be something super easy."

"It better not be," Deacon said as Walker nodded.

"It's probably all sweet as pie," Pierce said, making Matt and all the in-laws frown. They'd had to fight every step of the way. "Tammy's been talking about a spa day with the ladies. I imagine they're all sitting there getting manicures and talking."

"I don't know about that," Cole said even as Porter began to doubt the mani-pedi theory. "Paige is uber competitive and she did leave with her guns."

"Annie was sharpening her knives, so I too doubt it's all sunshine and rainbows," Cade told them.

Porter let out a deep breath and looked out into the darkness. Somewhere out there was the woman he was falling in love with in the company of his aunts and cousins, armed with weapons. What could possibly go wrong?

"Well, whatever they do it won't be as much fun as we have," Miles said, crossing his arms over his chest.

"It is fun after you've been initiated into the family," Deacon admitted.

"I kinda miss it," Walker said. "We haven't had a new boyfriend to torment in a while."

"Who do you think will be next?" Cade asked. "It has to be Greer, right? I mean, Cassidy is still too young."

"There's no way my daughter is next," Pierce said of Cassidy. "She's too busy babysitting for y'all to have a social life, thank goodness."

"That leaves Greer," Miles taunted Cole who leaned across the table and punched him in the shoulder.

"Greer has too much on her plate right now. She's going to head the FBI. Plus, no man is good enough for my little girl."

"Little?" Porter asked. "You do know she's closing in on thirty, right?"

"Like I said, little. Talk to me when she's forty-five and then maybe I might allow a man in her life."

"Yeah, I don't like the idea of Greer with a man," Jackson said, crossing his arms over his chest and frowning. Jackson and Greer's oldest brother, Ryan, nodded as he frowned.

"Aw, little Greer having a boyfriend for us to beat up would be fun," Lucas said with a floppy grin.

"I bet we could make him cry in under a minute," Talon said. "After all, Greer is like the entire FBI Hostage Rescue's little sister."

"Because Jackson threatened everyone who would have asked her out," Porter said, feeling the need to stick up for his cousin, who was also his best friend.

"Don't get all high and mighty," Jackson warned Porter. "You were out there giving Matt and Carter hell when they were dating your sisters."

Porter was about to say "true" when he saw a shadow move in the distance. He narrowed his eyes and scanned the area. "Hey, guys," he began to say.

"Nope, everyone has to earn their way into the family, especially the guys. I don't care if Aunt Annie or Bridget call me sexist, but what kind of big brother would I be if I didn't threaten my little sister's boyfriend?" Jackson said as he glared.

"I think we're about to be attacked," Porter said as he backed up from the window.

Miles was beside Porter instantly, looking out as Cy handed him a pair of night vision goggles. "It's a tactical team," Miles said excitedly. "This is not a drill! We got a standard two-by-two formation coming in the front and I'd also bet at the side and back. Get into positions!"

"Porter dear," his grandmother called out as his grandfather escorted her into the hidden shelter of the safe room Cade had put in thirty years ago. "Grab my nice dishes and the pie. Wouldn't want them shot. Thanks, dear."

The lights went out, night vision goggles were shoved into Porter's hands, and he ran to secure the pie and dishes. He bounded up the stairs to meet his brother. "You think you still got it in you?" Parker asked as he shoved a rifle and ammunition at Porter.

"Do I? I think the better question is whether you can keep up," Porter taunted as they opened the bedroom window on the backside of the house. The large maple tree provided cover and Porter climbed onto the tree and upward until he could easily jump onto the roof.

Porter's mind went straight to Willa, but before he could

get to her, he needed to take this team out. They were after him so hopefully Willa was safe for now. Porter lay on the roof with the chimney as cover while Parker did the same on the back end of the house.

Porter scanned the area and found the team using the cars to hide their approach. To his side he saw three dark figures break from the house and run low to the ground. That had to be Jackson, Talon, and Lucas moving in to flank the team coming approaching the front door.

Porter took a deep breath and waited as the men crossed into the open area before he started firing. He fired the first shot, then it sounded like an arsenal went off as the uncles and cousins joined in. The men who tried to retreat were met by Jackson and his team.

It was over in a matter of seconds. The team never stood a chance against the Davies family.

"Willa," Porter called out to Parker. "I have to make sure she's safe."

"We got it covered. Go!"

Porter raced across the roof, leapt into the tree, and in seconds was running off into the darkness to look for Willa.

"Did you hear something?" Willa asked as she held the knife she was using to compete with Sophie and Annie. She was currently trying to kill a straw dummy with the knife as Sophie and Annie attacked with foam pads. Layne was sitting back, watching them as she tapped a spoon menacingly against her palm.

"Hey, did you all hear something?" Katelyn asked as she, Tammy, and Sydney jogged up with their axes.

"I thought I did," Willa answered.

"Hey, y'all, did you just hear something?" Greer asked as

she and her mother joined the group with their guns in large carrying cases. "I could have sworn I heard gunfire."

"It was probably just the guys having a competition of their own," Layne said with a shrug.

Suddenly an arrow landed in the middle of the women.

"What the hell?" Annie muttered. "Cassidy isn't supposed to be shooting her arrows at us."

"Wait a second," Sophie said as she pulled out a gun from what looked like a diaper bag. She took off the protective cover from the scope and scanned the area. "Night vision. We have company."

Sophie handed the gun to Greer who did her own sweep. "Tactical forces. Call the others. This interrogation just turned real, Willa. If you survive, you're in."

"No!" Riley groaned as she, Reagan, and their mother, Gemma, jogged over. "I wanted my time in hand-to-hand combat with Willa."

"What's going on? We thought we heard something," Gemma asked, ignoring her daughter.

"We're under attack. For real," Greer told her as she looked around. "Is everyone armed?"

Willa grabbed a shotgun and nodded even as her heart beat a mile a minute.

"Hey!" Cassidy whispered as she ran forward with her older sister, Piper, and their aunt Morgan. All three were carrying bows and arrows. "Did you see them?"

"Yeah. Everyone break apart and hide among the dummies and targets. I need sharpshooters behind the mounds back there. They're elevated to keep the bullets in the range," Greer ordered. "Archers, fall back to where Cassidy was shooting at Willa."

Willa looked around as people nodded and then ran off into the darkness.

"We have to assume the sound of gunfire from the main house was hostile and not the guys just messing around," Greer told them. "Whoever these people are, they are willing to shoot so don't be a target. Knives and axes get behind the dummies. Throw and then fall back. The sharpshooters will provide cover."

Gemma grabbed the other shotgun. "I'll stay with Willa."

"Get behind the two hundred and fifty yard targets," Greer instructed. "We'll cover you if you need to run. Let's go."

Willa nodded and gave one last glance in the direction of the farmhouse. She just hoped Porter was safe. In this short amount of time she couldn't imagine her life without him.

"Thinking about Porter?" Gemma whispered as they ran. Willa could only nod. She couldn't put the fear she felt into words. "You love him, don't you? But you're scared."

Willa nodded again.

"I know the feeling well. Any woman who loves and is loved by a Davies is a lucky woman. Even if the force of the feelings we have can be overwhelming. Well, and you usually end up in a gunfight at some point. I didn't get to interrogate you, but that was going to be my question, whether you loved my son. If you do, that's all that matters to me. The love you share will only grow and develop until it's an unbreakable bond. You just have to be open to it."

Willa and Gemma ducked behind the target and Willa thumbed in two shotgun shells and snapped the barrel closed. "I'm ready to fight for it, that's for sure."

The two women sat in silence. They were on the ground, sitting with their backs against the large target. She looked into the darkness and could barely see the mound of earth Greer was behind.

It was eerily quiet. Even the footfalls she knew to be coming couldn't be heard. Then suddenly three shots boomed out from behind the earth mound. Willa's heart pounded as she heard people yelling in a language she didn't recognize.

"Fall back!" Annie yelled.

Willa heard the sound of running from all around them as Katelyn, Sydney, Tammy, Annie, and Layne raced by.

"Down!" Sophie yelled from where she was next to Greer.

The group fell to the ground and the sharpshooters began to return fire.

"Here!" Willa called as she reached for Sydney's hand and tugged her behind the target along with Sydney's mother, Katelyn. The others crawled behind the target ten feet away as a volley of shots was exchanged.

Willa took a chance and looked around the far side of the target. Three people dressed in black were crawling on the ground toward them.

"Gemma, there's three coming on the ground. Two are going wide and one is just to the right of the center path."

An arrow dropped from the sky and skewered the person in the middle.

"Okay, so now there's two," Willa said.

Gemma nodded. "You take the one on this side. Are you able to do that? If not, any of the girls can. We've had extensive training."

Willa thought about it. She could hand off her shotgun, but then a figure slowly rose behind the second target.

"Get down," Willa said as she shoved Gemma to the ground with one hand and aimed her shotgun over Gemma.

Willa didn't hesitate. She shot as the man pointed his gun at Layne. The blast hit the figure and sent him sprawling back. All of a sudden it sounded as if gunfire was everywhere, but then a shot boomed behind Willa.

Willa spun around ready to shoot only to find Porter standing over another body. "Willa!"

"Porter! Get down!" Willa cried, fear racing through her as he stood out in the open, rifle in hand.

"Gemma!" Willa heard Cy roar as men filled the area from all directions.

Willa choked back a sob as she realized it was over. They were safe and Porter was alive.

Willa scrambled to her feet and then she was in Porter's arms. His hands were on her face and his lips were on hers.

"Are you hurt?" he asked, his voice tight with worry.

Willa shook her head. "I was so worried about you."

They both talked simultaneously as they ran their hands over each other to reassure themselves they were not hurt.

"I love you. God, Willa, I love you and the thought that you were hurt or kidnapped aged me ten years. I don't think I have taken a full breath until now." Porter was talking in between kissing her.

Willa's heart had been pumping a mile a minute from fear, but now it was for a different reason. She speared her fingers into his hair and pulled Porter's head back until she could look him in the eyes. She needed him to know this wasn't a heat-of-the-moment thing. "I love you, too, Porter."

Willa slipped her arms around his neck as Porter leaned forward and kissed her so soundly it made her knees weak.

"This was an interesting beginning to family dinner. Never a dull moment for us," Grandma Marcy called out from an old pickup truck. "Now, I take it Willa has passed whatever test was thrown at her and we can enjoy our dinner."

"Willa saved my life," Layne told the group as she came

up to give her a hug. "Thank you. You have my vote, even if I didn't get to see you kill a dummy with a spoon."

"Is everyone okay?" Sienna, Ryan's psychologist wife, asked as she rushed forward. "The one dinner I was late for. I'd ask if y'all needed to talk, but you've done that. Willa, I'm here to talk if you need anything."

"How about some apple pie?" Willa joked.

Grandma Marcy honked her horn and people started to climb into the bed of the truck. "Come up here and talk to me, dear. Porter can tough it out in the back."

Willa reluctantly let go of Porter and climbed into the truck. Marcy pushed something across the seat at her and winked. "Something special for you."

Willa opened up the round Tupperware and was hit with the intoxicating aroma of apples and cinnamon. "Have I died and gone to heaven?"

Marcy chuckled as she drove back to the farmhouse. "I think you deserve it after the night you've had. Welcome to the family, dear. You give me a great-grandbaby before I die and I'll give you more pies."

"Are you bribing me with apple pie to get pregnant?" Willa asked with a giggle, feeling the tension melt away.

"After you taste it, let me know when I should place my bet at the café," Marcy said with full confidence in her baby-making pie.

"Are all family dinners like this?" Willa asked.

"Would it bother you if they were?" Marcy asked instead of answering.

Willa thought about it. "It was scary being under attack, but the rest was fun. There's a lot of teasing, but it's because they care."

Marcy nodded as they approached the farmhouse. "You're a good girl, Willa. I'm glad I picked you."

"Picked me?" Willa asked even as she broke off a piece of the flaky crust and popped it into her mouth.

"To have you over for dinner, dear," Marcy said with a smile. "You sure livened it up. Now, let me tell you a thing or two about my grandson."

Willa laughed as Marcy launched into a story about three-year-old Porter running around the farm naked because horses don't have clothes so he shouldn't have to have them either.

22

Willa had survived a shoot-out and the family dinner. Porter couldn't believe he'd just spouted out that he loved her in front of everyone. However, when he saw that soldier reaching for her his emotions had taken over.

"Two separate countries attacked the dinner?" Willa asked as they walked up the stairs to his house.

"North Korea attacked the house and Iran attacked you ladies. We don't have identities yet, but Cassidy heard the men attacking you all and recognized their dialect. She speaks a million languages."

Porter held the door open as she walked in—a house that would seem empty when it was time for Willa to leave. The thought weighed on him as she tossed her purse on the counter.

The high of being in love was colliding with the reality of who they were and that fact that they lived many states apart.

"Porter," Willa said as she fidgeted with her fingers. "I know you might have said you loved me because of the life-

or-death situation. If you did, I understand. It's only been a week."

"Is that what you're worried about?" Porter asked with a laugh. "Not the assassins from North Korea and Iran? Not the interrogation the ladies put you through? Not the thirty-minute lecture Uncle Miles gave you on the use of a spoon as a deadly weapon?"

He watched Willa's lips twitch on that last one. Uncle Miles had practically launched a Power Point presentation on the versatility of the spoon while they ate apple pie. However, Porter also saw the nervousness.

"I'm not a teenager anymore, Willa. I'm a decade past lust and love being confused as only teenagers can. I love you. You, Willa. The horse-loving, smart as hell, funny, slightly dirty-minded woman," Porter said before wrapping his arms around her, bending down, and capturing her lips with his.

"I love you, too," Willa managed to say between kisses.

Porter soared. He knew how lucky he was to be loved by Willa. He was even luckier when she reached down and yanked his shirt from his jeans and said, "I want you. Now."

"Yes, ma'am," Porter said with a grin as he lifted her into his arms and she wrapped her legs around his waist.

Their lips clashed, their tongues caressed, and their bodies pressed tightly together as he carried her down the hall toward the room they'd been sharing. Only this time, it was different. There would be no stopping tonight. Tonight Porter was going to love her, body and soul.

The second Porter set Willa down she was pulling the clothes free from his body. Porter didn't waste any time. He had her black shirt up and over her head as fast as he could. Willa was already working on his boxer briefs when he tackled the black running pants she had on.

"Did you paint these on?" Porter muttered as he fought to get hold of them.

Willa laughed and pushed down his boxer briefs. "See, easy."

Porter finally wedged a finger under the tight compression band of the running pants and grunted. "Not easy."

Porter gave up and used the palms of his hands to try to roll down the pants. He made it until he had to get them over the flare of her hips and the curve of her beautiful ass. Then the pants seemed to stop.

"You want me to do this? I thought it was bra clasps that gave men problems, not pants," Willa teased.

"These aren't pants," Porter said seriously. They were modern day chastity pants. "These are suctioned to you, but I have a solution."

Porter reached down to his discarded jeans and pulled out a knife.

Willa gasped. "No way! These are my favorite pair of running pants. You have thirty seconds to get them off or I'm sleeping alone tonight. I will have serious doubts about a man defeated by running pants."

"Never doubt me," Porter told her as he knelt down, grabbed the slightly rolled waistband, and yanked down as hard as he could. Willa put her hand on his shoulders to steady herself as he yanked and pulled the tight material down past her knees. Willa was giggling but she wasn't laughing anymore when he pushed her back onto the bed and grinned down at her.

"I don't even need ropes to get you where I want you. It's a shame. I'm very good with ropes," Porter said, peering down at her pants around her calves, trapping her. "No underwear? I like it, Miss Aldridge."

Willa's breathing hitched in a way that made him even harder than he thought possible. Porter got on the bed next to her, grabbed Willa's wrists and pulled them above her head to prevent her from pulling the running pants all the way off her legs. "I take back every bad thing I said about those pants."

Porter trailed his fingers to the sports bra covering her breasts. His lips followed and soon Willa was breathing heavy and moaning his name. "I hope you're not too attached to this bra. I'm not wasting any more time on Satan's clothing line. I let you keep the pants, but this contraption is dangerous. Your breasts are suffocating and need to be rescued."

"What?" Willa muttered from her lust-induced haze.

Porter took the knife, wedged it between her breasts, and in one quick motion sliced the sports bra open.

"Porter!" Willa said in surprise as she sat up.

Damn, Willa was perfect. The curves of her breasts, the flare of her hips, her muscled legs . . . and he was the man lucky enough to have her love.

Porter pushed the straps of her torn sports bra off her shoulder and used his body to push Willa back into the bed as her anger over the destroyed sports bra melted from the heat of his kisses.

"I take back everything bad I said about Satan's clothes. Now, Willa, let's see what you think about ever sleeping alone again."

Willa's eyes shot open as she realized she was bound by her own clothing. Her pants kept her legs in place and Porter had used her sports bra to tie her hands together. "What are you—?"

Porter ran his tongue over her nipples and all talking stopped. Willa groaned as Porter took his time exploring every inch of her body. He learned what every gasp, every moan, and every change in breathing meant.

When he finally finished undressing Willa, her body was sated and she had a satisfied little smile on her lips. "I don't know how much better it can get," Willa said on a sigh as Porter rolled on a condom.

"Let's see about that. Wrap your arms around my neck," Porter told her. He reached down and hooked her legs around his waist. A second later they were standing and he had her back up against the wall.

"Oh my God, it gets better," Willa gasped.

Porter tried. He really did. When he entered the café for lunch the next day with Willa on his arm, he tried not to grin like an idiot. It didn't work. One look at his goofy smile and Willa's satisfied one and bets went flying.

Porter was too happy to even care that folks were placing bets on him and Willa. Porter pulled out a chair for Willa at a table for two in the back. He walked around to his chair and sat down. He saw the Rose sisters move to turn up their hearing aids to eavesdrop and decided to have some fun.

"Do you think we should get one of those blood tests done to see if you're pregnant yet? I've heard you can tell as soon as six days if you're pregnant," Porter said quietly.

Willa's eyes went comically wide. "You used a condom, right?" she said, not realizing Porter was playing it up for the Rose sisters.

Porter pulled out his phone and sent her a quick text.

"The first one broke, remember?" Porter said, pointing to his phone to tell Willa to look at hers.

She read the text about the Rose sisters and grinned.

You're bad, Willa texted back, but played along.

That's not what you said last night. Or this morning. Or later this morning. Or right before we left to come here, Porter wrote back. Yeah, that was the reason for the goofy grin.

The door to the café opened and a man walked in. His suit was dove gray, his shirt a bright pink, his tie mint green. His hair was cut to perfection and his face was shaven.

"Bonjour," he said with a smile to the Rose sisters.

"Qui es-tu?" Miss Violet asked who he was in perfect French. Porter knew through Landon's time with the Rose sisters teaching him the old traditional recipes that Miss Violet had gone to culinary school in France and was already fluent when she married her French chef husband, Anton.

"Ah, the lovely lady speaks French," the man said in heavily accented English as he reached for Miss Violet's hand and brought it up to his lips for a kiss. "It makes this Frenchman's heart happy to hear. What should I order from this quaint café?"

Porter watched Miss Violet recommend the special and told him he'd enjoy the soufflé for dessert. Porter didn't like the way the man oohed and aahed in surprise that someplace as small as Keeneston would have anything French.

Poppy sat him at a table near the front door and Porter caught him looking around like a tourist, taking everything in.

"He doesn't seem dangerous," Willa whispered. "Do you think he's here to kill us?"

"Right now I'm going with the assumption everyone new is trying to kill us," Porter told her as Poppy brought them their food.

"I don't like the looks of him," Poppy whispered. "He gives me the creepy crawlies."

Porter and Willa ate in silence as they watched every move the visitor made. The Frenchman seemed relaxed as he chatted with those around him, asked about the town's history, and exclaimed over the tour of the bourbon distillery owned by Cady Woodson.

"I think we'll go out the back," Porter said, dropping his voice as Poppy set the soufflé in front of the man.

The man cocked his head as he examined the soufflé and tentatively put his spoon into it. His smile fell into a frown as he tasted it. "Such a shame. It's a bit flat, but only the most talented French cooks can truly make a perfect soufflé."

Porter stood and walked to Willa's chair. He put his body between her and the Frenchman as they prepared to walk out the back.

"Bless his heart, he's a dead man for insulting Miss Violet's soufflé and he doesn't even realize it," Pam Gilbert said with a shake of her head. "Miss Violet never has a flat soufflé."

"The soufflé was excellent," Willa agreed. "Maybe we can snag another one as we sneak out the kitchen?"

"Gun!" Pam yelled suddenly.

Porter shoved Willa down as Pam flipped the table over, but no gunshot rang out.

Thunk.

The sound echoed around the café even as weapons were pulled. Porter covered Willa with his body and slowly looked over his shoulder from where he lay on the ground. The table blocked his view so when no gunshot rang out he peeked over the table.

Miss Violet stood with a crepe pan hanging from her hand. "My soufflés are never flat, *connard*."

"Miss Violet, I thought the crepe pan was too heavy for you now," Zinnia called as she ran out from the kitchen.

"I switched up to a lightweight one. It's a good two pounds lighter. Doesn't have the same deep resonating thunk as the heavier one when you hit it against someone's head, but for a one-pound pan, I think it does the job well enough."

"Dog-gonnit!" Pam said angrily. "That's the third assassin I've missed. My Hummer is right outside and I didn't even have a chance to run him down."

"We could have the boys toss him out onto the street for you to run over," Miss Lily offered.

"No," Pam sighed. "That's cheating."

Porter turned to see that Willa was already standing. This time there was no fear in her eyes, only laughter and a trace amount of anger. "It's one thing to try to kill my boyfriend and kidnap me," she said with her hands on her hips. "It's quite another to criticize the best soufflé I've ever had."

Miss Violet preened under the praise. "You're such a dear. Why don't you grab another soufflé?"

The front door opened and Parker, Kale, and Brian Aldridge walked in. Parker looked down at the unconscious man sprawled onto the floor, to the gun that had been kicked away from his hand, and to Miss Violet with the crepe pan in her hand, then he smiled. "Good to see you back in action with the crepe pan, Miss Violet. So you walloped another assassin. What is this? Number three? Four?"

"I'm sure I'm up to six by now. But he got walloped for

saying my soufflé was flat," Miss Violet said with anger and looking ready to wallop the man again.

Parker bent down and cuffed the man. "Your soufflés are never flat. I'll take him to Desert Sun Farm with the others. Maybe he'll fall down the stairs for his bad manners."

Porter saw Kale sending a message and soon Deputy Luke Tanner arrived with his cruiser to haul the man away with Parker. Brian was talking to Willa as Greer and Tilly rushed inside. Everything was back to normal in a matter of minutes.

"I missed it again! I'm only one for three kidnapping attempts," Greer grumbled.

"I completely understand," Pam said, sending Greer a sympathetic smile.

"Is everyone okay?" Talon asked as he shoved through the door with Jackson and Lucas. "We got a text from Miss Lily."

Talon's eyes searched the room until they landed on Zinnia. Lucas's floppy, good-natured grin was gone until he scanned Poppy to make sure she was safe.

"They're getting bolder," Jackson said to Greer as they joined Porter to discuss what had happened. "The farm and now broad daylight in a packed restaurant."

"How are things going at Desert Sun?" Porter asked Kale when he joined them.

"It's going. We've seen the contract for your death and for Willa's kidnapping. I already have that guy's phone. Mr. Aldridge and I will work on further infiltrating The Panther's network. I'm not going to lie. The Panther is a computer genius and I'm in awe. He's so far ahead of my knowledge, but I'm assembling a little team and we're determined to get to the bottom of it. We just need more time, so try not to get killed this week."

"Ha-ha," Porter said dryly at his friend.

"What do you have planned for today?" Jackson asked.

"We need to go to the barn. I'm bringing Miss Trix home, but Willa needs to practice with Apollo for a little while. That's all we've planned."

"I think it's safe to say her bodyguards standing duty outside her rented house is no longer fooling anyone. We'll have them meet us at the barn and bring them back to Keeneston," Greer told him as she pulled out her phone and sent them the update.

Porter looked over to where Willa was talking with Tilly, her father, and a mix of the townspeople. She fit in Keeneston and in his heart. It was time to get her safe and see what their relationship could really become.

"Do whatever it takes to find the person behind this. I won't stop until Willa is safe," Porter told Kale.

Kale nodded and went to get Brian. It was time for the computer geniuses to do their thing while Porter did everything possible to stay alive and keep Willa safe.

23

Willa patted Apollo on the neck after dismounting. It had been a good practice. Yesterday they'd only done a small one after the Frenchman tried to kill Porter. Today was a little longer. Tomorrow was her last practice before show jumping began, so she made sure to push Apollo today so tomorrow could be a light workout before show time.

"It's been quiet," Greer said with a frown as she and Porter met Willa right outside the eventing area. "I don't like it."

"You don't like much these days," Porter pointed out. "Are you okay?"

Even Willa had noticed the happy Greer becoming snippier.

"Yeah, just work stuff. For years I thought leadership was my goal, but the more I get a taste for it, the more I hate the red tape and bureaucracy. I got a call from DC. They are going over every case of mine and questioning every decision I made, even though most of them have never been in HRT. They say it's to prepare themselves and me for any 'issues' but some of the things they're bringing up have nothing to do with my cases. Who I sleep with and how many times has nothing to do with my competency as leader of my hostage rescue team."

"Have you thought about just staying with HRT?" Willa asked as they walked back to the barn with her three bodyguards forming a triangle around her.

"I'm so torn. I don't want to put up with this, but I'm one of the first women to make it this far. I could change the landscape of the FBI for women," Greer told her.

"So you feel guilty for not charging ahead," Willa said with understanding. It was hard being the one to break through glass ceilings.

"I understand the conflict you're feeling," Porter told her. "However, I worry about you. My friend. My cousin. I don't want the glass ceiling you're shattering—again—to fall and crush you. Let us help. How can we support you?"

Willa fell even more in love with Porter right then.

"You help just by listening to me complain," Greer said with a smile that showed the strain she was under.

"You don't have to stay here and help me. If you need to go to DC or anything, I think the town has me covered," Willa told her. She didn't want to add any more stress to the situation.

"No, this helps me. If I were in DC, I'd strangle someone."

"You know," Willa said slowly, broaching a topic she wondered if Greer would even want to hear. "You don't have to do it. You don't have to become director and play the DC game. There are lots of private companies that would pay you a fortune to work for them. Or you could start your own."

"Porter said the same thing the other day," Greer told her and looked back at Porter to give him a smile. "I'll give it a little while longer and then maybe I'll explore my options. Thanks, you two. Sometimes I just need to express my frustration with this process."

"Whatever you end up doing, you'll always have my support," Porter told her as he slung an arm around his cousin's shoulders.

Willa smiled at them as they entered the barn. Here was a man who listened, who tried to understand, and who supported the people he loved. He never tore them down, only helped them soar. How did she get so lucky?

"I don't care that you don't like it!"

"Is that Tilly yelling?" Greer asked.

"It can't be. Tilly never yells," Willa said, but they were already picking up their pace to see what was happening.

Parker and Tilly stood toe to toe, both with their hands on their hips and both glaring at each other.

"Fine!" Parker bit out.

"Fine!" Tilly shouted back before spinning around and storming toward them. "I need a night without any dicks around and a big margarita."

"Whoa, Til, what's going on?" Willa asked as her friend almost ran by them in a huff.

"That man." Tilly took a deep breath and looked at Porter. "I like you. You're nice and you take care of Willa, but right now if I see another man I'm going to use that spoon on their balls."

"Got it," Porter said as he reached for Apollo's reins. "I'll rub him down and meet you at the stall."

"What did my cousin do?" Greer asked with a bit of amusement. Willa was glad to see the sadness in her eyes start to fade.

"He's a big, stupid man. That's enough, isn't it?"

Willa nodded absently. She'd never seen Tilly so worked up.

"How about a girls' night?" Greer asked. "We can go over to Desert Sun Farm to Abby's. We'll all be very safe there. Have some drinks, some good food, and just unwind for a night."

Tilly flung her arms around Greer in a surprise hug. "Bless your heart! That's just what I need. Willa? You'll come too, right?"

"Of course," Willa promised. She loved Porter, but Tilly was like her sister and when your sister is in need of getting drunk and venting about men, you bring the bottle, pour the drink, and agree with everything she says.

"Have Porter drop you off at six. The guys can hang out together at his place. I'm sure Dylan will be smart enough to head out as soon as we arrive. Come on, Tilly," Greer said as she tossed her arm around Tilly's shoulders. "Let's go clear out the ice cream aisle."

"You guys want to go to the guys' night or stay with the us girls?" Willa asked the bodyguards as they headed toward her setup.

"Our job is to stay with you, Miss Aldridge," Reggie said as he swallowed uncomfortably.

"But we'll stay outside," Barry told her. "Abby Mueez Davies scares the shit out of me."

"She's a legend," Deshaun told them. "I'll stay inside with you. I have three sisters. Ain't nothing you ladies are going to say that I haven't heard before. And maybe I get to have an actual conversation with Ahmed. I was too nervous to say anything to him the last time I saw him."

"Then we have a plan," Willa said as she approached Porter talking to a very heated Parker.

Parker lifted his eyes away from his brother and speared her with a hard look. "Your friend is insufferable."

Willa's hackles went up instantly. "Don't you dare say anything bad about Tilly or I'll use that spoon on you myself."

"Whoa," Porter said, holding up his hands. "Everyone calm down. Parker, what happened?"

Parker's jaw clenched. "It doesn't matter. If she wants to get herself hurt, then that's her choice."

"No one is going to be hurt," Porter said calmly, but Willa saw Parker's physical reaction to whatever went down and wondered what Tilly could have done to have the strong lawman practically shaking.

"Good thing we have a girls' night planned," Willa told them. "Porter, Greer asked that you drop me off at Abby's at six. My detail is going with me, but Greer said I'd be safe there for the night. Then Dylan can hang with you. I'm sure Parker can join and you all can have your own guys' night. Won't that be fun?"

"Only if I get to shoot something," Parker muttered.

"It's settled. I'll send a note to the guys. It'll be good for all of us to take a night to relax a little." Porter stepped closer to her and dropped his voice. "I'll pick you up at midnight. I don't care what happened between them, it's not keeping you from my bed for even a single night," Porter told her.

"Good. I don't intend to be away from it for even a single night."

"I love you," Porter whispered to her and Willa felt her body heat from the look he was giving her.

"Ugh. Give me that spoon so I can gag on it." Parker turned around and stormed off. "I'll see you at six-thirty," he called out to his brother before leaving the barn.

Willa held out her glass and Abby poured more bourbon into it. The women had moved to the back patio after Rahmi soldiers swept the area for intruders. Now the women sat under the patio lights laughing, drinking, and enjoying a wide variety of desserts.

"I swear, how can men be so smart yet so dumb?" Greer asked as the others giggled.

Willa was having a great time getting to know the women better. Abby wasn't as scary as she first had seemed and was actually very nice. Their royal highnesses, Ariana and Mila, were sweet and friendly and not at all what Willa had expected. Then there was Cassidy, the youngest Davies cousin except for little Cricket. Willa learned that Cassidy's mother, Tammy, had thought she'd gone through menopause when she'd been surprised by Cricket. Cassidy was in her early twenties, trying to find her way in life and that life with Dylan as an older brother was making it harder than it should be.

Then there was Cady Woodson, the master distiller. Willa had been fascinated by her story of loss, perseverance, and determination to be taken seriously as a young woman in a male-dominated field. Willa could instantly relate and when this was all over, Willa wanted to talk to Cady about investing in her distillery.

"Are we too late?" a blonde knockout in a red pencil skirt and four-inch heels asked as she strode across the grass as if she were on a catwalk.

Next to her Aniyah staggered along. "Veronica, you're not human. How can you walk in those shoes and not get stuck in the grass?" Aniyah said as she yanked her own heels out of the lawn before removing them altogether.

"It's all about walking on your tippy toes but staying upright so you don't look like the Leaning Tower of Pisa as you walk," the blonde answered.

"Welcome!" Abby called out. "Willa, Tilly, you both already know Aniyah, but this is Veronica. She basically runs Rahmi," Abby said of the blonde.

Veronica held out her hand and Willa shook it. "I don't run it. I'm just the royal families' executive assistant."

"Executive badass," Aniyah said as she grabbed the bottle of bourbon and poured two glasses before handing one to Veronica.

"Where's Blythe?" Mila asked Veronica.

"Who's Blythe?" Tilly asked, clearly tipsy from the bourbon.

"My significant other," Veronica responded before taking a sip of her drink. "But the purpose of the night is to get drunk, eat junk food, and complain about them, right?"

"You got that right," Tilly said.

"So, Blythe and I flipped a coin. I got this group and Blythe got the guys."

Tilly giggled. "That's awesome. Maybe she can give them some insight on women."

"Well, not if it's about putting dirty plates into the dishwasher," Veronica said with a roll of her eyes.

The women dissolved into laughter.

"So, what did happen with Parker?" Greer asked Tilly after the laughter died down.

"Yes, tell us everything," Ariana said, leaning forward to make sure she didn't miss a word of it.

Tilly frowned and shook her head. "He's a stupid man. Stupid, stupid, stupid, hot, sexy man."

A laugh escaped Willa's closed mouth in the form of a snort.

"What?" Tilly asked. "He is! We were talking, laughing, and he was being all flirty and then, bam! He locked it down. No more flirting, no more accidental touches, nothing. Now though, he won't let anyone else flirt with me either. This super sexy rider from Spain was talking to me this afternoon and Parker scared him off. Called him a 'threat to my person' when I asked him why he did that."

"Carlos? Carlos was flirting with you?" Willa gasped.

Tilly nodded. "After all this time of thinking myself invisible, I'm now getting attention from all these guys."

"It's because you're carrying yourself differently. You're more sure of yourself," Greer told her.

"If it is, it's because of your help," Tilly said, staggering over to Greer to give her a hug.

"I want to know more about Carlos," Aniyah said as the ladies laughed.

Willa pulled up Carlos's cologne campaign and showed it to her.

"He's not as muscled as my Sugarbear, but that is one fine man," Aniyah said as she fanned herself.

"Oh, I know him," Ariana said once she saw the picture. "Super hot. Way to go, Til!"

"Only it didn't go. Parker literally scared him away and sent him running with this laser glare thing he does. Then Parker yelled at me for not being smart enough to know when a man is only after one thing."

Willa, along with everyone woman there, sucked in air.

"Oh, girl. You didn't let him get away with that, did you?" Aniyah asked.

"No. I yelled at him," Tilly said defiantly. "I told him that was okay because there was only one thing I wanted from Carlos and I didn't care if he approved. Then he told me to go ahead and go after Carlos if I just wanted a man who was only interested in sex. I yelled fine, then he did too, and then I stormed off. Why does Parker even care?"

"It's because he likes you," Deshaun said from the corner of the patio. Willa had forgotten he was even there.

Everyone else seemed to have forgotten, too. Half of them jumped in surprise. Aniyah pulled a gun. Then everyone screamed and fell to the ground.

"He has a weird way of showing it," Tilly said from where Greer was lying on top of her.

When Aniyah put the gun away, everyone got back up.

"Dating is hard. It's scary to open yourself up to a person, especially if you already like them," Deshaun told her.

"Parker's had tons of girlfriends, though," Greer said, confused.

"Then they didn't matter to him. Obviously Parker has more serious feelings for Tilly and doesn't know how to process them. That's why he backed off but why he also won't let anyone flirt with her. He's scared to address those feelings, but at the same time the idea of another man with you scares him even more," Deshaun told them.

"Who are you?" Mila asked into the silence that followed as the women pondered what he'd said.

"Deshaun. I'm Miss Aldridge's bodyguard."

"Ever thought about going into the field of therapy?" Ariana asked and then the ladies laughed again. Except Tilly. She wasn't laughing. She was deep in thought.

"Since you decided to make your presence known," Greer said to the lone male in attendance, "why are men so chickenshit?"

"How so?" Deshaun asked as he moved forward and took a seat in the circle of women.

"Well," Greer said, standing up and doing a slow spin.

"I'm no Veronica, but I don't think I'm that bad-looking. I'm nice, except if you're a bad person. Yet no one wants to get me naked."

"You're very attractive. I'd totally get naked with you. I don't understand the chickenshit part," Deshaun said.

"I'm FBI Hostage Rescue and my brother Jackson put it out that he'd kill anyone who asks me out. Everyone, HRT, FBI field office, *everyone*, has fallen in line with them. No one will ask me out."

Deshaun suddenly got quiet and nodded. "I won't lie. I'd ask you out until you told me that. Jackson is one scary-ass dude. Someday, a man will be strong enough or lust-filled enough to get over the fear of having his balls cut off and will ask you out. Maybe go away from the military and law enforcement fields. Either that or go for a Delta Force or DEVGRU guy who could take Jackson on."

"Out!" Greer yelled at Deshaun who nodded and quickly scampered around to the front of the house. "This, this is what I'm dealing with."

"Have you talked to Evie about it?" Ariana asked, referring to Jackson's wife.

"Yes, and she's spoken to Jackson about it. It did no good. Instead, he doubled the threat," Greer said, crossing her arms over her chest. "What does a woman have to do to get laid?"

"Exactly!" Tilly said, saluting Greer with her almost empty glass of bourbon.

"Why do you think I went overseas so much?" Cassidy asked them. "If Dylan was your older brother, you'd know. Maybe you just need to take an assignment outside of Jackson's reach."

Greer leaned forward and put her elbows on her knees

and thought it over. "That's a good idea, Cass. Like, a really good idea."

"I have a friend getting ready to go on maternity leave," Abby said suddenly. "What about being loaned out to us?"

"Who's us and can I be loaned out?" Tilly asked.

Abby smiled innocently at Tilly and not for the first time Willa wondered what Abby did for a living.

"I need a break from this bureaucratic bullshit. I bet your department doesn't deal with that, do they?" Greer asked.

"Yeah, we don't do red tape," Abby said. "Think about it. Three months with no Jackson oversight."

"I'll let you know," Greer sat back with a contemplative look on her face.

"Well, that's great for Greer, but what about me? Do you have some government agency that will help get me laid?" Tilly asked as they all broke out into giggles again.

24

Porter tossed a case of beer into the cooler and carried it onto the back porch where his brother was sitting. Parker hadn't been talking much since he arrived ten minutes earlier.

"Hey guys," Dylan said as he didn't bother knocking. He'd just walked around to the back of the house as if knowing they'd all be hanging out back, drinking beer.

"So, that little minx kicked you out of your own home?" Parker asked before reaching for a beer.

"Are you talking about my wife? Because if you are, I might have to break something of yours."

"Tilly," Parker spat. "I'm talking about Tilly. She's a troublemaker with a capital T."

Dylan's brows rose as he looked over at Porter who just shrugged. He didn't know what was going on with his brother.

"I brought bourbon," Jameson said as he and his brother-in-law, Zain Ali Rahman, joined them.

"I got chips. I hope you don't mind, but I brought the

guys," Colton said as he joined the group with some of his firemen.

"Where are Kane and Nolan?" Porter asked the other two firemen.

"They're on call tonight. So am I, so I can't drink," Colton said, "but Flint, Conley, and Jack have the night off.

"Since there's not a lot happening in Keeneston, we figured this was a good way to spend the night," Flint said as he grabbed a beer.

"Well, except for all those assassinations," Conley said in his thick Eastern Kentucky accent.

"I brought food since I figured you'd only have beer and chips," Landon said as he walked onto the patio with an enormous tray of sandwiches and beer cheese for the chips.

"You're hands down the best cousin," Dylan said, snagging a sandwich as Landon said hello to his brother, Colton.

"Well, this spread looks better than I anticipated. I brought brownies."

Porter turned quickly at the sound of a woman's voice. "Blythe? What are you doing here?"

"We were invited to girls' night, but when you date a girl it's better to separate for the trash talking portion of the night. Veronica and I flipped a coin. She got the ladies and I got y'all."

"You got the better end of the deal," Parker said, tossing a beer to Blythe a second after she set down the brownies.

"I don't know. The way I see it, I'm surrounded by y'all and my girlfriend is with a bunch of sexy women talking about wanting to get laid, so . . ." Blythe held up her hands and Porter laughed out loud.

His brother didn't find it amusing. "They better not be getting laid," Parker muttered.

"I can guarantee my wife is getting laid tonight. It's nearly impossible to keep my wife off me," Jameson said with a smirk.

Zain groaned. "I don't want any details on my sister's love life."

"Abby's the same," Dylan said with a satisfied smirk as he toasted Jameson.

"No, dude, that's just wrong," Kale said as he joined them at exactly the wrong moment.

"Dude?" Dylan joked back. "Have you been talking to our mutual friend again?"

"It's better than talking about my sister's sex life," Kale said.

"I don't mind," Blythe said with a grin. "I'd love to hear all about your sex life."

"That's because you get to have sex with Veronica while I'm stuck with my hand," Kale grumbled as he grabbed a beer. "My dad has me working at the farm day and night. Now this Panther thing. I'm never going to get laid."

"What is it with getting laid?" Parker snapped. "Do women now just sleep with any Tom, Dick, or Carlos that gives them a pretty compliment?"

"Dude," Kale said slowly as he shook his head. "What is going on with you?"

"Tilly," Porter answered for his brother.

"Aw, damn. She's finer than frog hair split four ways," Conley said.

Parker crumpled the beer can with one hard squeeze.

"Okay, so you like her," Blythe said as the voice of reason. "Why are you going all caveman?"

"Caveman?" Parker asked incredulously.

"Well, you're not using your words, only grunting, and

now you've killed that poor, defenseless little beer can," Blythe pointed out.

"I can't talk about it," Parker grumbled.

Blythe just raised her eyes as if to say told you so.

"Oh, he really likes her," Colton said, giving Parker a punch to the shoulder. "Just ask her out already."

"It's complicated," Parker said with a frown a second before the beer can was shot from his hand. "What the fu—"

Porter shoved his brother to the ground. "Could we not just get one night off?" he yelled over the gunfire that was currently destroying the sandwich table.

Porter reached behind him and grabbed the rifle he'd left leaning against the side of the house. He didn't have time to aim before Dylan shot rapid fire into the woods with a massive gun.

"Where did that come from?" Porter yelled over the gunfire.

"Sophie invented it. It's foldable," Dylan said as he reloaded. Sounds of yelling filled the night as men poured from the woods.

"I got the axes in my truck," Conley said. "I'll be right back."

Conley and Flint raced into the house and out through the front door.

"Well, I did say I wanted to shoot something," Parker muttered as he lined up his shot and took it.

"Did everyone bring a gun but me?" Zain asked.

"Got extras in my bag," Dylan called out. "I figured this would happen."

"I am so glad I got tails. I bet the girls aren't having this much fun," Blythe said as she took down a man running right at her.

"Behind you!" Jameson yelled and Porter swung around to find men closing in on each side of the patio.

An ax swung and the man dropped. "I thought moving to Keeneston would be boring," Flint said, pulling the ax free.

"So did I," Blythe called out as she moved to hand-to-hand combat.

Parker knocked a man out with one punch. "This is making me feel better."

"What's this?" Conley asked, coming back through the house with the Acid Gun of Death in his hands.

"*No!*" Porter, Jameson, and Kale yelled, but it was too late.

A man punched Conley and the Acid Gun of Death fell from his hands. Porter leapt forward with his hand outstretched. He caught the gun a second before it hit the ground.

"This is such a great night," Blythe called out as the group gave up on any guns and moved to hand-to-hand. They didn't want to accidentally shoot a good guy at such close quarters. "I needed this after Veronica's lecture on putting dishes into the dishwasher. You don't hear me saying anything about her leaving her makeup all over the counter."

"Huh," Parker grunted before taking another man down. "Women."

"What the hell?" Porter heard Jackson yell. "We're fifteen minutes late. You couldn't wait another ten minutes to start the fight?"

Talon sliced his way through the outer perimeter. "Are those Zinnia's brownies? She makes the best brownies."

"I made them," Blythe called out. "But Zinnia did give me the recipe."

"Aw, shucks," Lucas said from where he had a man in a bear hug. "This sure makes me miss my Bertha."

"Zain, duck!" Porter yelled as a man came at Zain with a knife in hand. Zain dropped to the ground and Porter fired the Acid Gun of Death.

The acid bomb stuck to the man's shirt. He was surprised when he was still alive and smirked at Porter. Then he wasn't smirking. The acid bomb released and he melted.

"Oh my God," Zain screamed as he leapt up. "It's on me! Get it off me!"

"What's on you?" Dylan asked.

"The melted bad guy. He melted all over me." Zain spun around and sure enough, there was melted bad guy all down his back. "Ew! I stepped in it!"

Zain began to strip as he cursed. The surviving assassins looked to their melted teammate and took off while Landon tied up the ones who were injured.

"I missed all the fun," Jace said as he came around the side of the house with a bag of chips in his hands.

"The women," Porter said, filled with worry as Kale took the Acid Gun of Death from him.

"They're fine," Jace said. "I just dropped Stella off there. There's so many Rahmi guards, there's no way anyone could sneak in. So, who pissed off Tilly and why is Greer muttering about not getting laid?"

"She better not be getting laid," Jackson snapped. "Whoever touches my sister has to answer to me."

"I'd totally help her out if I weren't in a relationship with the love of my life. Even if my love has way more makeup than any woman should have," Blythe said with a grin.

Flint groaned at the image a moment before Jackson's fist met his face. "Don't even think about my sister like that."

"Tilly's mad that Parker won't make a move," Jameson told Jace as they tied the last of the men up.

"Interesting. Parker's never had a problem asking girls out before," Jace said. "One last question. Why is Zain naked?"

"Don't worry, reinforcements are here!"

"You're too late, Dad," Porter called out as his father and brothers ran around the house fully armed.

"Dammit!" Cy cursed. "I told you we should have had guys' night at my house instead of Cade's. Why is Zain naked?"

"Oh my gosh!" Veronica gasped.

"What?" Willa asked.

"Assassins from Iraq just attacked the guys," Veronica told them. "But everyone is okay. Well, except Zain."

"What happened to Zain?" Mila asked as she rushed forward. Veronica turned the phone around to show her. "Why is my husband naked?"

"The better question is why am I not naked?" Greer grumbled. "The guy who even admitted he wanted to see me naked ran to the front of the house as soon as he heard my brother's threat."

Willa was already sending a text to Porter when one from him came through. She relaxed as she read that they were all safe and they didn't need to hurry back. Guys' night was still going strong.

So relieved no one was hurt. Why is Zain naked? Willa typed.

He's fine. Just got something on his clothes.

Like he spilled a drink or like blood? Willa asked.

Kinda both.

Um, okay. "Mila, apparently Zain got something on his clothes. That's why he's naked."

"Huh," Mila said with a shrug. "That's kind of disappointing. I was hoping for a better story. Now, where were we?"

"We were talking about men being intimidated by independent women," Cady said, holding up her glass in salute to Greer. "I don't even need to get laid. I have a vibrator. I just need these men to stop patting me on the head like I'm a little girl."

"Chop that hand off and they won't do it again," Greer told Cady.

"I might have to do that."

"I'll help," Willa said to her. "I was going to talk to you later, but I'd love to invest."

"Me too!" Tilly said, jumping off the subject of stupid men. "Tell me all about what you want to do with the distillery."

Willa and the ladies sat back and talked business. They'd already decided they couldn't fix men, but they could help Cady fix her business. Women lifting women up were unstoppable.

25

Porter looked over the chessboard and didn't show so much as a flicker of emotion. After the captured assassins were taken back to Desert Sun Farm, Ahmed returned with Brian to enjoy guys' night.

Brian dropped the challenge of a chess match and Porter had accepted. Now everyone stood silently around the chessboard to watch the final moves of the heated game play out.

Porter played a ruthless match and Brian countered. Neither said one word to the other. Porter pretended to be relaxed as Brian fell into the trap Porter had laid. Then, with a single move on the board, it was over. Porter had captured the king. "Checkmate."

Brian blinked and his lips thinned as he realized he'd been beaten. Then he shook his head and sat back in the chair as Blythe handed him a bourbon.

"Very interesting," Brian said with a little smile. "You play like a spy. I should have seen that trap, but you hid it well. You're aggressive but not egotistical about it. You're confident and smart. I see why my daughter likes you."

"Does that mean you approve of me dating your daughter?" Porter asked as he masked the bundle of nerves he was feeling.

Brian let out a sigh. "I saw what Callum did to her self-esteem. I thought you might be taking advantage of her, but you're not. I'm seeing her grow under your love. You have my permission to date her. Heck, if you play chess like this, you have my permission to marry her if you show me how you cornered my king."

Porter laughed as did everyone else. Then his father took a seat across from Brian and a new game was set up as the two men talked. Only Porter wasn't listening. Marry Willa? He knew he'd loved her and he wanted her in his life, but the second he heard that word from Brian's mouth, it settled in his heart. Married to Willa. His whole body warmed and hummed at the thought. He was so lost in the idea of marrying Willa the rest of guys' night flew by in a blur.

"You look happy this morning," Tilly said accusingly.

Willa tried to temper her smile. When Porter picked her up the night before he'd had given her that hungry look that made her whole body respond in an instant. They'd sped home and had barely made it into the house before they were kissing. After last night, riding had a whole different meaning.

"Maybe it's because you and I are now both five percent owners of a distillery," Willa said, trying to steer the subject away from sex with Porter and Tilly's lack of sex with Parker.

Tilly grinned. "Yeah, I am part owner of a distillery. It's the first major investment I've made on my own without running it by a roomful of stupid male bankers telling me what I should or shouldn't do with my own money."

"Watch out, world. Tilly is taking the reins."

"Damn straight I am. Now, let's practice and then get me a bottle of aspirin for this hangover."

Willa smiled at her friend as they walked into the ring. They spent time walking the jumps to make sure they got the order down before they brought their horses out for a light practice.

"Great job," Porter said, giving her a kiss the second Willa dismounted from Apollo. Greer stepped forward and took the reins as her groom.

"Thanks. He feels really good," Willa said as she saw Aniyah and her husband, DeAndre, walking toward them with Piper and her husband, Aiden.

"I see you're wearing my jacket," Piper said happily as she hugged Willa. "I brought you something for the competition."

Willa took the bag from Piper and pulled out the tissue paper. Inside was a lightweight white show shirt. She had a million of them. "Thanks."

"I made it for you. It's with a new material I'm working with. These synthetics work great with my nanotechnology," Piper told her.

"Wait, is this bulletproof like my jacket?" Willa asked, holding up the shirt to get a better look.

"It is. That way you can be safe in the show ring."

"Thank you so much." Willa hugged Piper and turned to Tilly. "Here's another company for you to invest in."

"I don't even know what it is, but I want in if Willa says so," Tilly said, joining them from her practice ride.

"That was really amazing," DeAndre told her. "I'm on duty tomorrow so we decided to come watch practice."

"Thank you," Willa said. "That's so nice of you all to do. If you want, I can put Apollo up and meet you back here to watch the rest."

"That would be great," Aniyah said with her large smile.

"Porter, you can stay here. Tilly, Greer, and I will be right back." Willa turned to motion to her bodyguards to follow. She'd only be a minute and Aiden was already talking to Porter so she didn't want to make him leave.

Porter still leaned over and kissed her. "Hurry back."

Porter watched as Willa, Greer, Tilly, and three bodyguards headed back to the barn. He didn't like letting her out of his sight but felt she was safe here. Even Callum had been giving her wide berth recently.

"I can't believe I missed guys' night," Aiden said.

"Who keeps giving you that acid gun?" DeAndre asked, but Porter was interested in the man walking toward them.

The man was completely average-looking besides his deep tan.

"G'day," he said in an Australian accent.

"Oh, oh, I can talk like you. Aiden's taught me everything. Tally-ho, chap!" Aniyah said as the man looked thoroughly confused.

"What's this drongo talking about?"

"Would this bloke like some fish and chips? Some bangers and mash?" Aniyah went on happily spouting British sayings.

"Does she have a roo loose in the top paddock?" the man asked DeAndre, who no longer looked amused. "I'm looking for Porter Davies."

"I'm Porter—" Before Porter could finish, a knife was shoved into his gut and the man ran.

"Bloody hell!" Aniyah yelled as the man took off.

DeAndre and Aiden took off after him as Piper picked up the knife from the ground. "Told you my jacket worked."

Porter looked down and saw the blade hadn't even nicked the jacket he was wearing.

"Get down!" Aniyah yelled as she pulled a large pink gun from her purse. "I'm going to shoot that tosser!"

Folks around them might have missed the quick, prison-style attempted stabbing, but they didn't miss Aniyah waving her gun around.

People screamed. Security came running. DeAndre and Aiden dropped to the ground like bags of sand and lay flat as Aniyah fired off her shot.

"Oh my gosh," Piper said in disbelief.

"Holy crap," Porter said at the same time.

"I shot him!" Aniyah yelled as she jumped up and down. "Right in the arse."

Aiden and DeAndre were on the man, handcuffing him as security tackled Aniyah.

"US marshal," Parker called out, running over as Porter was trying to convince them Aniyah was the good guy in this scenario. "She's with us. She helped apprehend an attempted murder suspect."

Security backed off and Porter reached down to help Aniyah up.

"I sure hope that was a nightstick pressed against my leg or my Sugarbear is going to be real mad," Aniyah said as she brushed dirt off her jeans. "But did you see it? I shot him! And not on the toe!"

"You're my hero, Aniyah," Porter said, lifting her hand and placing a kiss on her knuckles.

"Baby!" DeAndre called out as he dragged the would-be assassin along. "Are you okay?"

"I'm great, Sugarbear. Now hand that wanker off to Parker because I am so hot for you right now." Aniyah completely ignored the assassin and kissed her husband.

"I think we need to have a little talk," Porter said, bending down to where the handcuffed man was on his knees moaning.

"Porter!" Willa cried as she ran forward with Greer and Tilly.

Tilly took one look at Parker holding a man moaning about being shot in the ass and asked Aniyah if she could borrow the gun. Parker narrowed his eyes at her and glared.

"Are you okay?" Parker asked Tilly. Willa ran to join them as a large group of people began to form a circle around them to see what was going on.

"As if you care," Tilly said as she rolled her eyes at him.

"Well, I don't see any blood on you so I better take this guy to get medical treatment." Parker turned and walked away as he dragged the Aussie assassin behind him.

"What happened?" Willa asked as she looked him over for blood.

"He tried to stab me, but the jacket worked great. I'm fine. Parker will take him to Desert Sun Farm and Jace will treat him either before or after they interrogate him."

"Can't we go one day without someone trying to kill or kidnap us?" Willa asked with frustration.

"I think it's kind of fun," Greer said with a grin. "Keeps life interesting."

"It's been a while since I got to tackle someone. All in all, I thought it was a great morning so far," Aiden said in his British accent.

Porter had Willa in his arms and had to agree; he was getting pretty used to these attempts.

"I don't know whether to be frightened or proud about

the fact that I'm recovering from these attempts a lot faster," Willa said as the audience began to disperse after Parker took the assassin away.

Porter saw it first. The bad news crew was strutting toward them with Callum in the lead. Willa groaned when she saw them. "Just what I need."

"Wow, your boyfriend is so unpopular someone tried to kill him. Not surprising since you like him and we all know how bad your judgment is," Callum said with a snicker.

"Who's this wanker?" Aniyah asked as she joined them and Aiden gave a little chuckle.

Callum looked over Aniyah with distaste, though Porter didn't know why. Aniyah was a knockout. She was barely five feet tall, but she had the kind of curves that went on forever.

"My, how you have fallen," Valentina laughed. "You can't find any respectable friends so now you're with the country bumpkins."

"Worse," Cyril said, glaring at Greer. "Uptight, frigid bitches."

"Now, you're not bad to look at. I'd let you carry my luggage," Marguerite said to Aiden.

She was reaching toward Aiden when Porter heard, zap, zap, zap, zap in quick succession followed by a chorus of farts.

"Now," Willa said with a smile as she put the fart taser back into her pocket. "Someone get some video with sound and then let's watch some jumping."

"Way ahead of you," Aniyah said as she filmed the musical gastro number the four were performing.

Willa stepped over the four as she linked her arms with Porter's family and walked away while talking to them about the jumps and the scoring.

"So, five days, right?" DeAndre asked as he came to walk next to Porter.

"Five days? Oh, yes, the last day for Willa's show jumping is in five days. Are you planning on coming more?" Porter asked.

DeAndre shook his head. "That's not what I meant."

"What did you mean then?" Porter asked.

"I'll let it be a surprise," DeAndre said cryptically as they headed into the stands to watch the rest of practice.

Willa's life might have changed drastically, but her preshow routine did not. Porter had somehow known to let her do her own thing this morning. He'd risen early, made her breakfast, and simply told her to let him know if she needed anything.

Willa had eaten, meditated, and gotten dressed in silence. While she was quiet on the drive to the barn, her mind was not. Mentally she was going over every jump, every lead change, every squeeze of her thighs, and every lean of her body.

"I'm sorry I haven't talked much," Willa said to Porter as they walked into the barn.

"It's no problem. You're in the zone. I get it. Just tell me if you need anything. Otherwise I'll just hang out and give you a little peace."

Willa stopped walking and Porter turned to see what had happened. Before he could ask, Willa kissed him. It wasn't the kind of kiss that made you hot and bothered. It was the kind of kiss that was a slow burn of feelings. "Thank you. Thank you for understanding and for being so supportive."

"I might not fully get what you do for work, but I get horses and I get competition," Porter said as one side of his lips tilted up into a smile. "You're going to do great. You know the course, Apollo is on his game, and you're one hell of a rider."

Willa gave him another quick kiss. "Thank you. You know exactly what I needed to hear."

Willa linked her fingers with his as they walked the rest of the way to the stall. Greer and Tilly were already there and talking. Tilly had moved her horse to what had been Miss Trix's stall after practice yesterday to make it easier for Greer and the rest of Keeneston to keep an eye on both of them. Today the barn had a whole new feel since it was show day. The entire barn was alive with the anticipation of competition.

"Did you see?" Tilly called out as she bounded forward.

"See what?" Willa asked.

Tilly turned her phone around. "It went viral," she crowed in delight.

Willa stared down at the video of the fearsome four farting. Aniyah had added some music and graphics to really make it pop. Willa was speechless.

"They've threatened to sue everyone involved, but they can't prove you or anyone did anything. After all, there's no such thing as a fart stun gun," Tilly giggled.

"They're going to be so mad and take it out on us," Willa realized. The funniness of the video was going to be replaced with them going on a bullying rampage. That used to leave her worried, but not any longer. Instead it was just an annoying distraction. She didn't need them and she sure as hell wasn't going to put up with their intimidation anymore.

Tilly shook her head. "Nope. People started commenting on the video with their own videos and stories of the four being abusive bullies. Former grooms, current competitors, barn staff, everyone! Their parents have all called them home because of the PR nightmare."

Willa took a deep breath. "We're free of them? For real?"

Tilly nodded her head excitedly. "At least for now and I'll take it. Today is going to be a very good day."

Willa smiled largely. "Yes, I believe it will be."

"Good luck. I love you."

Willa took a deep breath and looked down at Porter as walking beside her toward the ring. He'd been such a support for her this morning. "Thank you. Love you too."

"Go get 'em, boy," Porter said to Apollo before looking up at Willa and giving her a wink.

Willa turned her entire focus on the jumps as she entered the ring. Porter faded away. The gossip about Callum and his crew, now called the "farting foursome," all faded away. The crowd was no longer there. It was simply her and Apollo and the jumps. She felt the way Apollo's skin shimmered with anticipation. The way his muscles bunched, ready to take the jumps. And the way his breathing slowed as if he, too, were mentally preparing himself for the course.

"Let's go, sweetheart," Willa said a second before she squeezed her thighs and trotted Apollo into the ring.

Willa knew the obstacles from her walk-through. The oxer with its numerous standards and poles to create wider jumps, the fake wall, the vertical with the single standards and only one pole wide but very high, and then the combinations for multiple jumps with just a few strides between them.

Willa took a deep breath and, with a squeeze of her legs, sent Apollo into a canter. Together they sailed over the first vertical. Willa brought Apollo into an immediate canter and into the second jump, an oxer a couple feet wide. As she cantered around the ring, she kept an eye on the time. When she cut across the diagonal of the ring, she pushed Apollo to lengthen his stride into a hand gallop. Not a racing gallop but a fast canter since today was the Speed Competition. Willa was going to take every split second she could get.

Willa and Apollo were in sync as they approached the final jump. Willa went up into her two-point stance as she squeezed her calves and asked Apollo to fly.

When they landed, she heard the cheers. She'd made time and Apollo had a clean round. Not a single hoof touched any of the jumps. She smiled and patted his neck. Apollo tossed his head and shook his mane, making the many braids dance. He knew he'd done well.

"You were fantastic!" Porter called up to her as she walked from the ring.

"It felt fantastic. Apollo is really on point today." Willa dismounted right into Porter's arms.

"So were you." Porter kissed her quickly and Willa felt as if she'd just won it all. Apollo was on, she nailed it, and she had a boyfriend who was proud and excited for her.

"Great ride!" Tilly said, giving her a hug.

"That was so cool," Greer said, coming up and hugging her before taking Apollo's reins. "You made that look easy and those jumps are crazy high."

"That was insane," Bodyguard Barry said with a shake of

his head as he fell into line slightly behind her as they headed back to the barn.

"There's no way you could get me to do that. I think I'd rather jump out of a plane," Deshaun told her.

"What about between jumping or asking Greer out?" Willa said, giving Greer a wink. Reggie and Barry laughed so Willa knew Deshaun must have told them about girls' night. Greer rolled her eyes and Willa was pretty sure Greer flicked her off, too.

"Greer, you're fine and I appreciate you, but if it's between facing your brother or jumping over a five-foot fence on the back of a horse, which I don't know how to ride, I'm taking my chances with the horse. A broken neck would be better than what Jackson would do," Deshaun said without hesitation.

"My freaking brother," Greer groaned. Porter knew Jackson was overprotective, but geez, maybe it was worse than he thought. "And Deshaun, you're a wimp. I don't care about all those muscles. You're a wimp. All men are!"

Porter grinned at his cousin as they entered the barn. "Yet you love us."

"At this point, I think I'd have more luck getting laid by her," Greer said with a head nod to a tall woman with dark hair up in a ponytail and wearing the standard jumping attire.

"Who is that?" Tilly asked Willa.

"I don't know. She's very pretty," Willa said and Porter had to agree as a group of women riders walked in from the other side of the barn. They were all tall and gorgeous.

"Damn, those women are fine and I bet they don't have a scary ass brother," Deshaun said, teasing Greer.

Porter laughed as Greer rolled her eyes.

"Did you just finish?" the woman Greer had eyed asked as the other women joined her.

"I did. They're on the sixteenth rider right now," Willa told them. "I'm Willa Aldridge. Are you all new?"

"We're the riders on the Israeli team," the woman told her.

"That's neat. Good luck today," Willa said as the group parted for them to walk between.

Porter gave them a friendly smile and a tip of his hat. In return he got a punch to the face.

Porter staggered backward at the unexpected blow. Reggie, Deshaun, and Barry tried to converge on Willa to protect her but the women were on them. One took out Barry's knee, another was beating the crap out of Reggie, and a third was fighting with Deshaun.

"Still thinking of asking her out?" Deshaun yelled to Greer as the woman Greer had joked about dating attacked her with a knife.

"This only makes me like her more!" Greer yelled back as she and the woman were locked in a lightning-fast battle of knife slices, blocks, and punches. "Tilly, take the horse!"

Tilly stopped screaming as she grabbed Apollo's reins and ducked out of the grasp of a woman to move him out of the fray. The bodyguards had their hands full and the last thing they needed was to lose control of a horse his size. Willa fought off two women trying to kidnap her and Porter was face to face with an Israeli-trained super soldier.

Porter ducked an elbow intended to break his jaw. "So, is it sexist to hit her or not to hit her?" he yelled out.

"It's sexist to not hit her," Greer called back as she took the woman with a knife down and two more went after her.

"I agree. I can take any man, but I appreciate you asking," the attacker told him.

With that settled, Porter got to work. No longer only on the defensive, he went on the offensive and fought with all the training his father and Ahmed had taught him since he was a child. Hit, block, punch, duck, elbow . . .

"You're very well-trained. Our intel says you've only been with the CIA a week," the woman said as she jumped back to avoid a punch.

Porter made his move now that she'd given him room. He didn't leap forward to continue the fight with the woman. Instead, he leapt sideways and tackled the two women who had Willa by the arms and were trying to pull her away.

They went down in a heap on the rubber mats of the barn floor. Porter kicked out and sent one of the women rolling backward. "Get onto Apollo!" he yelled at Willa as he leapt up and put himself between the now three attackers and Willa.

He didn't look back to see if she did what he told her. Instead he was embroiled in a three-on-one fight.

"Okay, enough playing around," he heard Greer mutter as he heard the hoofbeats of Apollo galloping away from them. Good, Willa was safe.

Greer grabbed the closest woman soldier fighting her by the collar and head-butted her. The woman she'd been fighting crumpled to the ground and then his cousin was by his side. "You know what I'm craving all of a sudden? Bread pudding with a caramel bourbon sauce," Greer said.

"Are you serious right now?" Porter ducked a punch and slammed his fist into the woman attacker's face. Her nose broke under his hit, but she hardly blinked. "They're like super soldiers."

"Your training is superior. It's a shame after this we can't collaborate," Greer told the two women she was fighting.

Porter took a punch to the gut and swore it was just as hard a hit as a fall from a bull. Time to pull out the move he used to beat Parker.

Porter took a step back and then dropped to the ground as if he were sliding into home plate. The woman jumped his lead leg, thinking he was trying to sweep her feet out from under her, and never saw the hook with the other leg coming. His leg, strong from rodeo, hooked behind her knee and brought her crashing down. Porter had her in a headlock before she could regain her balance. He squeezed just enough to send her into unconsciousness.

Porter glanced around and saw security running toward them yet again. Tilly and Willa were on Apollo at the back of the barn, watching to see if they needed to run or not. Barry hobbled around, barely holding off his attacker, Reggie was unconscious, and Deshaun was about to be knocked out.

Greer was in full badass mode, taking on two at a time. She also didn't need his help. Porter glanced around, found a lead rope hanging near a stall, and grabbed it. He snapped it quickly, whipping it through the air like a bullwhip. It slashed into the back of the head of the woman fighting Deshaun. It gave him the time he needed to take her down with an uppercut.

Then Porter went down and dirty and tackled the woman fighting Barry. It was a short battle on the ground with her, but then Deshaun and Barry leapt in and pinned her down.

Porter felt pretty good about the number of soldiers he took down until he turned to see Greer wiping her hands on her pants with four unconscious women at her feet. "So, about that bread pudding."

·　·　·

Willa held Tilly's hand as the fighting continued. Her heart was pounding and she was doing everything she could to keep Apollo calm.

"Do we need to help them?" Tilly asked, her voice full of fear.

Willa saw Greer head-butt a woman and Porter break one of their noses. "I think they've got it, but run for security." Tilly slid down off Apollo's back and hit the ground running.

Willa heard Tilly screaming for security. A second later she was back. "They're on their way."

Willa reached out for Tilly and removed her foot from the stirrup. "Jump back on behind me in case we need to make a quick getaway."

Willa was sure she didn't breathe until it was all over. Porter had been a beast, but Greer had been next level. Where Porter moved with power, Greer moved with lethal grace. As security rushed the building, there was nothing left but a pile of unconscious women and Reggie moaning as he tried to get up.

Greer flashed her FBI badge, had security zip-tie the women, and then they were loaded into the back of a horse trailer Greer was "borrowing." Willa was pretty sure Callum's staff gleefully handed it over and even told her not to bother with returning it.

Porter had Willa in his arms as soon as the soldiers were fully secured and off to Desert Sun Farm. "Is Apollo okay? Are you okay?"

"I love you for asking about my horse first," Willa told him a second before she kissed him. "We're fine, but I'm going to need to stay here for a while and calm him down."

"I'll stay with you. My family is on their way. Deshaun needs to take Barry and Reggie to the hospital. I think

Barry's knee is busted and Reggie has one hell of a concussion."

Willa looked up and saw Parker striding into the barn sending people running for cover at the thunderous look on his face. "Is anyone hurt?"

"No, we're all fine," Willa assured him.

"Where's Matilda?" Parker asked even as his eyes scanned the barn.

"She had to go up to the show ring to check on how much longer she has before her ride," Willa told him. "You do know she hates that name, right?"

A slow, wicked smile spread across his face. "I know."

Willa shook her head. Whatever was going on with them was between them. Tilly would tell her eventually. In the meantime, she had her own troubles to worry about.

Willa spent the next hour making sure Apollo was rubbed down and cleaned up from his time in the ring. The familiar routine calmed the horse. By the time he finally decided to eat an apple, Abby, Dylan, Aiden, Walker, and Jameson were sitting outside his stall and Jackson and his FBI team had the barn exits covered.

"So, badass women kidnappers. That's a new one," Dylan said, winking at his wife.

"They were pretty awesome actually," Willa said, taking a seat on the stool by Apollo's stall. "If I were to be kidnapped by anyone, I'd want it to be them."

"Kale said they were getting closer," Abby told her. "Although he says it's like finally moving an inch when you still have a mile to go."

Willa let out a long breath of frustration. "So, we're doomed to do this day in and day out until we've either killed every assassin and kidnapper in the world or my father and your brother find a way to take down The Panther."

"Basically," Abby said with a shrug. "But look at all the people from around the world you're meeting."

Willa snickered and then laughed out loud. Apollo stuck his head over his door and nuzzled her hair as she laughed. "Very true, Abby. And I got to meet Porter."

Porter walked over and put his hand on the base of her neck. His thumb ran over her skin and caused it to warm. "It's worth it because of you," Porter whispered to her before kissing the top of her head.

Teasing, laughing, stories, and conversation flowed around Willa as she began to feel part of this crazy Keeneston world, even if Dylan and Abby didn't tell her who they worked for. Maybe when she and Porter married . . . whoa. Marriage? That thought just snuck in and exploded in her mind. Marrying Porter refused to go back in the bottle. It was all Willa could think about now.

27

The next night, Porter lay in bed with Willa curled up against his chest. She'd scored well for Team Competition Day. Luckily Callum and his cohorts, who were no longer competing, were on a separate team. Tilly and Willa had stepped up big time to help lead their team into fourth place. They had always been second to Callum's team at previous events. Willa was exhausted and had fallen asleep after a quick dinner at the café.

Porter turned the page of his reading app on his phone with one hand and held Willa with the other. It was only nine at night, but he enjoyed holding her while she slept and didn't even think about sneaking from bed to go into another room.

You might want to get to the café, was the text that came from his father.

Willa is asleep. Did something happen? Porter typed with his thumb as he began to pull himself free from Willa.

Trouble at the Café. Meet me there in five. Blythe is at your door.

Of course she was. His father would have everything all lined up.

Porter slid from bed, pulled on his jeans, and yanked a T-shirt over his head before picking up his boots. He carried them from the bedroom to the front of the house and opened the door to find Blythe sitting on the front step.

"What's happened?" Porter whispered.

"The café is in an uproar. There have been some incidents. I was sent here to watch Willa."

"Alone?"

Blythe just narrowed her eyes at him. "Is everyone okay?" he asked.

"Of course they are. Keenestonites aren't your average citizens. Jackson and Talon are on their way to walk the perimeter," Blythe told him as she stood up and dusted off her pants. That's when he saw the gun at her hip, the one strapped to her thigh, and the assault weapon she had leaning against the stairs.

"Keep her safe, Blythe. Please," Porter practically begged as he trotted down the stairs and out to his truck.

The drive to the café was fast in the middle of the night when there were no tractors, horse vans, or giant trailers moving rolls of hay. For just after nine at night, the place was hopping. Well, it was a Friday night and the café was literally the only place to go in town.

Porter didn't care that he double-parked outside the door to the café. He'd talk Matt into dropping any ticket he got. Not that his brother-in-law or friends would even write a ticket at a time like this.

Porter flung open the door and rushed inside. He expected worried looks and panicked conversation from the people inside. Instead, he found people laughing and teasing Pam Gilbert, who looked like a pouting teenager.

"What's going on?" Porter asked as his father came forward.

"Well, there's a regular United Nations convention going on in the Desert Sun Farm holding cells," his father said. "There are people from China, France, Australia, North Korea, Iraq, Iran, and Israel."

"I know this. Did Kale find something?" Porter asked. "Is this what's going on?"

"Everyone found something," his father said dryly. "Walker and Layne were on a date night when a man stopped and asked for directions to your house. He claimed to be a friend of yours. Walker took him out and added Pakistan to the Assassins' UN Assembly. Then Nash and Sophie were on their way to the café for their date night when they found a car hidden along the side of the road near the farm. They leapt into action and captured an assassin from Saudi Arabia."

"How many countries spy on the US and would want this information?" Porter asked with a shake of his head.

"All of them. Just like we have spies in every country. And don't think just because we're allies with someone that we don't have spies in their country and vice versa. Heck, allied spies in the US probably outnumber all of our enemies two to one," his father told him and his father would know since he had been one of those spies.

"So, two more countries have been caught?" Porter asked.

His father shook his head and held up a third finger. "Matt, Cody, and Luke found an Italian assassin trying to hide in the upstairs courtroom with a sniper rifle aimed at the café door." His father held up a fourth finger. "Ryan and

Deacon caught Spain trying to cut through the neighboring farm." Then his father stuck out his thumb as well. "And Dylan, Abby, Greer, Jackson, and his team got into a shoot-out on Main Street, taking down a large cell of Russians. My brothers and I got to help with that. Good times for a Friday night." His father gave a little grin and Porter shook his head. His father had a strange idea of fun.

Porter took a deep breath and let his head fall back. "Please tell me there weren't anymore. We're running out of countries."

His father grinned then. "I saved the best for last. Cassidy was babysitting everyone's kids for date night. She had a baby strapped to her front and was pushing that large multi-baby stroller toward the café to pick up dinner to go before putting them all to bed. We were all in here celebrating taking down the Russians when a German assassin came up behind her and grabbed her. He intended to hold her and the children hostage in exchange for you and Willa."

Porter quickly scanned the café. Cassidy was sitting at a table talking to Sophie and Nash, bouncing their daughter, Emersyn, on her knee. "Who saved them?" Porter asked.

"Cassidy had the situation handled by the time Greer got to her," Cy said with a grin.

"Cassidy?" Porter looked at his little cousin with question. "She's good with a bow and arrow, but close combat?"

"No one knew it, but she's been training with Abby and Dylan. Dylan insisted after Cassidy told them she intended to travel on her own more with her language work." Cassidy had a knack for languages. She could learn a new one at a drop of a hat. Right now she was fluent in eight different languages and conversant in several more.

"What happened then?" Porter asked.

"She strangled the assassin into unconsciousness with the diaper bag as she cussed him out in whispered German. She took him down without waking the babies and now Germany is with the rest of the International Brotherhood of Assassins at Desert Sun Farm. Plus, she's just been deemed the best babysitter in the world. She's throwing around the idea of a business training babysitters for combat for diplomats and celebrities," his father told him.

"It's not fair!" Pam suddenly yelled as she jumped up from her chair. "I've been driving around town all day trying to spot someone to hit. *Six* countries! Two right here on Main Street while I was sitting in here with my keys in my hand and at the ready. I'm literally the only person who hasn't caught a bad guy yet."

Pam's face was red, her bottom lip trembled, and the keys to her military Hummer hung limply from her hand.

Porter walked over to her and wrapped her up in a hug. "I really appreciate you looking out for Willa and me."

"I just want to help. I want to be part of the team again. I used to hit bad guys all the time, but now it's like I've lost my touch," Pam said with a sniffle.

"Your time will come, Pam," her sister, Morgan Davies, said soothingly, coming over to hug her too. Pam nodded her head slowly and sat back down in her chair.

"Kale and Brian have all their phones and passwords. Each assassin is being interrogated right now and we'll hopefully have some news soon," his father told him as he joined Porter over by Pam.

Porter's phone rang and he looked at the unlisted number. He flashed it to his father. "Put it on speaker," his dad said before quieting the café.

"Who is this?" Porter asked instead of saying the customary greeting.

"Birch Stratton, President of the United States."

"Prove it," Porter said, not believing the president was on the phone.

"Abby Davies gave me your number. She's currently interrogating some Russian assassin with Dylan and her father, Ahmed," the person claiming to be the president told Porter.

"Yeah, I'm going to need more than that. You could be a Russian trying to get them free," Porter said.

"The last time my wife and I were in Keeneston was for Ariana's wedding and I found a pair of panties in my limo that didn't belong to my wife," he said flatly.

"Ah, the panty dropper struck again. What can I do for you, Mr. President?" Porter asked.

"I'm sending three people to help Kale and Brian Aldridge to try to track down The Panther. You'll know one of them. Don't bother asking about the identities of the other two. I'm also authorizing you to do whatever is necessary to apprehend The Panther. He or she has been selling government and corporate secrets for too long. Abby and Dylan have my number . . ."

"I do too, Porter," his grandmother called out. "Hello, Birch dear."

"Hello, Mrs. Davies. The pie this month was the best yet."

Yup, definitely the real president. Porter's grandmother was known for sending out pies once a month to all her friends and family who didn't live in Keeneston.

"My reinforcements will arrive soon at the airport. I'd appreciate it if you could take a security team and pick them up. They'll be staying at Desert Sun Farm," the president instructed.

"How will I know who to pick up?" Porter asked.

"Private airfield. You won't miss them. Good luck at capturing The Panther. Goodbye, Mrs. Davies. We'll talk soon," the president called out to Porter's grandmother. Then the line went dead.

Porter still couldn't believe the president had just called his phone. However, it shouldn't shock him with who lived in Keeneston. Royalty. Spies. America's Sweetheart. Horse racing champions.

"I'll go with you," Greer said as the room went into a full debate over who the president was sending to help. "Jackson and Talon are at your house keeping an eye on Willa. Lucas is with Tilly back at the apartment."

"Okay, then. Let's go pick up our mystery guests." Porter turned to the café crowd. "Thank you all for keeping us safe. I really appreciate all you've done."

Pam sniffled again. The others smiled as if it had been a fun Friday night.

"Best date night in a long time," Nash called out as Porter headed out of the café.

Porter and Greer sat in the pickup truck and waited for their mystery guests to arrive. Porter kept his eyes roving the night sky as they talked.

"I think I'm going to take a leave of absence from the FBI and work with Abby and Dylan for a couple of months. I might even ask Aiden if I could work private security for a short trial period. I want to see what my options are before I make my decision regarding going into the FBI leadership," Greer told him.

"Sounds like a good idea. I'm sure there are lots of private options for someone with your experience," Porter said. "There's our plane."

Porter watched as a sleek private jet landed on the runway and taxied toward them. The plane was nicer than Mo's and that was saying a lot since he was a prince of a very wealthy island nation.

The plane came to a stop and the door opened. Porter and Greer got out of the truck and walked forward quietly. Greer was fully armed even if you couldn't tell. Her eyes were less on the plane and more on scanning the surrounding area.

A woman was the first one off the plane. She looked to be in her mid- to late-twenties. Her brunette hair was in two buns that looked like little ears on the top of her head. Her brown eyes were lined with dark eyeliner and she had more than a few piercings on her ears.

Next out was a man about Porter's age. He had wide shoulders but was still lanky-looking. His shaggy dark brown hair hung over his eyes and his slightly darker Latin skin made the woman's alabaster skin seem to glow.

"Dude, this is Kentucky? Are there horses? I've never ridden a horse," the man said to Porter with a floppy smile.

"Yes, this is Kentucky. I'm Porter Davies and this is Greer Parker," Porter said trying to take in the exuberant man.

"I'm Alex and this is my wife, Roxie," the man said with a big grin as he held out his hand.

"Luv, you weren't supposed to tell them who we are," Roxie said to her husband with a very London accent.

"Dude, they're friends with Abby and Dylan." Alex shrugged it off as if it were no big deal.

"We're Dylan's cousins," Greer supplied as she shook hands with Alex and then Roxie. "Great T-shirt."

Porter looked at the shirt. It was black with Byte Me written in white block letters. Porter snickered and looked to Greer. "I think Kale has some friends."

"You know Kale too? Dude!" Alex said, slapping Porter's shoulder.

"I've told you before," a tall man in an expertly fitted suit said from the door to the plane. "Keeneston is so small they know everyone."

Porter had seen the man before at Abby's wedding and then again more recently at Ariana's. Sebastian Abel was hard to forget. He was best friends with the president and carried a gigantic chip on his shoulder. From what Porter had heard about Sebastian, he had been a kid from the bad side of town who happened to be a computer genius. He started out in the tech industry with SA Tech and then branched out to form a massive conglomerate. He was a self-made billionaire before he turned forty. Then there was the fact he'd been Abby's semi-date before she and Dylan finally committed to each other. However, in a strange twist, the three of them turned out to be great friends.

Sebastian held out his hand to Porter after joining them at the base of the stairs. "Sebastian Abel."

Sebastian was an inch taller than Porter and his handshake was firm. "Porter Davies."

Sebastian turned his hard gray-eyed gaze to Greer. "Miss Parker," he said, giving Greer a slight bow of his head. "I hear you're joining Abby and Dylan for a couple of months."

"Dude!" Alex exclaimed with delight and even Roxie smiled at that.

"I'm thinking about it," Greer said, not giving away the surprise Porter was sure she felt. The town knew Abby and Dylan did some black ops type things, but now it appeared there were more people on the team who had previously been unknown. Jackson had met a couple of the team members and then Ariana had met two others. Sebastian, Alex, and Roxie appeared to round out the group.

Sebastian took Greer in from the tip of her head to the bottom of her boots, but didn't say anything. Then he looked up and his eyes landed on the pickup truck. "Is this our ride?"

"Yeah," Porter said, taking Sebastian's suitcase in one hand and Roxie's in the other.

"I call shotgun. I get sick riding in the back. It's bad, dude. Around the city is one thing, but I saw Keeneston is in the country and, dude, I don't want to hurl," Alex said, putting his luggage in the back of the truck and then leaping up into the front passenger seat.

Porter almost laughed at the look of disbelief on the billionaire's face when he realized he was going to be riding in the backseat of the truck since Roxie was already climbing in to take the seat behind her husband.

"After you," Greer said sweetly and Porter had to cough to smother his laugh.

"Oh no, after you," Sebastian said, laying on the manners.

Greer pulled a rifle from the floor of the truck and smiled. "I have to keep your ass safe. Get in the truck, Sebastian."

Sebastian's smile fell as he grumbled and got into the middle seat of the truck. He seemed to take up most of the backseat and Greer had to wedge herself into what space was available.

"Let's go, Porter," she called out when she was in position.

The ride back to Keeneston was interesting as Alex said

dude twenty-three times and Roxie asked questions about Keeneston.

"I'm in the main house," Sebastian finally said when Porter drove up the long drive of Desert Sun Farm.

Porter dropped Sebastian with Dani and Mo and then took Alex and Roxie to where Kale and Brian were still working at the security center. The door to the security building opened and Kale came out with a huge smile. "Dude!"

"Dude!"

"I am so sorry," Roxie whispered to them. "Dudenese is contagious. Thanks for the lift."

"This was a very interesting night," Greer said with a chuckle as they got back into his pickup.

"I don't think Sebastian likes you very much," Porter joked.

"I'm crushed. I don't know how I'll manage to carry on," Greer said sarcastically.

Porter laughed as they left Desert Sun Farm. Now if these tech geniuses could track down The Panther before he or Willa were killed, he'd say dude as much as Alex wanted.

28

Willa had a big smile on her face and patted Apollo on the neck as they walked from the ring. He'd sailed over his jumps today and Willa knew their names would be at the top of the individual scoreboard going into the individual championship the day after tomorrow.

Porter was beaming at her and Greer was jumping up and down as she dismounted outside the ring. "You were breathtaking to watch," Porter told her before kissing her.

She'd slept so soundly last night and when she had woken up Porter had been holding her in his arms. It had been the perfect, peaceful night she'd needed. They'd wrapped up the team competition and she kept her fingers crossed for the results. Tilly still had to jump, but right now they had a real shot at second place in teams.

"I just needed one uneventful night of sleep," Willa joked, but she stopped laughing when Porter's smile fell.

"About that," Porter said as Greer shook her head and hid a smile.

"Don't be too mad at him," Greer said to her as she took Apollo and gave his cheek a friendly scratch.

"Mad about what?" Willa asked as they began to walk back to the barn.

"So, about last night . . ."

Willa's mouth opened, then her jaw dropped, and somehow managed to drop again by the end of the story. "I slept through all of that?"

"I knew today was a big day for you. Should I have woken you?" Porter asked.

Willa stopped and thought about it. She wouldn't have been able to do anything but worry. "I guess not. I know the good night's sleep is what allowed me to be on today. So I guess, thank you?"

"I'll take it. Now, want to watch Tilly and then see how your father is doing on the case?"

"Yes. I hope this is over soon. I'd really like to get back to my old life without fear of being kidnapped."

Willa didn't think about what she'd said until Porter frowned. "Yeah, I bet you're missing Florida."

Willa stopped and grabbed his arm. "Oh, Porter. I don't know why we haven't talked about this, but I'm not going back to Florida. Well, I am, but not for forever."

Porter's brow creased and Greer hurried off with Apollo to give them privacy. "If we can catch The Panther and continue our contract with the government, the team I'll be leading will be headquartered here in Lexington. So, yes, I'll go back to Florida, but only to pack."

Suddenly Porter grabbed her up in a hug and twirled her around. "Are you serious? You're staying in Lexington?"

Willa cupped his face with her hands and kissed him. The joy she saw in his eyes was contagious. "Yes. If we can catch The Panther and can safely continue our contract. I even found a place to live, but it's nowhere near being completed so I may have to stay with you for a while."

"I hope it's never completed. I'd love for you to live with me. Let's get to Keeneston and do whatever we can to catch the son of a bitch," Porter said, full of determination.

Willa laughed as Porter put her down, placed her hand in his, and ran for the barn.

Less than an hour later they were pulling up to the security complex at Desert Sun Farm. "So, this is like a consulate?"

"It's considered Rahmi land and the US government can't operate here unless invited," Greer answered Willa's question. She'd spent time as Ariana's bodyguard and knew all the legal ins and outs of diplomats.

"That explains all of the armed soldiers," Willa said as she looked around.

"Dani and Mo are on high alert with your father here and our guests from last night. It wouldn't look good if anything happened to your father and the president's crew while they were guests of theirs," Greer said bluntly before pressing the button on the door and looking up at the camera. She gave it a little wave and the door buzzed open.

Willa followed Porter and Greer down a hall into a cavernous computer room. There were more people in there than she'd thought. Not only were her father and Kale there, but so were Nash and someone who looked like an older version of him. Then there was Ahmed, a drop-dead sinfully sexy older man, a girl who looked like a rocker, and a shaggy-headed younger man.

"Willa!" Her father was the first to see her. He jumped up and had that same smile on his face that she saw every time she walked into a room.

"Hi, Dad." Willa hugged her father and wondered how much longer they could go on like this. Her father may be smiling at her, but there were dark circles under his eyes and he looked very pale.

"How did today's competition go?"

"Great. Apollo was really on. Our team finished second and I'm in the top three for the individual championship day after tomorrow," she told her father.

"That's wonderful, honey. I knew you could do it. Rest up tomorrow and then knock 'em dead."

Willa looked around the room and at the giant television screens on the walls that people were looking at. "How are things going here, Dad?"

"We have a good team. Come meet everyone," Her father turned to the room. "You know Kale, Nash, and Ahmed. This gentleman is Nabi. He's the current head of security for their highnesses."

"Miss Aldridge," Nabi said with a bow of his head. He looked to be between Nash and Ahmed in age.

"And this is Alex and his wife, Roxie," her father said, indicating the shaggy-haired man and the rocker chick.

"Dude," Alex said with a welcoming grin that reminded her of a happy puppy.

Roxie smiled kindly and then they went back to work. Mr. Tall, Dark, and Handsome stood up and held out his hand. "Sebastian Abel."

"SA Tech," Willa said, shaking his hand. "What are you doing here?"

"A favor," Sebastian said before sitting back down behind a computer.

"And here I thought you were just some billionaire who sold and bought companies," Greer said to him with a little smirk. The look Sebastian gave her made Willa take a step back but just made Greer's smirk grow.

"I made SA Tech myself. The tech part usually means

I'm good with computers, Miss Parker," Sebastian said coolly.

"Did they have computers back then?" Greer asked with faux curiosity.

Willa took another step back. Sebastian didn't seem like a man to tease.

"You do realize you're only ten years younger than I am, right? I'm just a year older than your brother, Ryan." Sebastian asked.

A twinkle lit in Greer's eye as the smirk turned into a smug smile. "You've been checking me out, Mr. Abel?"

"I check out everyone I have to deal with, Miss Parker."

"So does Ahmed. I wonder which of you gets a more in-depth background check? Should we whip them out and measure them? You know, for length. Of the reports that is." Greer said, mimicking Sebastian's dismissive tone.

"Sure. Ask him to pull out the stone tablets he has to use and we can compare background checks," Sebastian said dryly.

Greer burst out laughing and Ahmed narrowed his eyes. "You have a sense of humor, Bash."

"No one calls me Bash. It's Sebastian."

"That's not true. Abby refers to you as Bashy," Greer taunted. "Would you prefer Bashy?"

"Now who is checking up on whom?" Sebastian said with a dangerous smirk that Willa had to admit made danger look really good.

"I got it!" Kale yelled suddenly.

All teasing stopped. Everyone looked to where Kale sat. He wasn't saying anything else. Instead, all his focus was on the computer.

"Put it on the screen," Brian told Kale, and all the

television screens turned into one giant computer monitor. "Jackpot!"

Willa was suddenly looking at a roster of stolen goods, auction prices, and who bought them.

"That son of a bitch," her father cursed. "I knew Oliver had stolen the coding for our last program. He sold it to The Panther who auctioned it off and our competitor bought it," he said of one of their lead coders.

"Could he be the one who told The Panther about the skeleton key?" Willa asked as her father was already at work on his computer. One of the screens turned to mirror her father's computer.

"There!" her father said. "A fifty thousand dollar deposit one day before that man showed up in Florida harassing you."

"We'll take care of it," Sebastian said as he picked up his phone and sent a message. A second later he set his phone down. "Oliver will be picked up and taken to a black site for interrogation in less than four hours."

Willa didn't feel bad about the fact there was a good chance Oliver wouldn't ever be free again. She saw his name popping up multiple times as she looked at thousands and thousands of stolen items ranging from corporate intellectual property to blackmail pictures to lists of government agents.

"I'm saving it all," Sebastian said.

"I'm planting a tracking device," Roxie said. "The next time The Panther enters data, I'll log his keystrokes and follow him online. Hopefully, it'll lead us to his identity."

Willa's father kissed her cheek. "We're closing in on him, honey. I have to get back to work."

Porter put his arm around her and nudged her from the

room. "Let them do their thing. We can grab dinner at the café and have a quiet night at home."

"I'll grab something for Tilly and the bodyguard recovery ward I have going on at my apartment," Greer said with a roll of her eyes.

"You offered to take care of them," Porter reminded her cousin of Willa's injured bodyguards.

Greer shrugged. "It lets me leave Tilly behind safely when I want to do things. They'll be fine in a couple of days. Well, except Barry. They moved him to the rehab center to start PT for his knee after surgery."

"I think you're doing it just to torture your brother," Willa said, calling her out.

Greer smiled largely. "Maybe. It's fun to torture Jackson. He deserves it. Now, torturing my bother is making me hungry. I think I want a hot brown and then I'll tell Jackson I'm hand-feeding half of it to Deshaun."

Porter shook his head at his cousin. Greer had a devilish streak in her that had gotten him and the younger set of cousins in trouble more than once as children. "This is going to end worse than the time you got us in trouble for stealing Jackson's car."

"You stole a car?" Willa asked in shock as they drove toward the café.

Greer chuckled at the memory. "When Jackson was seventeen, he worked all year to save up and buy his first car. I had just turned thirteen and was asked out on my first group date. Well, Jackson went and threatened my date that if he touched me he'd make sure my date swam with the fishes. He'd just watched The Godfather for the hundredth time." Greer rolled her eyes.

"So you stole his car?" Willa asked.

"The date was horrible and to make it worse, my date told all the boys in the seventh grade what Jackson said and no one would ask me out for years. Porter, Parker, Jace, Colton, and Landon helped me get a little revenge." Greer stopped and laughed at the memory before continuing with the story. "Colton and Landon distracted Jackson while Porter, Parker, and I stole the car. We drove it down to the lake and filled it with all the fish Jace had caught for the last two days. Then we left it for Jackson to find."

"What happened next?" Willa asked.

"Uncle Marshall was the sheriff then, and he found the car. It smelled awful. Jackson was beyond pissed and knew it was Greer who had done it. But, there was no evidence of it until he planted a bug on her and caught us all laughing about it. Then our parents made us clean the car until there was no smell left," Porter told her.

"The worst part was that Jackson didn't get into any trouble for what he did to my date," Greer said, clearly still bothered by this.

"Surely you didn't let that go?" Willa knew Greer enough by now to know she wouldn't sit back and take it.

Greer grinned as they pulled into a parking space down the street from the café. "Of course not. I told Jackson's prom date not to worry about the sores on his penis. That they'd probably be gone by prom night."

Willa started to laugh but then noticed a second later no one else was laughing. Instead, Porter and Greer were staring out the window at the couple a short distance ahead of them on the sidewalk.

"Who's that?" Willa asked.

"The man is Henry Rooney. He and his wife are the town's defense attorneys. Their daughter just married the

King of Bermalia and now she's a queen. There's a rumor they're going to retire so they can spend more time in Bermalia with their daughter," Greer told her.

"His wife is stunning," Willa said, taking in the Latina woman with legs for miles, silky hair, and breasts that would make any woman jealous.

"That's not his wife," Porter told her as he rolled down his window.

The woman ran her hand over Henry's chest. "I bet a man like you knows every location in town."

"I know I don't need a map to read your body."

Willa scrunched her nose up. "Is he cheating on his wife?" she whispered.

"No," Porter whispered back. "Henry only speaks in pick-up lines. Neely Grace tolerates it, but only to a point."

The woman's hand faltered on his chest before she slowly began walking her fingers downward. "I bet you could give me a map right to Porter Davies."

Greer, Willa, and Porter shared a look.

"You're so hot you make habanero peppers look like candy. Look, you're making my zipper melt."

"I can do other things to your zipper if you tell me where Porter Davies is," the woman practically purred.

Henry stepped back and looked her over. "You must be made of sugar because you have a sweet ass."

The woman reached down and grabbed Little Henry. Henry sputtered for a second but regained his composure as he tried to disentangle himself to take a step backward. "Stop, drop, and roll. You're so hot you're on fire."

The pick-up line didn't have the same heat to it as the others, but the woman didn't let go of Little Henry and Big Henry was starting to just spout random lines. "Looks like you are lacking in vitamin D."

"Give me Porter Davies and I'll give your D a pull."

"I'm not feeling myself today. Can I feel you?" Henry asked, sounding a little nervous.

The door behind the woman opened and Porter and Greer cringed.

"Uh-oh," Porter whispered. "That's Neely Grace."

Neely Grace took one look at the woman who had Little Henry in a death grip, raised her leather briefcase, and swung it hard against the woman's head. The woman stumbled and went down on her knees.

"That's one way to get her to go down on me," Henry said with a big smile for his wife.

Neely Grace rolled her eyes. "Not one more word, Henry."

"I think this is where we need to step in," Porter said, pushing open the truck door. "What's going on, Neely Grace?"

Willa saw all the heads turn their way. The woman on her knees had cartoon eyes that still seemed to be shaking from the impact. That didn't stop her from trying to pull a gun, though.

Willa jumped back, but Greer and Neely Grace were already in action. Greer pulled her gun but Neely Grace bashed the woman with her briefcase again. "I always told Henry his pick-up lines would kill someone."

Greer snorted as she reached into her back pocket and pulled out a zip tie. "She'll have one hell of a headache when she wakes up. Nice shot, Neely Grace."

"My lioness has claimed the king of the jungle, now let's see how she can attack my snake."

"Oh no," Neely Grace said, shaking her head at her husband. "You've been ticketed for trespassing on your pants. You're going to have to get on your knees and get the judge to give you a pass."

Neely Grace strode off with Henry chasing after her.

"This town es loco," the woman Greer was holding muttered, shaking her head and blinking furiously.

"And what country are you from?" Porter asked.

The woman closed her mouth as a black SUV with tinted windows pulled up. The window rolled down and Abby looked out. "Hello, Carmen."

Willa shivered at the innocent tone that was anything but innocent.

"Dios Mio!" Carmen snapped out of her daze and practically leapt into Greer's arms. "You're law enforcement? You arrest me, yes?"

Abby got out of the SUV and walked over to them. "I'll take this little Venezuelan seducer off your hands. Did you try to seduce Porter so you could kill him? Didn't work for you this time either. I told you the men in my life were smarter than most."

"Did she try to seduce your husband?" Greer asked, making sure not to use their names.

"Tried and failed."

"Well," Porter said with a grin. "She tried to seduce Henry and Neely Grace took her out with a briefcase."

Abby burst out laughing. "Was he giving her his best lines?"

"You know it," Porter said as Abby hauled Carmen into the back of her car.

"That might be punishment itself. Have a good dinner. Carmen and I are going to have some girl time together."

"Help me, please!" Carmen yelled before Abby shut the door on her.

"So, dinner to go?" Porter asked, turning back toward

her as if the strangest scene she'd ever witnessed hadn't just happened.

"That may be a good idea after how today is shaping up." Porter reached for her hand and together they headed to the café as she hoped for a very quiet night at home. "Plus, maybe I'll try some of those lines and see if I can get lucky," she whispered to Porter.

"Men are simple creatures. Just get naked. We can figure it out from there," Porter whispered back.

Willa laughed as they entered the café and knew no matter what, their lives together were going to be interesting in the best possible way.

29

"See, I told you all you needed to do was get naked," Porter said, still breathing heavily. Willa rolled so that her cheek rested in the crook of his shoulder and her hand rested against his chest.

Willa laughed and he loved the sound of it. Making her laugh was one of his favorite things to do. Well, not number one. They had just finished his favorite thing. Making Willa laugh probably fell to number two.

"What would you like to do tomorrow on your day off?" Porter asked as he absently ran his fingers up and down her bare back.

"I'd love to go riding around your farm," Willa told him.

"We can do that and have a sunset picnic," Porter suggested. "There's a great spot at the edge of the property. It's a small climb up and then you can look out over the farm as the sun sets."

"That sounds like the perfect way to spend my day off from the show ring. We can check on Apollo in the morning and then do that in the evening."

Porter pulled Willa on top of him and brushed back her

hair from her face. "Let me show you the perfect way to spend a night."

Porter was happy. The computer crew was making progress. Last night with Willa had been perfect. Apollo was happy this morning and Willa looked gorgeous as they stood hand in hand, waiting to cross the street to the café.

"How do you feel about tomorrow's championship?" Porter asked as Pam made a slow drive-by in her Hummer.

"Really good. I'm nervous, though. I've never been this highly ranked going into the last day before. I'm usually a solid fifth, but now I'm up in third. If I can get a top three placement, I'm going to be over the moon."

Porter looked both ways, but before they crossed the street a large black SUV pulled into the lot and honked at them.

"Looks like the Desert Sun Farm crew," Porter said, turning to smile at his friends.

The door opened and a clean-cut guy stepped out with a big smile on his face. "Porter Davies and Willa Aldridge, eh?
"

"Do you know him?" Porter asked Willa. Porter was already suspicious of anyone asking after him, even if this man looked to be nice.

"I don't think so," Willa whispered back.

"Do we know you?" Porter asked him.

"I'm Jared Dales. I don't want a kerfuffle, but I need you to come with me, eh?"

Porter blinked at the man with the Canadian accent who was still smiling at him. "For what?"

"I'm here to get the key, if you'd be so kind." The man

opened the back door to the SUV and indicated they should get in.

Porter just shook his head. "No. I think we'll pass. But thank you for asking."

The man's smile slipped a little. "Please, I don't want to mess aboot and have this turn into a real gong show. Let's just keep this easy peasy."

"I don't know what a gong show is, but it sounds fun. Let's go that route," Porter said to him as he moved Willa behind him. "Run to the café," he whispered to her.

Willa turned and ran as Porter was only a step behind her.

"Don't be a hoser!" Jared yelled as he pulled a gun out and aimed it at Porter. "Stop or I'll shoot, Mr. Davies. I have a clear headshot."

Porter wasn't going to stop, but Willa slid to a stop in the middle of the street and he was forced to stop or run her over. Willa raised her hands as she turned slowly back to face Jared. "Please don't shoot him."

Jared smiled again. "That's what I'm talking aboot. Thank you for being reasonable."

Jared reached into his pocket with one hand and pulled two pairs of handcuffs. He began to walk toward them as he held them out. "Please put these on, Mr. Davies and Miss Aldridge."

Porter held out his hand for the cuffs. "Willa is too scared to move. She's shaking like a leaf," Porter told Jared. "Just hand them to me and I'll put them on us."

Porter watched Jared step out into the street and then pause in the middle of the lane. He tossed the handcuffs to land at Porter's feet. Porter reached down and felt the street vibrate as an engine roared. A Hummer barreled down the street and even as Jared turned in surprise, Porter was shoving Willa aside.

"What's this then, eh?"

The answer to Jared's question was the grille of Pam's Hummer slamming into him like the most powerful slap shot of all time. Porter watched Jared being punted into the air as Pam drove on. He got a good fifteen feet into the air before landing on Pam's roof and rolling off the back. He landed hard on the pavement as Pam spun the giant Hummer on the street and put Jared's body right in her sights.

The café door was flung open as people rushed out and Pam leapt from the Hummer. "I got him!"

"Are you okay?" Porter asked Willa, who was watching Pam now standing over Jared trash-talking him.

"Yeah, I'm great. He was the nicest hitman so far."

"But not a good one," Pam taunted. "Now that's how you carry out a hit. Boom!"

Jared groaned and rolled over. "I was just trying to do my job and serve my country. I am sorry I got in the way of your vehicle. Are you okay, ma'am?"

"See, nicest hitman ever," Willa said, looking down at the man Jace was running toward with a medical bag in hand.

"I'm fine, but you've been Hummered," Pam tried to gloat, but her smile was faltering.

Jared groaned again. "I should have looked before I crossed the street. I sure hope there's not much damage done to your vehicle."

"Both legs are broken and I'm guessing several ribs, too," Jace told them.

"Ma'am, are you sure you're not injured, eh?" Jared asked Pam.

"Darn it!" Pam stomped her foot. "I finally get a good hit to save the day and sending him bouncing over my car. And I have to hit the only nice hitman."

"I'm Canadian, sorry aboot that."

"No! Don't be sorry. You were going to shoot them, right?" Pam asked, bending down and getting into Jared's face.

"Well, only Mr. Davies. And I would have hated every second of it."

"Aha! I did save the day."

Jared went to open his mouth but Pam shook her head. "Not another word. You were going to kill Porter and I stopped it. Bad guy down. Somebody get me a drink. We're celebrating."

"Your order is ready, Porter. Or do you want to eat in now?" Poppy asked as the onlookers began to file back inside. Cody and Luke were there. They could transport Jared wherever needed.

"To go, please," Porter said, turning back to slip his hand into Willa's. "I could visit Canada after this. Several of these countries are now on my do-not-travel list, but Canada seems nice."

When they got inside, Pam was on top of a table reenacting the hit and using a spoon to demonstrate how Jared bounced over the Hummer.

Porter paid, and as they walked out Dylan was there with some Rahmi guards putting Jared into the back of a truck.

"They'll be nice to him, won't they?" Willa asked.

"Jace is going with them. He'll help Jared's injuries as best he can."

"Goodbye, Jared!" Willa called out. "Hope you feel better soon!"

"Thank you, Miss Aldridge. It's been a pleasure to meet you. I hope you're still alive when I recover so I can bring you in," Jared yelled back to her before he groaned again in pain.

Porter opened the door to his truck for Willa and then placed the food in the back. He had a blanket and a basket ready to go for when they arrived at the picnic site.

"Is it bad that I'm no longer scared when someone points a gun at me?" Willa asked as they drove out of town. "I almost corrected you when you said I was scared. How could I be scared of Jared?"

"I actually feel bad I didn't let him shoot me," Porter said with a laugh. They'd had tactical teams, snipers, hand-to-hand, seduction, and now Jared, who'd tried to kill them with kindness.

"Can you tell me anything about your company headquarters in Lexington?" Porter asked Willa. He turned into the farm but drove past his house and only stopped when he reached the small ridge between his house and the property he wanted to buy. The woods and land separating the two parcels of land weren't quite a mountain but more of a hill range with limestone outcrops and thick woods.

Porter lifted the basket and blanket from the back of the truck. He slung them over his right arm before reaching back with his left and taking Willa's hand in his as they entered the woods.

"Yes, I found this nice new office development in Lexington near the airport. I still haven't learned my way around here yet, but I think it's on the side closest to Keeneston."

"I know the development. It's about twenty minutes from here," Porter told her as they began the short climb. He let

Willa go first; if she slipped he could catch her. "See that rock sticking out up there? That's where we're going."

Porter followed Willa up the trail as they talked about the new headquarters and how it was to look like a generic company. "We're going to say we do data entry," Willa told him as they reached the rock. "Oh, wow," Willa said as she looked out.

Porter followed her gaze. The view never got old. The rock jutted out about eight feet over the hillside, but what made it perfect was a natural break in the tree line that gave an unobstructed view of the pastures below and the setting sun.

Oranges, yellows, pinks, and purples were painted across the sky as they sat and ate their dinner.

"Do you think you'll stay with the CIA?" Willa asked him as he held her in his arms. She sat between his legs and leaned against him as they watched the last of the sun set below the horizon.

"No. I've ever only wanted to have a horse farm. There's land on the other side of this ridge that's going up for sale. I'm thinking of buying it and putting a path through the woods to connect the two farms," Porter told her.

The sun dipped below the horizon and darkness began to fall even as the last bits of color lit the horizon.

Porter's phone buzzed and he was tempted to ignore it, but with all the action going on, he never knew if Pam hit someone again or if Kale found The Panther.

Where are you?

"It's my dad," Porter told Willa, who'd looked over her shoulder with worry. She relaxed and turned back to the sky.

Rock Ridge, he typed back.

Sensors have gone off near the woods there. We're on our way. Hide.

"What is it? You went rigid?" Willa asked even as Porter moved to cover her mouth with his hand.

"Shh," he whispered. "They found us."

30

"What do we do?" Willa whispered even as Porter slowly looked around.

"We get into the woods. We're too exposed here."

Porter reached into the picnic basket and pulled out a gun before tucking it into the waistband of his pants. "Leave everything here. Let's go."

"Is it bad to hope it's more Canadians?" Willa whispered as she placed her hand in his. Porter hoped like hell it was the case as he led Willa off the rock and began a quick walk upward into the thick trees.

"We go up, then along the ridge, and back down closer to the house," Porter whispered to her as the terrain grew steeper.

A rock falling behind them had Porter freeze. It wasn't close, but it was close enough that he knew whoever was after them was on their tail. He looked at the worry on Willa's face and with a silent nod of agreement, they began to rush upward.

Porter stopped at the last rock outcrop and knew he'd have to help Willa up. "Like mounting a horse," he whispered as he looked back down the hillside. Through the trees below, a shadow moved as the woods fell into darkness. "Hurry," Porter ordered as he laced his fingers together.

Willa put her booted foot into his hands and he lifted her up. She clawed at the rocks as dirt and small rocks broke free and fell onto Porter. With one last boost, Willa pulled herself up.

Porter jumped up, grabbed the rock, and pulled himself up as the bullet slammed into the rock beside him.

"Hurry!" Willa yelled frantically as she grabbed his hand and pulled, helping him up and over the rock ledge.

"We have higher ground," Porter told her as he grasped the gun and lay on the ground. "I'll provide cover. I want you to run a quarter of a mile that way," he said pointing along the ridge. There's a break in the rocks and you can slide down that way. Just head straight down and it'll spit you out near the back of my house. Don't go to the house. Go to the barns and hide. Reinforcements are on the way."

"I don't want to leave you," Willa told him as she shook her head.

Porter saw the shadow moving toward the rock ledge and fired off a shot, but the shadow disappeared behind a tree. "Go, Willa! Now."

Willa's bottom lip trembled and she looked as if she were going to argue, but at the last moment she ran. The darkness swallowed her in a matter of seconds and now it was up to Porter to distract the assassin long enough for Willa to get to safety.

Porter saw the figure dart toward the rocks, but he couldn't get a shot off before it disappeared under the rock ledge.

Porter held his breath as he listened. The assassin was

coming. Porter backed away and waited. A hand appeared and Porter fired off a shot, sending pieces of rock flying. A second later the man's other hand came into view. Only it wasn't to grab onto the rock. He had a gun and began spraying the area with gunfire.

"Shit," Porter cursed as he rolled away and leapt up. He had no choice but to run. He was too exposed. He wanted to run after Willa, but he couldn't risk leading the man to her. Instead, he ran a few yards in the opposite direction and fired off a shot. He knew he couldn't hit the assassin, but he needed the man to follow him and not Willa.

"Follow me, Willa!" Porter whispered harshly in the direction of the ledge. Then he took off. "Come on, hurry!" Porter said just loud enough for his voice to carry.

Porter waited until he saw the figure pulling himself up and raised his arm to shoot. In the dark it was hard to tell the difference between the man and shadows. The man pulled himself up and over and rose, firing his own weapon. Porter ducked and got off one wild shot before running down the ridge with the man hot on his heels.

Willa's lungs burned. She was breathing hard from running, but she was also scared to breathe in case they heard her. Then she heard the gunshots. The break in the trees came into view and she stopped. She turned to look back and wondered if she could help Porter.

"Please be safe," she whispered before doing as he ordered and racing down the grassy hillside.

Momentum shot her forward and then she was falling. She wanted to scream, but the impact with the ground prevented any sound from coming out as she rolled head over heels a couple of times until her body was flung like a rag doll down the rest of the hill.

Willa felt every rock, stick, and divot in the ground as she logrolled the rest of the way down the hill. Then suddenly she wasn't rolling anymore. She lay flat on her back with her legs and arms sprawled out as she looked up into the starry night sky.

She had to run. She had to get help for Porter and she wasn't any help lying in a heap at the bottom of a hill in the woods. Willa grimaced as she staggered to her feet.

There was no time to assess any of the aches and pains. Instead, she ran. She ran as if her and Porter's life depended on it, because it did.

The house came into view and she swung wide of it and headed straight for the barn even as she saw the headlights off in the distance. She didn't know if they were friends or foes and she wasn't going to stand in the open to find out.

Willa darted through the barn door and then shut it behind her. Horses snorted and stomped their feet. They knew something was wrong and it was making them nervous.

Willa passed an empty stall and instead opted for a stall with a horse in it. "Shh, I won't hurt you," Willa whispered as she opened the stall door. She kept herself relaxed as she stood still and let the horse size her up.

Willa latched the stall door closed as she heard the barn door slide slowly open. The galloping heartbeat she'd had running was nothing compared to the sprint her heart was doing now.

A shadow slipped into the barn and melted into the darkness. Willa ducked down and pressed herself against the stall wall right under the feed bucket and hoped that the man would just glance inside and move on.

The horses grew nervous. The stomping and snorting grew more impatient as the assassin moved through the barn. She should have grabbed a pitchfork, then she'd be armed . . . wait.

Willa reached down to her boots and slid her fingers inside. She'd worn them for their afternoon ride around the farm. Inside was the spring steel blade Sophie had given her. Willa tightened her fingers onto the hilt and silently slid the blade free. She clutched the knife in her hands and held it against her chest.

"Willa Aldridge. I won't hurt you if you come with me. Otherwise I'll be forced to hunt you down," the deep voice said quietly but firmly from somewhere in the barn. Yeah, she wasn't born yesterday. Like hell she'd go quietly.

Light flashed through the stall windows as the sound of vehicles screeching to a stop at Porter's house echoed in the barn. She wanted to scream for help, but she couldn't put them in danger.

"Come out or I'll kill them," the man said. He was closer now and she heard the soft footfall of his feet coming closer to the stall she was hiding in.

"Willa! Porter!" she heard Cy yell.

Willa had to bite her lip to stop from calling out.

"Where are they?" she heard Dylan ask.

"Porter told us to get lost until dark. I shouldn't have listened," Willa heard Jackson say with anger and worry in his voice.

"Tick-tock, Miss Aldridge. Either you come with me or I kill them all."

Willa's whole body trembled as she held herself quiet.

"Walker, your team clears the house. Dylan, you're with me in the woods. Jackson, your team clears the barns. Let's move," Cy ordered.

"It's now or never, Miss Aldridge. I don't mind killing a few more people, even if I'm not paid to," the man said in a low voice. He wasn't the least bit concerned and that's what worried Willa the most.

Willa held up the knife. Sophie's words echoed in her head, "You can do anything when your life is on the line."

"I'm here. I'm coming out. Don't kill them, please," Willa whispered back as she slowly stood up. She moved the knife so that the blade pressed against her forearm and out of sight.

The man moved quickly and was by the stall before she'd finished talking. He was tall and lean. His face was covered with a trimmed beard and he looked normal in almost every sense. Nothing shouted psycho killer.

He slid the stall door open and reached inside. Willa gasped as he grabbed her upper arm and yanked her from the stall. He pressed her back to his chest. He anchored her to him with an arm around her waist and a gun pressed to her head.

"We are going to quietly step out the back of the barn," he whispered into her ear. "You make a sound to warn them and I don't care how much I'm being paid to bring you in, I'll kill you. Nod if you understand."

Willa gave a single nod as he walked her quickly to the back of the barn as Jackson and Talon entered the barn from the side closest to the house.

"Move." The man shoved her through the small opening in the back door and out into the night.

"You're holding Miss Willa like my Bertha holds a seal," Lucas said from beside her. A gun appeared in Willa's peripheral vision as the FBI Hostage Rescue Team member slowly approached them. "Let Willa go and I won't kill you."

Relief flooded Willa, but it was premature as the man

flung his arm around and shot. Willa screamed as Lucas went down.

Porter leapt down the rocky slope making his way around the thick trees that proved cover from the man chasing him. He was close to the bottom of the hill when he heard a gunshot followed by a scream. The noise was unmistakable. Willa was in danger.

"My associate has your girlfriend. I don't need you anymore," a man called out some fifty yards behind him.

"Which country are you from?" Porter called out as he hid behind one of the last trees on the hillside and searched the darkness for the assassin. He glanced down at his gun and cursed. He was out of bullets.

"Country? Nah, I'm more of an independent contractor."

"Did The Panther hire you?" Porter asked.

"No," he answered. "There's more than one player in the world who wants the information Miss Aldridge has."

A competitor to The Panther. Interesting. "The enemy of my enemy is my friend, right?" Porter asked. "How about you give me information on The Panther and I'll take care of the competition for you?"

"Nice try, but my job isn't to eliminate The Panther. It's just to get the girl." The man was closer, but Porter couldn't see him as he moved from tree to tree to protect his own cover.

Porter closed his eyes and opened his ears. He took in every sound of the night and then he finally heard it—the sound of grass being flattened no more than five feet away. The man was approaching the tree Porter was hiding behind.

Porter bent low and waited. When a dry leaf rustled just

two feet away, he propelled himself around the tree. He lowered his shoulder and rammed it into the man's gut, sending them both careening to the ground.

The man's gun dropped from his hand, but before Porter could grab it, the man was punching Porter's face. One thing Porter was good at was taking a hit. No matter how tough this man thought he was, he wasn't tougher than a pissed-off bull.

Porter's head didn't even snap to the side. Instead, he smiled and slammed his head into the man's and then the battle was on. Close combat fighting was hard because you couldn't pull your arm back enough to get the full impact of a punch, but that didn't mean you couldn't do damage. Porter let loose a flurry of punches to the man's side near his liver.

"Ah!" the man yelled in pain as he used all his energy to shove Porter to the side.

However, Porter had a grip on the man's shirt. The shove sent him rocking to the side enough for gravity to take over. Locked together, they rolled down the hillside. Porter exhaled in hopes of not have the air knocked out his lungs from either hitting a tree or from the assassin slamming into him as they rolled. Porter could tell when they hit the bottom of the hill as they were flung apart on the last bounce.

Porter scrambled to his feet, sucking in a deep breath. The assassin did the same and then they faced off as they circled each other. Porter didn't wait for the man to make a move. He was never the sit back and let it happen kind of guy. Fear for Willa, anger over having countless assassins coming after them, and the need to get to Willa now propelled Porter forward.

The man blocked Porter's punch but not the head-butt

followed by a hard uppercut that connected to his chin. The man went down like a sack of bricks.

"I won't mention the head-butt to Jace so you can avoid another concussion lecture if you don't tell Abby I came without her. Deal?" Dylan asked as he tied the man up and hoisted him over his shoulder.

Willa looked at where Lucas lay groaning on the ground. Rage filled her as her kidnapper began to drag her toward the next barn even as they heard people running toward them.

"The Panther won't get anything from me," Willa said angrily.

"I don't work for The Panther," the man said, surprising Willa.

"Who do you work for?" she asked as he shoved her into the next barn and locked the door from the inside.

"I go where the money is, babe," he told her as he dragged her toward the far exit even as someone tried to open the front door.

"I can pay you. I can pay you more than anyone else can."

The man chuckled as he slid the back door open. "You don't have enough money to match what she's paying me."

"She?" Willa asked.

"The Panther is nothing compared to a Lioness," the man said knowingly.

When Willa looked up, she saw an SUV hidden behind the equipment barn. There was no way she was going to get into the SUV. However, she didn't need to worry as Greer materialized between the equipment barn and the SUV with her gun raised.

"Let her go and I let you live," Greer said in a voice that Willa didn't even recognize.

The man gave a little snort of disbelief. Willa had seen what he did. He shot with no warning. Willa's hand tightened on the knife before loosening her grip so the knife swung like a pendulum down and forward. Then she tightened her grip on the hilt. She kept her eyes on Greer and when she gave the slightest nod of her head, Willa made her move.

Willa turned to dead weight and dropped down. As she forced the man to hold her upright, she turned and stabbed upward. The blade stuck into his side under his armpit. It slid between his ribs, through the muscle, and into the lung as if it were sinking into butter, thanks to the sharpness of the blade.

Willa didn't have time to find out if it killed him. Greer fired and the man dropped to the ground with his arm still around her. Willa fell back against the man and instantly went into fight or flight mode.

"Willa!"

She heard her name being calling but was too deep into the battle to free herself for the sound of Porter's voice to penetrate the fight or flight response.

"Willa! You're safe, sweetheart. Stop fighting." Strong arms went around her and lifted her up into a reverse bear hug.

She struggled, but then his lips were next to her ears whispering to her, "I love you, Willa. It's okay. I got you. You're safe."

"Porter!" Willa cried as the tears came. Porter set her down and she spun to leap into his arms. "I was so scared for you. Are you hurt? Are they dead?"

"This one is," Greer said, no longer feeling for a pulse.

"Ugh. That felt like one of Bertha's playful hits," Lucas groaned as he staggered over while ripping his bulletproof vest off.

"Are you hurt?" Cy asked, running over to Willa with every Davies—young, old, male, and female—behind him.

"I'm fine, thanks to Lucas, Porter, and Greer," Willa said with a sigh as she smiled at Greer and squeezed Porter's hand.

"Porter Davies," Jace said with his hands on his hips. "Why is there a bruise forming on your forehead? Did you head-butt someone? Do you I need to remind you of the damage concussions can do to your brain?"

"No, Doctor Jace. I'm good. Dylan saw—I didn't head-butt anyone. Did I, Dylan?" Porter asked as his cousin loaded an unconscious man into the back of an SUV.

"Nope. Not a single head-butt. Just like I wasn't here," he said as he got in and drove off.

"Abby's going to be so mad she missed this," Annie said with a low whistle.

"Ahmed is, too," Bridget, Ahmed's wife, said. "So, y'all didn't see me either. I don't want to watch him pout."

"I'll drive you. I'll say we were having girls' night," Annie said as they ran to a car parked down the drive.

"Girls' night?" Cade, Annie's husband, called out. "Hey, wait a minute. You said you and Bridget were having a girls' spa weekend two weeks ago. What were you really doing?"

Annie turned with a confused look on her face. "We were at the spa, darling. Where else would I be?"

Then she got into the car and drove off, leaving a trail of dust.

"Wasn't there a huge drug bust two weeks ago involving a shoot-out as two boats raced down the Kentucky River?" Marshall asked the group as all the men's brows creased.

They were all quiet for a moment, then Cade chuckled. "Nah. It wasn't them. Right? Didn't the boat crash after a sniper shot out their engine?"

"Yeah, no way was it Annie and Bridget. Can you see them in a boat race while engaging in a shoot-out?" Miles asked. "They're in their sixties, for crying out loud."

The husbands all chuckled and Willa noticed the wives were awfully interested in the ground and even saw the smiles they were hiding when Gemma looked up and caught her eye. "The important thing is everyone is safe, right?" Gemma asked.

"Of course, honey. I forgot you were at the spa with them. You all were," Cy said as he slung his arm over Gemma's arm.

"Yes, it was very relaxing," Paige said with a far too innocent grin that mirrored the one her daughter, Greer, gave sometimes. It was then Willa saw Paige hide the sniper rifle she was carrying behind her back.

"I feel as if we're missing something," Porter whispered to her. "But as long as you're safe, I don't care. I love you, Willa."

"I love you, too." Willa said, turning her head and kissing him. She didn't care if the entire family was there. She was madly in love with Porter and she didn't care who knew or how many bets were being placed right now.

31

"Lioness?" Kale asked with pursed lips. "I know her."

"So do I," Sebastian said, crossing his arms over his chest.

It was late and all Porter wanted to do was take Willa home and make love to her. But as soon as things started to calm down, Kale and his team flew up the drive. Roxie hurled when she got out of the extended SUV. Brian staggered a little. Sebastian wiped a wrinkle from his suit. Alex just said, "Dude."

Then they spent ten minutes filling everyone in on the capture of the assassins and the news that they were hired by a woman going by Lioness.

"She gives women hackers a bad name," Roxie said with a sneer of disgust.

"She thinks she's as smart as The Panther, but she's nowhere near it," Kale said as he went through the assassin's phone. "See, she left a trail."

A second SUV drove up and Abby and Dylan jumped out. "What did we miss?" Abby asked. Everyone went quiet and found their boots very interesting.

"I stabbed someone," Willa said into the silence.

"Way to go!" Abby said, giving her a high five.

"Found her," Kale said, handing the phone to Brian who nodded and handed it to Sebastian's outstretched hand.

"I've had run-ins with her, too. She's not particularly good at hacking, but she's good at getting other people to do her dirty work," Brian said. "I didn't think she'd gotten this powerful or had this kind of financial backing."

"I know where the money comes from," Sebastian said cryptically, but didn't expand further. He looked back at his phone and nodded. "Abby, Dylan. Humphrey is on the line for you."

"Humphrey Orville? President Stratton's chief of staff?" Porter asked.

Sebastian didn't reply. Instead he handed the phone to Dylan and Abby. A second later Abby snagged the assassin's phone from Sebastian and headed for her SUV.

"We have a quick errand to run. We'll be back in time for the show tomorrow. Good luck, Willa!" Abby called out with a smile as she got behind the wheel.

"Who do they work for?" Willa asked, turning to Sebastian. "You or the president?"

"I'm curious about your role in this, too," Greer said, looking at Sebastian with narrowed eyes.

"I'm here because I'm good at everything I do," Sebastian said cockily as he crossed his arms back over his chest and blatantly checked Greer out.

Porter had to hold Jackson back, but then Kale got their attention. "Oh, the reason we're here. We found The Panther. Well, we found all his or her assets and servers. We took them out. The Panther has lost everything. They have no money, no servers, and no network. And that means no power."

"What does that mean for us?" Porter asked.

"No money to pay assassins. You're safe for now while we track him or her down in person," Kale told them.

"Wait," Willa said from where Porter held her to his side. "Does this mean it's over? We're safe?"

"As safe as you were before The Panther entered your life," Sebastian told her.

"Dude, you're good," Alex said, giving them two thumbs up.

"I'm more than good," Porter whispered into her ear before swinging her up into his arms. "You'll find out as soon as we can get rid of them all."

Willa yawned loudly. "All this chasing, shooting, and stabbing has really worn me out. What a relief it's over. I have to get to bed. Tomorrow is a big day. You have a Panther to hunt, I have a horse to ride, and boy, am I exhausted."

"And I have a grandbaby to get ready for," Porter heard his mother whisper.

"I have another wedding to help plan," his father whispered, and it only made Porter smile because the words wedding and baby were the best things he'd ever heard.

"Willa can—" her father began to say, but Porter's mother cut him off.

"Get right to sleep," she finished for Brian. "Everyone, we can retire to our house for some champagne."

In an expert move, his mother had the area cleared in less than a minute.

"So, your parents want a wedding and babies?" Willa asked with a little laugh as they walked back to his house. "How do you feel about that?"

"I think words are overrated," Porter said, scooping Willa up into his arms. "I'd rather show you."

And he did.

Porter held his breath. This was the most nerve-wracking moment of his life. No bull could worry him as much as watching the woman he loved leaping over fences almost as tall as she was.

His hand gripped the box in his jeans pocket as Willa guided Apollo into the last jump. He held his breath until she was over the jump and her beaming smile reminded him to resume breathing.

Brian and Porter hugged each other as they cheered for Willa.

"Are you going to do it now?" Brian asked.

"Or at the barn?" his mother asked.

"I'd run out into the middle of the ring and do it," his father told him.

"I have a plan if y'all will hush and not spoil it," Porter hissed. What was he thinking about being traditional and asking for their permission to marry Willa?

The final rider, who was currently in first place, began the course and everyone went quiet again. If the leader had a clean ride, Willa would finish second. Porter couldn't watch. He kept his eyes on the ground, but then he heard it. The hollow sound of a hoof hitting a pole.

Porter's head shot up as the arena groaned in disappointment as the pole was knocked to the ground. His eyes shot to where Willa was standing with Apollo near the ring and her face said it all. Willa was going to win.

The rider finished and people applauded as he left the ring. "Wait for it," Brian said, gripping Porter's upper arm as they all stared at the scoreboard. The number flashed up and Brian let out a whoop.

Willa had done it! She'd won! Porter raced over to her and wrapped her up a hug while spinning her around. "I'm so proud of you!"

Willa laughed with happiness as he set her down. "Medal ceremony and then we'll all celebrate!" Willa went up on her toes and kissed him before the top-place finishers walked into the middle of the ring as the press set up their interview station.

Porter watched as Willa was handed an enormous ribbon rosette the size of a turkey platter and then stepped from the podium to head over to be interviewed. Porter looked over at his brother who gave him a smile and a thumbs-up.

Porter moved in closer to hear the interview as friends, families, trainers, coaches, and staff all began to mingle around the ring. Porter came up behind Willa, but stayed out of camera shot as she talked about Apollo's championship jump.

"It was a championship ride for sure. You must be thrilled. How are you going to celebrate?" the reporter asked.

"With a bottle of my sponsor's champagne, of course," Willa said with a laugh.

"There are reports you are dating rodeo star Porter Davies, who also finished second here in the roping event."

Porter saw Willa scanning the crowd looking for him. "Um, yes. I am."

"I thought you might also celebrate with a marriage proposal from your very handsome boyfriend," the reporter said.

Willa laughed again and Porter saw the reporter point to

him. Willa turned around to find Porter waiting behind her on one knee. He smiled up at the shocked look on her face as he lifted up the ring box. The entire arena had gone silent as he spoke to her. "Willa, I have fallen so deeply in love with you that I can't imagine a day without you ever again. Your humor, your intelligence, and your love are more than this cowboy deserves. But I'll spend every day showing you how honored I am to have it. Willa Aldridge, will you marry me?"

Porter saw the tear slip from her eye as she nodded her head. "Yes! There's nothing that would make me happier."

Porter felt clumsy from nerves as his large fingers took the delicate ring from the box and slid it onto her finger. The second he got it on, Willa dropped down into the dirt of the show ring and threw her arms around him. "I love you," she whispered into his ear.

"Kiss! Kiss! Kiss!" The crowd chanted.

"I'll forever kiss you every chance I get," Porter said with a grin, making the arena cheer by giving Willa a kiss that might have to be censored for the broadcast.

EPILOGUE

Four weeks later . . .

Porter held Willa's hand as he looked at his bride. Happiness couldn't describe the feeling of overwhelming love he had for this woman at his side. The last four weeks had flown by as his father and Brian helped plan their wedding. Brian had pushed for a giant wedding at an exotic location, but Willa stood firm. She wanted her wedding in Keeneston. So her father had surprised them with a two week trip on a private yacht for their honeymoon instead of the giant wedding.

Now, with the setting sun as their backdrop, they stood in a flower-covered gazebo that Porter, Parker, and his cousins had built in the meadow behind his house. Wildflowers filled the meadow and Willa looked lovely with them in her hair.

"I now pronounce you husband and wife. You may kiss the bride," Father Ben said beaming at them.

Porter cupped Willa's smiling face with his hand and

dipped her back for a kiss that showed her how excited he was for the rest of their life together.

Hand in hand, they walked down the grassy aisle to the cheers of their friends and family. Tonight the air, the town, and their hearts were all filled with love.

Greer smiled as her cousin danced with his new wife. She hadn't been back to Keeneston for three weeks and it felt good to visit for a couple of days. She had flown to meet Abby and Dylan in the Bahamas two days after Porter proposed to Willa and hadn't been back since.

They'd found what was left of The Panther's operation in an obscenely large oceanfront Bahamian mansion. He was in the wind. However, Abby and Dylan had already caught the woman trying to climb the ranks as the Lioness before Greer started her time with their team.

The president had had some backroom talks with the countries that had sent assassins. He worked out deals with some and not with others. Either way, Greer had spent the last three weeks deep in the thick of black ops with Abby, Dylan, Dalton, and Lizzy. And even Sebastian had been there.

Greer let out a deep breath as the object of her annoyance strode toward her looking sexier than any man had a right to. Tonight was one of the rare social events Greer had seen him at without the ever-rotating lineup of models on his arm.

That wasn't what annoyed her, though. Okay, maybe it annoyed her a little. What really annoyed her was his superiority complex. Ariana and Abby swore he was a good guy under the stony stares. But that wasn't what Greer had found so far. In the last three weeks, they'd butted heads on everything from his questioning her ability to be part of the team, his disinclination to share information, her moral compass, and consequently his lack of one.

"Miss Parker," Sebastian said as he handed her a glass of champagne.

"Mr. Abel," Greer said back in the same cold formal tone Sebastian used.

"I hear congratulations are in order. Your team did well in Venezuela."

"Thank you." Greer took a sip of the champagne and kept her eyes on the dancers.

"I was hoping to talk to you about something," Sebastian said as he turned to stand next to her, similarly looking out at the dancers.

"Why do you act so high and mighty?" Greer asked with innocence.

"Because I am. Remember who you come to when you need a private jet or fake documents to get into a country," Sebastian said with his same cold tone.

"Which makes me wonder, Mr. Abel."

"Wonder what?" Sebastian asked, turning to face her.

Greer looked up into his steady gray eyes that seemed to peer into her soul. "Whether you're the good guy or the bad guy?"

Greer watched as Sebastian's lip twitched, but just as fast as it appeared, it was gone and his serious stare was back. "What do you think of your cousin Ryker Faulkner?"

Greer hid the surprise she felt at the question. "What's it to you?"

Sebastian took a sip of his drink, but didn't answer. Greer knew enough to realize he wasn't going to answer any question he didn't want to. And this was obviously one of them. She'd never met a man who played his life so close to the vest. Even Ryker shared more than Sebastian, and that was saying a lot.

Greer looked across the reception to where Ryker was talking to her family. "He's a loyal cousin who would do anything to help his family."

"That's what I needed to know. Thank you, Miss Parker."

"You're welcome, Mr. Abel."

Greer watched as Sebastian turned on his heel and crossed the reception area. Ryker's head turned as Sebastian neared. They didn't smile as they shook hands. They were two powerful billionaires with more secrets than the CIA.

"Ladies," Gemma said, raising her champagne glass. "Another one for the books!"

Dani opened the old worn matchmaking notebook the Rose sisters had handed down to them and put Willa's name with Porter's.

"Look at how well we're doing," Kenna Ashton said with a smile as they turned the pages of all the matches they'd made.

"Porter and Willa are so perfect for each other," Katelyn said to Gemma. "You'll have more grandbabies in no time."

"Now the question is, who's next?" Dani asked as she held the pen to a blank page. It was just another love match waiting to be made.

"Cassidy is still coming into her own and Cricket isn't out of preschool," Tammy said with a little frown. "I fear it'll be a while for me."

"I'm out. I got them all married off," Kenna said with a smirk as she looked to her children, Sienna and Carter.

"Me too," Dani added as her children Zain, Gabe, and Ariana were happily married.

"Me three!" Katelyn laughed. Sydney and Wyatt were blissfully happy with their spouses.

"I was a one and done," Morgan said as she looked at her daughter, Layne.

"I still have Parker," Gemma said. "He's settling down with the marshals so his time is nearing."

"I have Colton and Landon," Annie told them. "Landon is far too busy trying to establish his restaurant. Colton? I don't know. He's settled in Keeneston now, but the firehouse sure has a bachelor pad feel."

Bridget nodded her head. "I think that's where Kale is. Total bachelorhood."

"Kale sure has changed this summer," Annie said to her friend.

"He's been working out with Ahmed and Nash. He's put on twenty pounds of muscle. I also know he's thoroughly enjoying becoming eye candy to young women. I fear he'll be out of the marriage game for a while," Bridget said with a sigh.

"What about Greer?" Tammy asked Paige.

All eyes went to where Greer stood with Porter, Parker, Jace, and Ariana.

"Maybe," Paige said. "I just feel as if something is still off. Her future isn't clear and she doesn't like that."

"Well," Dani said, looking at the book. "Why don't we just put down Greer on this page and Parker on the other page. Then we can't go wrong."

"Great idea. We'll work on them both to determine which is next," Kenna said with a nod of finality. She raised her glass again to her friends. "To more love, marriages, and babies."

. . .

"Your father-in-law went all out for the reception," Parker said as Porter finally got a moment alone with his closest family and friends.

"It's beautiful," Ariana told him as she gave him a welcome-to-the-married-club smile.

"Brian and my dad could open a wedding planning company. They did all this in four weeks. Willa, Sydney, and Tilly designed the dress and came up with the theme," Porter told them.

"What did you do?" Greer asked, looking lovely in her bridesmaid dress that matched Tilly's.

"I showed up. And I picked the music." Porter grinned as the hottest country band played on the stage. "It's good to have friends in the biz. Even Brian was impressed Holt hooked us up with his friends."

"Well, he did open for them a couple of years ago," Jace said as they all glanced around the happy reception filled with laughter and dancing.

"What are you doing about the farm?" Greer asked as they watched Nikki grinding on some tech billionaire who was mesmerized by Nikki's enhanced booty. Porter turned away to look at his wife talking to Tilly, Lucas, and Talon.

"I'm going to ask Mr. Habisher if I can buy the land behind me," Porter said as his eyes connected with the elderly man talking to the Rose sisters. "Excuse me."

Porter had a grand plan. He was going to buy the farm, expand the rodeo breeding program, and still have enough space for Willa and him to build a house, her own barn, and even a practice arena. He just needed to buy this land first.

"There's our handsome groom," Miss Lily said when he joined their group.

Porter greeted the sisters and then shook hands with Mr.

Habisher. "Mr. Habisher, I was hoping to have a moment of your time."

"Of course," he said as they excused themselves from the Rose sisters who immediately went and turned up their hearing aids. Nothing was private in Keeneston. Not their love lives or their business plans. "What can I do for you, Porter?"

"I know you've talked about putting your farm up for sale. I was hoping I could buy it from you when you were ready." Porter waited for the smile to come, but it didn't. Instead, Mr. Habisher frowned.

"Porter, I sold the farm five weeks ago. Some corporation bought it."

"They're going to develop it?" Porter asked as he felt his stomach drop.

"No, that was a condition of the sale. I don't know what they're doing with it. It was all done at arm's length and I was wired the money in full."

"Porter, is everything okay?" Willa asked as she joined them.

"Um, yeah," Porter said, putting on a fake smile. He wasn't going to let this ruin the happiest day of his life. "Willa, meet Mr. Habisher."

Willa held out her hand as her brow creased, then cleared. "It's nice to meet you in person, Mr. Habisher."

"You know Mr. Habisher?" Porter asked his bride with total confusion.

"Yes. My trust bought his farm the day I moved here. I'm embarrassed to say I don't know where it is compared to here. I got caught up with wedding stuff and getting the headquarters set up, and quite frankly, it just got pushed aside. But if you know Mr. Habisher, then you know where it is, 1784 Old Woods Road in Lexington. I was going to talk to you about selling it so we could buy that property behind you."

Porter tossed his head back and laughed. Then he grabbed his wife and swung her around. "Sweetheart, that *is* the property behind me. The ridge is the county line. You bought the property next to mine before we even met. Now that's fate!"

"Sure, fate," Marcy Davies said with a wink as she clinked her champagne glass to Lily's, Daisy's, and Violet's.

"As soon as I heard from Nora at the Fluff and Buff that her cousin, the realtor, had this big new client from Florida looking for a horse farm, I knew exactly what we had to do," Miss Lily said with a grin.

"Mr. Habisher was happy to listen to my idea of privately listing his farm with Kimberly. Then it was as good as done," Miss Daisy said with a smirk.

"And a little birdie passed it along to Brian," Miss Violet said of the random mailing Brian Aldridge received from her. One that just happened to be sent to Kimberly as well.

"Mrs. Davies?"

"Ah, Agent Naylor," Marcy said, looking up at the agent whose suit was still wrinkled. "How did you enjoy the pie I sent you last month?"

"It was the best pie I've ever had," Agent Naylor said and Marcy knew he was angling for another one. Well, he did do her a favor, even if he was a bit of an ass. "If you stop by tomorrow, you can pick one up."

"I'd love that! Thank you, Mrs. Davies." Naylor turned and then bowed his head quickly. "Mr. President. Mrs. Stratton."

"Agent Naylor," Birch Stratton said in a dismissive tone

that Marcy had used herself a time or two. It worked as it sent Naylor scampering away.

"Just how extensive is your spy network, Mrs. Davies?" President Stratton asked.

"Wouldn't you like to know?" Marcy smiled up at the president. "Now, about that favor you owe me, Birch dear."

Marcy glanced across the room. They thought they were being sly with their glances, but they weren't. They couldn't keep their eyes off each other. Sometimes tension was foreplay. Sometimes it was a way to hide your feelings. Sometimes it was because the feelings you felt were too great and tension kept them at bay so you didn't have to face them. Marcy was sure this was a case of all of the above.

"Are you sure about that?" Birch asked her, not sounding sure of it at all.

Marcy stomped his toe with her cane. "Don't make me stop your pie order, young man."

"Do what she says, Birch!" his wife, Tate, cried as she smacked his arm. "You will not deprive me of my pie when I'm in this condition."

"Congratulations, dear," Marcy told the First Lady as the Rose sisters made a fuss over her.

"Thank you. Keeneston is lucky for us. I got pregnant when we were here for Ariana's wedding," Tate said, resting her hand on her stomach. She then looked across the room and nodded. "I see it, too. I'll do whatever I can to help."

"Such a dear," Marcy said, patting Tate's hand. "Stop by tomorrow for an extra pie."

Marcy hugged the first lady and president before turning to her friends. She raised her glass in a toast. "To Greer and Sebastian."

"Bless their hearts, they'll never see it coming," Miss Lily said as they toasted and then laughed.

. . .

"Porter and Willa Davies?"

Porter turned to see a deliveryman standing awkwardly with a large arrangement of flowers.

"Yes?"

"These are for you. Congratulations."

He shoved the flowers into Porter's hands and hurried from the reception.

"Who sent us flowers?" Willa asked as he set them down on a nearby table. She pulled the card and read it out loud. "To a worthy adversary. Congratulations on your wedding. I'm happy to have played a part in it and for you doing me the favor of taking care of Lioness. As such, I've decided for this happy occasion a gift is in order—the gift of your lives. –P."

Willa looked up at him with surprise as she handed him the card. "What does this mean?"

Porter read the card twice. "I think it means The Panther isn't coming after us."

"There's no better gift than sharing my life with you. I love you, Porter Davies."

Porter leaned down and kissed his wife. "I love you, Willa Davies."

The nickering of a horse had him looking up. Apollo and Miss Trix were tied to the tent waiting for them to ride off into their future together. Wildflowers adorned their manes and tails and a pair of pale blue satin panties were hanging from Apollo's mouth as he chewed on them.

Porter laughed as he yanked them from Apollo's mouth. "The panty dropper strikes again."

"Hmm, that gives me an idea." Willa gave him that look and Porter held out his hand.

"Shall we, wife?"

"We shall, husband," Willa said with a laugh that made Porter's heart swell with happiness.

Porter placed his hands at her waist and lifted her into the saddle before he swung up into Miss Trix's saddle. He reached out and took Willa's hand in his as their friends and family gathered to wish them well.

"I love you," Porter told his bride as they rode into their happily ever after.

THE END

Forever Concealed

Forever Devoted

Forever Hunted

Forever Guarded

Forever Notorious

Forever Ventured

Forever Freed

Forever Saved

Forever Bold

Forever Thrown

Forever Lies (coming Jan/Feb 2021)

<u>*Shadows Landing Series*</u>

Saving Shadows

Sunken Shadows

Lasting Shadows

Fierce Shadows

Broken Shadows

Framed Shadows

Endless Shadows (coming Oct 2021)

<u>Women of Power Series</u>

Chosen for Power

Built for Power

Fashioned for Power

Destined for Power

<u>*Web of Lies Series*</u>

Whispered Lies

Rogue Lies

Shattered Lies

Moonshine Hollow Series

Moonshine & Murder

Moonshine & Malice

Moonshine & Mayhem

Moonshine & Mischief

Moonshine & Menace (coming Nov 2021)

Moonshine & Masquerades (coming Dec 2021)

ABOUT THE AUTHOR

Kathleen Brooks is a New York Times, Wall Street Journal, and USA Today bestselling author. Kathleen's stories are romantic suspense featuring strong female heroines, humor, and happily-ever-afters. Her Bluegrass Series and follow-up Bluegrass Brothers Series feature small town charm with quirky characters that have captured the hearts of readers around the world.

Kathleen is an animal lover who supports rescue organizations and other non-profit organizations such as Friends and Vets Helping Pets whose goals are to protect and save our four-legged family members.

Email Notice of New Releases

https://kathleen-brooks.com/new-release-notifications

Kathleen's Website
www.kathleen-brooks.com
Facebook Page
www.facebook.com/KathleenBrooksAuthor
Twitter
www.twitter.com/BluegrassBrooks
Goodreads
www.goodreads.com

15000954R00189